"Hi, Kara. Looking good."

"Jace. You've changed. Not for the better. Excuse me."

Something flickered in his eyes and he mouthed an apology. "Sorry," he whispered so low she wasn't quite sure she'd heard him correctly.

"You. How about a drink for old times' sake?" he asked in a much louder voice.

"Jace... Please..."

Jace circled her like a lion stalking a gazelle. His stance was predatory, not even a flicker of the tenderness and emotions from the past, when they were each other's everything.

"Or a ride. You used to ride a long, long time and never get tired with me."

"You're despicable," she muttered.

Jace pulled away, but in his deep blue eyes she saw a hint of something of the old Jace. Shame.

He took her hand, unfurled her palm and gestured to the bikers.

"Anyone got a pen?"

Hoots and whistles as a biker rushed over with a pen. A thrill of awareness and fear rushed through her as Jace scribbled a phone number on her open hand.

"Here's my number, sweetheart. Give me a call if you want a nice long ride all night long."

Dear Reader,

Motorcycles have always fascinated me. I have friends who ride and expressed how free you feel in sensing the world around you more than when you are boxed in in a car.

When I set out to write *Escape from Devil's Den*, I knew Jace and Kara would be special characters. Jace loves his motorcycle and escaping on his bike. Kara loathes and fears motorcycles after a tragedy involving one when she was younger. Motorcycles are one reason Kara and Jace broke up years ago.

When FBI agent Jace has the chance to infiltrate a notorious outlaw motorcycle club that's stealing high-value jewelry, he grabs it. Little does he know, Kara will get involved when the gang targets her store.

It will take all Jace's fierce resolve to keep Kara safe while not blowing his cover, and all Kara's strength to trust Jace as she rides with him on this dangerous journey.

Special thanks to the motorcycle enthusiasts who helped me: Joy Kenyon Allen, Jill Blonder, John Burden and Matt Mastrony.

Happy reading!

Bonnie Vanak

ESCAPE FROM DEVIL'S DEN

BONNIE VANAK

Harlequin

ROMANTIC SUSPENSE

If you purchased this book without a cover you should be aware that this book is stolen property. It was reported as "unsold and destroyed" to the publisher, and neither the author nor the publisher has received any payment for this "stripped book."

Harlequin® ROMANTIC SUSPENSE™

Recycling programs for this product may not exist in your area.

ISBN-13: 978-1-335-50244-5

Escape from Devil's Den

Copyright © 2024 by Bonnie Vanak

All rights reserved. No part of this book may be used or reproduced in any manner whatsoever without written permission.

Without limiting the author's and publisher's exclusive rights, any unauthorized use of this publication to train generative artificial intelligence (AI) technologies is expressly prohibited.

This is a work of fiction. Names, characters, places and incidents are either the product of the author's imagination or are used fictitiously. Any resemblance to actual persons, living or dead, businesses, companies, events or locales is entirely coincidental.

For questions and comments about the quality of this book, please contact us at CustomerService@Harlequin.com.

TM and ® are trademarks of Harlequin Enterprises ULC.

Harlequin Enterprises ULC
22 Adelaide St. West, 41st Floor
Toronto, Ontario M5H 4E3, Canada
www.Harlequin.com

Printed in Lithuania

MIX
Paper | Supporting responsible forestry
FSC® C021394
www.fsc.org

New York Times and *USA TODAY* bestselling author **Bonnie Vanak** is passionate about romance novels and telling stories. A former newspaper reporter, she worked as a journalist for a large international charity for several years, traveling to countries such as Haiti to report on poor living conditions. Bonnie lives in Florida with her husband, Frank, and is a member of Romance Writers of America. She loves to hear from readers. She can be reached through her website, bonnievanak.com.

Books by Bonnie Vanak

Harlequin Romantic Suspense

Rescue from Darkness
Reunion at Greystone Manor
Escape from Devil's Den

Colton 911: Chicago

Colton 911: Under Suspicion

The Coltons of Red Ridge

His Forgotten Colton Fiancée

SOS Agency

Navy SEAL Seduction
Shielded by the Cowboy SEAL
Navy SEAL Protector
Her Secret Protector

Visit the Author Profile
page at Harlequin.com.

In memory of John Blonder. Never forgotten.
Always loved by many.

Prologue

Twelve years ago

Time for a journey. Maybe a short one to test her sense of adventure.

No adults around, and she itched to take her birthday gift out. Forget the fact her father insisted an adult had to be with her because she only had her learner's permit.

I can do this.

As Kara Wilmington scampered outside, her little brother, Conner, followed. "Kara, where yah going?"

Rolling her eyes, she jingled the keys in her hand. "Nowhere. Get back in the house."

"Can I go?"

"No."

"Aw, c'mon, Kara!" His lower lip jutted out. "Dad says you can't take the car out alone. I'll tell!"

Kara scowled. Conner was an eight-year-old pain in her butt. "Snitch! What did I tell you about snitches? No one likes them!"

Then he got a sly look in his eyes. "If I go with you, you won't be alone."

She had to laugh at his cleverness. "No. I'll only be gone a minute. Get back in the house or I won't let you have that sleepover at Dylan's tonight."

His face fell. "Aw, Kara. Dylan's supposed to show me his new gaming system. Don't be a jerk."

"I won't if you won't. Now get!"

She herded her brother inside and closed the door. Conner was a perpetual thorn in her side. The kid was always trying to spoil her fun. Dylan, their cousin and his best friend, was the same. The two were closer than Kara would ever get to her little brother.

Her phone rang. Guilt speared her as she glanced at caller ID. Mom. Kara walked away from the car to the driveway's end, pretending to check on the mailbox.

"Everything's fine, Mom. No need to keep calling me."

"You know how I worry. We'll be home by eleven tonight. Keep an eye on Conner. I know he's a handful, honey. I wish we had hired someone to watch him..."

"We're fine, Mom. Don't worry." She hung up.

Grinning, Kara ran to the 2010 Mustang, climbed in and turned the keys in the ignition. Oh wow, that engine purred like a contented kitten. She backed out of the immense driveway of her family's house and headed down the quiet street, then hooked a left to access the main road leading to the bridge connecting to the mainland.

On the main road, she drummed her fingers, waiting. Now! Kara turned right and gunned the engine, hooting. This was bliss—new car, her life stretched out before her like the black ribbon of road. Sweet sixteen, indeed.

She pressed hard on the gas pedal and it responded beneath her foot. Kara laughed with joy. The light ahead turned yellow and she slowed, then stopped as it turned red. After counting five seconds, when the light turned green, she accelerated.

The motorcycle shot out of nowhere. Screaming, Kara heard a sickening crunch of metal and glass as the bike slammed into the passenger side. She braked, but the force of impact caused the car to fishtail and slam into a tree. Her seat belt pulled and the car's airbags deployed.

Jerked forward, she felt pain as the seat belt held tight. Her head hit the glass, cushioned by the airbag. Moaning, she felt blood trickling down her temple. Kara glanced over and saw the crumpled form of the biker against the back window, his face smashed against the glass—blood, God, so much blood! Her gorge rose in her throat.

As the paramedics lifted her out of the car, she saw a small child on the pavement. Still. So still...

"No," she cried out. How had her brother snuck into the car? She should have known he'd do it. Conner never listened to her...

"Stay still, miss," one paramedic ordered.

The collar around her neck prevented her from moving much, but she saw enough. Saw the paramedics attending to her little brother. Saw one shake his head with a grim look.

"Conner," she screamed.

It was a long time before she stopped screaming...

Chapter 1

Bad-boy biker coming through. Sure hope I look the part.

Wind in his long hair, sunshine overhead and nothing but road stretching ahead of him.

FBI agent Jason "Jace" Beckett smiled behind the windshield of his helmet as he roared on his Harley toward the Tiki Bar. Along with reputable motorcycle riders, the Devil's Patrol lunched there every Sunday. Jace stood on a knife's edge of acceptance into the outlaw motorcycle club. Infiltrating was key to his undercover assignment. Almost there. Today could be when Lance, the leader of the DP's powerful Florida chapter, tested his loyalty and then Jace was no longer a prospect, but a member.

But as he headed to the bar through a less than desirable area of town, past crumbling buildings and gang graffiti that decorated walls, he spotted an older couple standing by an expensive sedan on the side of the road. Didn't take eagle eyes to spot the problem—flat tire.

Or the potential problem. Their shiny, polished presence and their expensive vehicle made them stand out like diamonds in a trash heap.

Inwardly cursing, he pulled to a stop in front of them. Pulled off his helmet and placed it on the seat. Jace hurried over to them. If any Devil's Patrol riding to the Tiki Bar saw them, the couple would be robbed. Or worse.

If any DP saw Jace aiding them, they'd be suspicious. To stay in character, he had to act like a total prick. But no way in hell was he leaving Ma and Pa America stranded here in this part of town, ripe for violence.

As he neared them, the couple backed off. The white-haired woman put a hand to her throat. Jace stopped, realizing their fears. He wasn't a member of the Devil's Patrol yet, but the Prospect patch on his jacket indicated he'd embraced the outlaw lifestyle.

"Got a spare and a jack in that trunk?" he asked.

The man's shoulders relaxed, but the woman still shrank back. Jace gestured to the trunk. "Pop it."

The man obliged. Jace pulled out the spare and the jack, relieved they at least had the equipment, if they lacked the knowledge.

"We called the auto club, but they said it would be at least an hour." The woman, who had followed her husband to the trunk, had a quavering note in her voice.

"One hour in this place is not a good idea." Jace set about changing the tire as they stood by, wringing their hands.

In minutes he had the tire changed and the flat and jack tucked back into the trunk, which he closed with a firm hand. He glanced at the relief on their faces.

"Thank you, young man. May we give you something for your trouble?" The man pulled out his wallet and Jace glimpsed several bills.

He groaned. Why did people carry that much cash?

"No, thanks. Glad to help."

The woman gave a real smile. "You remind me of our grandson. He's a police officer. Always helping others."

Terrific. If the DP saw this display of kindness, their impression of Jace as a potential member would turn to suspicion. Mistrust. They wouldn't allow him into the club. Or worse, admit him and then when he happened to turn his back, slice him up and dump his body into the Everglades. Make him gator food so no one in his family could ID his body.

He almost laughed. What family? His father was serving twenty-five years in prison and his mother had moved on to her third husband, who'd made it clear Jace was not welcome at family reunions.

Jace offered a brief smile. "No problem."

The woman had finally uncovered her throat, only to display a diamond pendant.

He stared at it and her smile dropped. She put a hand to her throat again. He glanced up and down the road and heard the distant, but distinct, roar of motorcycles. Dammit. Had to leave. So did they.

Now.

"Ma'am, I highly advise you to put your jewelry away where no one can see it. And when you leave here, take the long route. This is not a good area." He gestured east to the growling engines approaching. "There are people who use this shortcut who wouldn't hesitate to rob and beat you."

Blood drained from their faces, but they hurried back inside the car. He scurried to his bike. The motorcycles drew closer, but the couple sped off, the man turning down a side street Jace knew led to the main road.

Too late for him, though, because the bikes were closer. He recognized the unmistakable cough of an engine. Lance, the leader of the Devil's Patrol.

Excuses. He needed one fast. Jace sighed, went to the side of a nearby building and unzipped his jeans.

He was just zipping up when they arrived, stopped and regarded him. He eyed them with the same interest they showed. Shrugged.

"Couldn't wait, prospect?" Lance lowered his sunglasses. "You raised in a barn?"

No, I was raised in a motorcycle clubhouse. "Had too many beers already. Building's a hell of a lot cleaner than the damn gas station men's room."

Lance smiled without warmth. Shorter than Jace, with bulky muscles and a beer belly that advertised his favorite beverage, Lance had a craggy face and slit brown eyes. Reptilian eyes. He was always squinting against the ever-present Florida sun. Ink covered his bare arms. Most prominent was a Devil's Patrol tat on his left forearm.

"Why you here ahead of us? You too good to ride with the pack?"

Jace pointed to his bike. "Damn, you know my bike needed a new tire. Wasn't going to slow you down, so I got it fixed and waited here."

The excuse might fly. Might.

Big Mike, hands on the ape handlebars of his Harley, shook his head. "Prospect, ride ahead of us and get me a damn beer."

As a club prospect, Jace was often disrespected and treated like an old lady. He put up with it, doing whatever they wanted. Sometimes they slapped him around. It was all to test his loyalty and see how he reacted. See if he wanted it bad enough to take a beating or two.

Jace endured everything and moved on.

"No problem," he said easily.

Lance laughed. "You'd better have a lot of cash, prospect. I'm mighty thirsty."

After tugging at his gloves, he climbed on his bike and roared ahead to the bar, hoping like hell no other people might blow his cover today.

Instruments of death crowded the parking lot.

Cold sweat trickled down Kara Wilmington's back, despite the heat. Her breathing hitched. Motorcycles. Two rows of them at least, gleaming in the bright sunshine like metallic beasts. Killer beasts, the same kind that killed her little brother. Nearly paralyzed with dread, she squeezed her damp palms and tried to force a smile at her client.

"Reggie, are you certain you want to eat lunch here? There are other places…"

"Not like this. Best catfish around. Bikers love it. Look at all of them!" He grinned, making him look younger than his 77 years. "If I weren't with you, Kara, I'd be here, anyway, jawing away with them. Every Sunday I come here for lunch."

You can do this. It's only lunch. Then you can leave.

If she balked, she could lose this deal, and Reggie was a client who could lead to bigger deals through word of mouth. *I need this. They're only bikers and not on their motorcycles. It will be okay.*

Kara took a deep breath, steadied her voice. "Shall we?"

The hostess escorted them through the Tiki Bar to a table. She tried to ignore the bikers as Reggie pulled out a chair for her. Why couldn't he have seated her facing away from them?

Kara felt as conspicuous as if she'd worn a bikini and flip-flops instead of a Chanel sheath dress and pumps. Much as she'd learned to ignore men staring at her—God, why did they always stare?—she hated this.

Hated being the center of attention, hated the motorcycles that reminded her of Conner's death…

She thanked the waiter as he handed her a menu, ordered iced tea with lemon and silently steeled her spine.

"Don't knock bikers, Kara. They're fun people. You should have fun, live a little instead of working all the time." Reggie shook his head. "No offense, but you're young and you drive slower than ladies half my age."

There's a reason for that.

Reggie was selling his entire estate and moving to California to be closer to his daughter and her family. Years of valuables sat in the luxurious house and he needed Kara's firm to liquidate everything, fast. Anything of personal or sentimental value had already been shipped out west. Kara had already appraised all the items and came up with a whopping two-million-dollar total.

The jewelry, passed down through two generations, would sell easily. Kara planned to keep the most expensive pieces in her store and sell them to private bidders.

The interior of the Tiki Bar was sticky, but ceiling fans stirred a sluggish breeze coming from the east. Kara's gaze flicked to the gathering of twenty or more men in jeans or leather, some with long beards and a few with gray hair. An eclectic collection, for certain. At another cluster of tables were bikers who looked rough and had leather jackets, despite the heat. She saw patches on their jackets and a chill rushed down her spine.

"What's a one-percenter?" she asked Reggie.

His gaze flicked in the direction of her gesture and he immediately looked away. "Ignore them, Kara. That's the Devil's Patrol. Motorcycle club. One-percenter describes outlaw MC clubs. The other ninety-nine percent of bike riders are law-abiding. These guys are not. They're criminals and dangerous."

A shiver raced down her spine. "Aren't most bikers skirting the edge of the law?"

Reggie bristled. "Most motorcycle enthusiasts are good guys. Stop clumping them all together."

Kara hid her surprise. "Sorry. I did not know."

Reggie nodded. "Let's order."

As the waiter brought their drinks and they ordered, Kara turned away and focused her attention on Reggie. He began talking about everything from fishing to motorcycles.

When he finally came up for air, she dove in and removed a sheaf of papers from her briefcase. "Reggie, the contract to hire my firm is all ready for you to review."

He took the papers, frowned as he scanned them while sipping his beer. "This part about the commission you collect…"

"My commission is thirty-five percent."

Reggie lowered his beer. Frowned. "Your website said twenty-five percent."

Offering a serene smile, she locked her gaze to him, ready to play hardball. "Willow Wind Estate Sales charges between twenty-five and forty-five percent to liquidate an estate. I have to charge you toward the upper end of the scale because you requested expediency. That means I must scramble to hire extra help the day of the estate sale, not only to handle sales but keep an eye on your valuables so people do not walk off with them."

He drank more beer. "I don't know. What if you don't sell anything?"

Kara's confidence rose. She knew how to push the facts without shoving. "Reggie, my firm pays all the expenses of the estate sale, and the items that do not sell can be donated and you can collect the tax write-off. I assure you, you will get more than a fair price for your treasures. I have buyers I will connect with your valuables so they get a private show-ing. These are clients who will pay more than a fair price."

As he squinted at her, she went for the kill, lowering her voice so no one could overhear. "My costs will be consider-able, and your net will be as well. Perhaps over one million."

Beer sloshed over the side of his mug as he set it down. "That much? Hot damn!"

Her smile widened. "It will be more than enough to fund your trip west, plus hire an attorney to set up a legacy for your grandchildren. I'm sure Miles and Macy cannot wait to see you."

Reggie nodded. "I thought it was a bunch of old junk. Well, you're the expert, Kara."

Expecting him to shake hands, she was shocked to see him grope for a pen in his pocket and begin to sign. Kara stopped him. "In your best interests, you may want to have your attorney review the contract."

"In my best interests, lawyers are a waste of time and I have no time to waste." The pen hovered in midair. "I can trust you. And the jewelry you plan to sell at your store will be guarded at all times?"

Thinking of the jewelry, which she'd appraised at more than one hundred thousand dollars if it went to the right col-lector, Kara nodded. "We have excellent security."

He signed.

Tucking the signed contract back into her briefcase, she allowed herself a moment of sheer relief. Their meals ar-rived—catfish for him, salad for her. She ate, enjoying the fresh greens and the homemade dressing, as Reggie talked with growing excitement about his plans for moving and en-suring his grandchildren received a generous college fund.

As he talked, her gaze drifted around the bar. The bik-ers were absorbed in their meals and drinks. Soon all but the Devil's Patrol left the bar and she heard the unmistakable roar of motorcycles. Kara fought the usual nausea she experienced when she heard a motorcycle, unable to forget the belch of smoke and the growl of the engine as the motorcyclist had headed straight for her new car...

The biker had been killed.

So had her little brother.

Throat tight, she forced herself to drink more tea and peeked at the Devil's Patrol gang. One man, who had his back to her, suddenly turned and laughed as he signaled to a nearby waitress. The salad turned to cardboard in her stomach.

Kara stared at the handsome face of her ex-fiancé. Jace Beckett. Clad in a tight black T-shirt that showed off the curves of hard biceps, and ragged jeans that hugged his amazing butt...

Swigging back a bottle of beer, he stretched out his long legs and plopped up biker boots on an empty chair. Jace laughed at something said by another at the table.

Jace. Here with a notorious motorcycle club. What on God's green earth was he doing here? He was a straight shooter, a white-collar pencil pusher who'd worked at an investment firm six years ago when they broke up.

Not a rowdy biker who shouted for another round for his pals, but that what he was doing right now. His dark brown hair had gold streaks and was curled at the edges. Hanging to the firm jawline of his once clean-cut face was a beard. A well-trimmed beard, but a beard just the same.

If not for his deep guffaw, she'd never have recognized him.

Confidence drained out of her like a deflated balloon. She fiddled with her iced tea, tracing a droplet of condensation on the glass. It felt like a teardrop. Like the damn tears she'd cried the day they broke up.

Motorcycles always meant more to Jace than she did. Not even the amazing sex they'd had, or the way they clicked on other things, like the theater, or their long conversations, had been enough to keep them glued together.

Filled with bitter memories and a sudden, sharp longing, she glanced up.

Only to see him pull a woman in denim short shorts and a sleeveless shirt onto his lap. The woman planted a big kiss on his mouth as Jace wrapped his arms around her. Stinging jealousy shot through Kara. She tried ignoring it, but there it was, like a cloud of gnats at sunset. She knew how Jace liked to do it—long, deep, intoxicating kisses, making her forget everything but him, and then they'd end up in bed together.

Kara bit her bottom lip, remembering his lazy smile, the way he'd cup the back of her head, holding her steady for those drugging kisses…exquisite, filling her with heat.

She dared to look at him again. The way he kissed this stranger on his lap wasn't the same. He kissed without the finesse he'd always displayed, kissed this woman as if she meant nothing.

Forget him. You've moved on.

Still, the ache for something she had and lost couldn't be fully ignored. Kara felt like a hungry diner staring inside an exclusive restaurant, knowing she could never dine there again.

Reggie finished his catfish. Time to go. She paid the check in a hurry and as she pushed back from the table, Jace glanced over.

He saw her.

Chapter 2

Kara. What the hell was she doing in a place like this?

Elegant five-star restaurants on the beach were her style. Not this laid-back bar in the middle of farm country.

He rubbed his bearded face, ruefully thinking of what he must look like. Not the clean-cut man in black tie she'd seen recently at a fundraiser for the turtle hospital. Seeing her at the gala had been the first time he'd encountered her since their bad break-up six years ago, and wow, that hurt. He hated what he had to do for this assignment, hated having to act like his old man. But the end surely must justify the means. He needed to nab the small fish—Lance—who was the president of the Florida Devil's Patrol, to get to the big fish.

The leader and holder of power in the Southeastern Division of the Devil's Patrol was nicknamed Marcus Aurelius, and he was a shadowy figure much like a mafia kingpin. Before Marcus came along, the Devil's Patrol was an outlaw biker club into petty theft.

A year ago, they began stealing, selling guns and even distributing drugs. Intel picked up chatter about a new mover and shaker in the DP and his name was Marcus, a biker wanting to protect his identity and avoid law enforcement.

Anyone could be Marcus. Little was known about him. They needed to nail the bastard. Surveillance chatter on social media indicated a possible domestic terror plot in the works. Marcus was going after something big and the public was in danger.

For more than three months, Jace had grown his hair and beard. This undercover assignment required him to look the part. Taking his motorcycle out every day, hanging in the places where the Devil's Patrol gathered. Using his old man's knowledge of the gang to make inroads, thankful his old man was still imprisoned. Getting a job as a motorcycle mechanic in the garage the club owned.

The Bureau had even set him up with a fake criminal record for assault on a police officer, fake jail time and fake fingerprints to loan him credibility with the DP.

Jace was close to acceptance. So close to gaining an inroad with the group he needed to infiltrate.

Kara might blow his cover. Then again, when they'd dated, he hadn't yet worked for the FBI.

He couldn't deny his attraction to her, the pull of longing when he saw her.

The woman on his lap turned his head toward her. "Hey, lover boy, pay attention. I asked a question. Stop staring at the eye candy. She's way out of your league."

Jace blinked hard, inwardly cursing. Seeing Kara had almost made him blow it. He looked up at the woman, gave a lazy grin and took a swig of beer. "What can I do for you, little lady?"

Allison Lexington was a female biker who hung around the Devil's Patrol. Unlike other DP female groupies, she was an experienced biker who eschewed the men's advances.

Lance, who regarded women as assets, gave orders that she wasn't to be harassed because Allison was also a trauma-room nurse who'd saved his life a few weeks ago. At a bike rally, Lance had taken a bullet to the shoulder and refused to go to the hospital, which had to report all gunshot cases to the local police. Allison, who witnessed the gun battle, brought Lance to a friend's veterinary office and patched him up. Lance never forgot a debt.

Or who owed him.

Allison brought over beer, groceries, did their laundry, did everything but sleep with the guys. Brunette, with big brown eyes and a pretty smile, she was as tough as the bikers. Probably tougher, since she'd seen a lot working trauma cases.

"You're awfully quiet, Gator," Allison cooed as she ran her red manicured nails down the front of his shirt.

Allison knew things. Last night while sharing a beer, she hinted Lance's boys on racing bikes had knocked over a jewelry store last week and the haul was small, but significant. Lance organized the heist. The burglaries began two months ago with a pawnshop.

So he'd told her everything about himself with the cover he'd created, to increase his rep and knowing the information would trickle down to Lance.

Speaking of the chief devil, Lance skirted the bar after returning from the men's room, and eyeballed Kara with interest. Too much interest. He planted himself in front of Kara.

"Hello, beautiful. Ain't you a sight for sore eyes," Lance drawled.

Every muscle in Jace's body tensed. He fought the urge to spring up, rush to her side and defend her from this prick. Maybe even punch him in the face. He used all the self-control he'd learned in the Army Rangers on missions to play it cool.

Kara looked him up and down as if Lance was a new species of cockroach. Her pert nose wrinkled. "If your eyes are sore, may I suggest an optometrist?"

Then she sidestepped Lance, her cool look of disgust

stomping on the man's ego as if she'd danced a flamenco in her designer heels all over the front of his dirty gray shirt. Jace silently applauded. *Atta girl.*

With a snort, Lance swaggered toward Jace's table.

"Jace Brown." Lance swung a leg over a chair. "We need to talk."

Without ceremony, silently apologizing to Allison for being a prick, Jace shoved her off his lap. "Beat it."

As she pouted and flounced off, he looked at Lance. "What's the deal with her?"

Jace jerked a thumb at the departing Kara.

Lance frowned. "Pretty, but snobby. Women are only good for cooking and screwing, and I can have all the ones I want."

Right. Keep telling yourself that, Lance. There was no shortage of women for club members, but not the kind Lance seemed to covet. Women like Kara—cultured, sophisticated and beautiful.

"Why you interested?" Lance demanded.

"Just asking."

"More than asking." Lance's brown gaze sharpened. "Seeing the way you keep staring at her, looks like you're into her. Or were into her. You know her? Who is she?"

Sweat trickled down his back. Damn. Lance wasn't foolish. If he denied knowing Kara, Lance could do a little more digging into Jace's past, and despite the cover story the Bureau set up for him, things could get dicey.

He was almost in with the DP. Lies only got him so far, and he couldn't blow it now.

"I did know her. We dated once." Jace took a long chug of beer. "You know that guy she was with, Lance?"

If he turned the attention away from himself, and Kara, maybe Lance would lose interest. Instead, the biker grew speculative.

"Reggie. Old dude who comes here every week. What's her name?"

"Kara. Why ask if you're not interested?"

Lance used his cell phone to take a photo of the bar. "You've hung with us for weeks, proved your worth and loyalty. You wanna join us?"

No application, no references needed, but Jace knew he'd have an initiation challenge to prove his loyalty. *Don't look too eager.*

He shrugged. "Thinking about it."

Lance glanced over at Kara, who was walking out of the bar with the older man who'd accompanied her. A sly grin touched his face and the knife scar stretching from his mouth across his cheek tightened.

"Go say hello to her. See if she blows you off like she did with me. Me and the boys could use some entertainment to liven things up."

His blood ran cold. He grinned. "Naw, I don't think so…"

Lance's gaze narrowed. "Do it, prospect."

His chest felt hollow, but he stood, giving a long stretch. "No prob."

Jace followed Kara to the parking lot, wondering how the hell he was going to do this.

As they left the Tiki Bar, Kara almost collided with a biker headed for the parking lot and staring at his cell phone. The man, covered with tattoos, apologized profusely.

"Sorry, miss. Wasn't looking. My wife says I'm on my phone too much. But got new photos of my grandson and couldn't wait to see them." He waved his phone.

Kara thawed a little and smiled. "No apology necessary. How old is your grandson?"

The biker beamed. "Two months. We're going to ride out to Utah see him soon. Can't wait."

She reached for his phone. "May I see?"

Like a proud grandfather, he showed her the photos. Kara's smile widened as she handed him back to the phone. "Thank you. He is adorable. Congratulations and good luck on your journey west."

Nodding at her, he walked toward his bike. Reggie gave her a knowing look. "See? Most bikers are friendly and love the open road. They're like you and me."

Maybe she'd judged too harshly. Something to think about.

Kara escorted Reggie to his Mercedes and waved as he drove off. Pure relief surged. With this new contract, if she did a great job, word of mouth would surely spread. The summer season was always slow in Florida, but this commission would tide over nicely.

She'd finally be able to give Dylan the raise he deserved, the one she knew he needed. Her cousin was a hard worker, and he brought every penny home to his mother. Even though they were family, he refused help and insisted on working hard.

Dylan had been Conner's best friend. A year younger than her baby brother, Dylan had worshipped Conner.

Kara tried to push back the guilt that always lingered in her conscience, like a slow winking neon sign.

As she headed for her sedan, she heard a noise behind her. The firm tread of boots. Motorcycle boots.

Jace ambled up to her with a swagger and blocked the path to her car. Several bikers wearing Devil's Patrol jackets and vests trailed behind him, rounding the corner of the building and standing close to their motorcycles. Watching Jace. Watching her.

Fear curdled her stomach. Kara swallowed hard, knowing

instinctively if she showed emotion, they would trample all over her. They could smell fear like a dog scenting a bone.

What happened to Jace, the man she once loved? Who'd once declared his love for her? Why was he acting like this?

"Hi, Kara. Looking good."

Summoning her coldest look, she lifted her chin. "Jace. You've changed. Not for the better. Excuse me."

Kara tried to sidestep Jace, but he blocked her way. She went the other way and he followed. Jace whipped off his mirrored sunglasses and grinned.

"What's your hurry, sweetheart?"

Glaring at him, she lifted her chin to tell him to get lost, but couldn't speak. Couldn't move. All she could do was stare at him with longing, caught in the past.

He got closer. She heard catcalls and laughter behind him. His biker friends, that gang. Why had Jace changed so much? What drove him to hang out with criminals?

Jace got closer. Closer still. Feeling like prey trapped by a much larger and more powerful animal, she remained motionless. Maybe he'd walk off.

"What do you want?" she asked, hating the quaver in her voice.

Something flickered in his eyes and he mouthed an apology. "Sorry," he whispered so low she wasn't quite sure she'd heard him correctly.

"You. How about a drink for old times' sake?" he asked in a much louder voice.

"Jace…please…"

Jace circled her like a lion stalking a gazelle. Kara's stomach clenched hard. His stance was predatory, without even a flicker of the tenderness and emotions from the past, when they were each other's everything. When he'd put himself between her and danger, and then they broke it off and became ghosts to each other.

"Or a ride. You used to ride a long, long time and never get tired with me."

The double entendre, reminding her of the times when they had made love for hours, made awareness rush through her. Barely aware of what she did, Kara licked her lips. Then as the other bikers laughed and hooted, she stepped back, horrified at her reaction.

"You're despicable," she muttered.

Jace pulled away, but in his deep blue eyes, she saw a hint of something of the old Jace. Shame.

He laughed and took her hand, unfurled her palm and gestured to the bikers.

"Anyone got a pen?"

Hoots and whistles, as a biker rushed over with a pen. A thrill of awareness and fear rushed through her as Jace scribbled a phone number on her open hand.

"Here's my number, sweetheart. Give me a call if you want a nice, long ride all night long." He released her hand, winked at her.

Clenching her fist, she turned and hurried to her car. Behind her, whoops and hollers from Jace's friends.

Jace had been different. Courteous, friendly and never this abusive. Always tender and passionate, and their sex life had been amazing, but never crude or base.

Her entire body went cold. The delight of closing on a major deal turned to bitterness.

She, who never drove fast, pressed her foot on the gas pedal and tore out of the parking lot. She needed to go home, where she'd be safe in her house, her world.

Leaving behind the new, ugly Jace and his world. *I hope I never see you again.*

* * *

It hurt to watch her drive away, see a glint of tears on those perfect cheeks, knowing he'd made her cry. Jace grinned and slapped Lance's back, hating himself. Why the hell did Kara have to show up now, of all times?

But he saw a new expression on Lance's face—respect. Lance admired him because Kara was his ex-girlfriend. *How screwed up is this?*

"Man, she's gorgeous. I saw the way she looked at you, like she couldn't wait to get into bed with you. I bet you five hundred dollars she calls you."

His grin slipped. "She won't."

Not if I can help it. I hope she goes on a business trip and doesn't return until after this assignment ends. I don't want her anywhere near you assholes.

Lance narrowed his gaze. "You never date. You don't have an old lady. What the hell is wrong with you?"

Jace sucked in a breath. Damn. He had to say something, quick. Excuses, excuses…

"You saw her." Jace shrugged. "Nothing compares to Kara. Hard to get over her."

"Huh." Lance slapped his back. "Go after her. Women can't resist bikers. They all secretly want us. But remember, club loyalty comes first. Show up at the den tonight at seven. Have the club rules memorized."

Jace's grin widened. He felt sick to his stomach.

My old man would be proud.

For that, Jace hated himself, hated this assignment. But he was in. Right now, all he wanted to do was race home, jump in the shower and scrub away all his disgust. Get clean.

He knew he could never erase the stain of his past. No matter what.

Chapter 3

Magnolia Shores, Florida
Two months later

This motorcycle was proving to need more repairs than the customer had indicated. Jace picked up a socket wrench. It was Thursday, and the customer wanted the bike by tomorrow for a big trip he'd planned for the weekend.

As a full-fledged member of the Devil's Patrol, Jace had made himself as useful as possible. The club liked his knowledge of bikes and how he had doubled business—legitimate business—at Al's Body Shop, the garage the club owned.

Thanks to his old man, he knew a lot about fixing bikes and cars. Not that Jace ever expected to see his old man again. Hell, he'd hoped as much. Considering Albert Beckett was imprisoned, his wistful thinking was valid.

All his hopes died a quick death when he went to get a part from a shelf and felt a strange prickling at the back of his head.

A warning.

"Hey, you work here?"

He'd know that deep voice, raspy from all those years of smoking, anywhere. The old man wasn't in prison anymore.

Heart hammering against his chest, he waited a minute.

Couldn't show any emotion. No anger. Certainly no fear. Jace nodded but did not turn around.

"Al's Body Shop. They named it after me, you know. I was damn good with fixing things when I was with the Devil's Patrol."

Jace's hand tightened on the wrench he'd grabbed off the shelf. His knuckles whitened. A chill ran down his spine. Knew his past would catch up to him, but did it have to be this soon? Why the hell did his old man have to get paroled early?

He headed back to the bike, keeping his head down.

"Any chance Walt's still around? He used to work here."

Squatting down, Jace pretended to be absorbed in the bike he was repairing. "Not familiar with that name."

"Walt worked here years ago, when this was my garage. I'm Al, like the Al on the sign."

Yeah, I know. The same Al who fought and killed a member of a rival bike gang and left me and Mom to fend for ourselves while you were supposed to rot in prison.

Al wandered closer into the garage. Jace's stomach tightened. Old man wasn't supposed to be in here, only employees, but he acted like he still ran the place. Why couldn't they have kept him locked up and tossed away the key?

"Garage looks good, same as it did when I was here. Some improvements." A deep inhale. "Still the same smell. Love that smell. Miss it. Oil and power."

Jace pulled out the carburetor and examined it, saying nothing.

Al began talking about the bikes he'd fixed, the machines he adored, while sweat trickled down Jace's back, banding in the waistband of his jeans. He wiped his forehead on the sleeve of his shirt.

"You don't talk much."

No kidding. Finally, Jace gritted his teeth. "Can I help you with something?"

"Came here to ask for a job."

"Not hiring now."

Al walked around the bike's other side until he stood directly in front of Jace.

"Who would I talk to about a job around here?"

Jace mumbled something.

"Look at me when I talk to you, son."

Now Jace did look up, the term sending him into a slow boil. *I'm not your son. I ceased being your son the day you killed that biker.*

He stood, wiping his grease-stained hands on a somewhat clean towel. "No work around here. Lance runs the place and he doesn't have any jobs open."

"Huh. You look like you know what you're doing. Experienced. Good for Lance, having you as a mechanic." Al's tone deepened. "Always good for a man to have a trade to fall back on. I always told that to my son. Damn, I haven't seen him in years. Wish I could find him, but I heard his mother moved out west. She probably took him with her."

Now he got a long look at his father. The dark hair, so similar to his own, had been replaced with a shock of iron gray. His cheeks were leaner, and a sense of weariness hung around him like baggy clothing. He looked presentable in clean, somewhat new jeans, a crisp white T-shirt and a denim jacket.

But his blue eyes, an echo of Jace's, held a sadness previously missing, edging out the hardness Al always exhibited.

Prison had done something to his father. Didn't matter. They were finished, and he only wanted the old man gone before he started sniffing out the truth.

"Anything else? I've got to get this bike fixed."

Al gave him a long, thorough look that made Jace squirm internally. Finally, he nodded. "I get it. Old biker like me, and you have no time for me. Got it. No worries. But if you run into Snake or Vic, tell 'em Diesel was here."

His father walked out the open garage bay doors.

Too close. No warning. No time for him to reel in his emotions, pretend he didn't care.

Good thing no one else witnessed this little interaction. Jace blew out an angry breath and saw movement out of the corner of his eye. He headed for the back door, saw a bulky, large figure disappear around the corner. It might have been one of the guys. Or not. Couldn't worry about that now.

At least he'd succeeded in driving away his old man, who hadn't a clue he'd chatted with the son who hadn't seen him since the day Al got hauled off to jail by the cops.

An hour later, he headed to the apartment rented for his undercover assignment. Home never looked so good to him, even though this temporary place was to crash. It was safe from prying, suspicious eyes. Here, in the privacy of this little studio, he could be himself.

As he pulled into his assigned space, he saw Oscar Porter, the neighbor who'd recently moved into an apartment on his floor. Oscar was in his assigned space, putting new wiper blades on his elderly sedan.

The man turned and pushed his glasses up his nose, grinning, as Jace roared into his spot, pushed down the kickstand and switched off the engine.

"Hey, Jace. Wow. I love your bike. Harley, right?"

Jace bit back a smile as he removed his helmet. "Yeah."

As if the bike's insignia wasn't already a clue, but Oscar wasn't bad. Guy kept to himself and didn't cause problems. Not too curious, either, which Jace appreciated after a long day of dodging questions and trying to act the part of some-one he was not.

Someone he'd vowed to never become.

"Great bike," Oscar continued, walking over and giving the motorcycle the same look some men gave an attractive woman. "Mind if I look her over?"

Jace dismounted. "No problem. Just don't touch the chrome."

Oscar whistled as he ran fingers across the hand-tooled leather seat Jace had specially installed. "Custom job, right?"

"Yep."

Oscar's dark brown hair was cropped short and spiky on top. With his button-down shirts, neatly pressed trousers and white socks with black shoes, he might as well carry a pocket calculator.

"You think I could get a bike like that?"

The wistfulness on his face gave Jace pause from reply-ing with the flip answer he'd intended. "Maybe. But you sure you want a motorcycle? Your car suffices. Plus, with the weather down here in Florida, in the summer, you never have to worry about sudden rainstorms."

For a mere few seconds, he saw contempt flicker in the other man's gaze. But the sun was setting in his eyes, so Jace rubbed his face and then put on his sunglasses. Must be a trick of the light.

"Sure. You're right."

Oscar's gaze traveled over Jace's arms and one of the tats inked on his right bicep. "Rise? What does that mean? Like in flour? Or sunrise?"

Jace grinned. "It's a reminder for me to rise above cer-tain things."

In truth, he'd gotten the ink shortly after he and Kara broke up. It served as a bittersweet reminder for him to get up each damn day and face the morning instead of wallowing in self-pity.

Kara had smashed his world when she'd left him. Hated to admit the truth, but though he'd told everyone it was mutual, he truly wanted to stick it out.

Work things out.

"Jace?" Oscar pushed up his glasses again. "Did you hear me? What kind of things?"

"Many things. Like rising above a situation, or a person. Especially in my job. Working with the public can be a bitch, but you can't let it get to you."

Oscar nodded, as if approving. "I get it. I go through the same stuff in my job."

He nodded, his mind elsewhere. Few details with this guy or anyone else. Rule of undercover work—it was best to stick as close to the truth as possible.

"I'm thinking about getting one. They make you look bad."

Jace nodded again. "Well, gotta get upstairs, lots of stuff to do before I go out tonight."

Oscar brightened. "You have a favorite biker bar you hang out at? Maybe I can join you sometime for a beer."

They would eat you up in a minute and spit you out in one sip of domestic beer. And then use their boots to kick out what was left. If anything was left.

"Maybe."

"Great. Thanks, man, really appreciate it."

With a wave, Jace dismissed his neighbor and raced up the steps to his second-floor apartment.

Even someone as innocuous as Oscar could prove dangerous if he learned too much. Best not to trust anyone.

Jace tossed his helmet and sunglasses on the worn sofa and closed his door. It had been a devil of a day, and he rolled his eyes at his own pun. Suddenly exhausted, he plopped onto the sofa and closed his eyes just for a minute.

He dreamed of Kara, her soft smile, her big blue eyes gazing at him with the love she once felt.

And then they clouded with terror as she gazed beyond him. Something yanked her away with extreme force.

Something dark, hidden in the fog suddenly swirling around them.

He saw her fading, her scream ringing in his ears as she vanished from his sight.

TGIF, but not for her. Today was already proving challenging.

On a bed of black velvet, the diamond necklace gleamed beneath the quartz light. Dylan Moore stared at the gems, his eyes huge in his thin face.

"Kara, what do you plan to do with it?"

Kara paused in checking off an item on her to-do list. So much going on at the Willow Wind Estate Sales that her head whirled. "I have a buyer from New York coming next week. He's offering the right price."

"What's the right price?" Dylan frowned as he set down the box on the glass case. "How do you know?"

"You know from research and experience in this business." She gestured to the box. "Off the glass, Dylan. You know the rules. Don't set anything on the display case."

"Sorry." He set the box on the ground. "What's the right price?"

"The diamond necklace is worth about two hundred thousand and he's offering one hundred seventy-five. Cash."

Dylan whistled. "That's a lot of dollar bills. Why the discount?"

"It's too risky for me to keep it here in the store. If I can sell the necklace sooner, I stand to turn a better profit." Kara wiped her forehead after setting down the clipboard.

He glanced around the shop. "You're installing the new security system day after tomorrow, right? Want me to come in early to help?"

Dread shot down her spine as she thought of how vulnerable the store might be, especially with the necklace. She'd purchased a portable safe with a sturdy lock, and planned to hide the safe, but the idea of having such expensive jewelry in her store troubled her.

Even more troubling was that her friend's husband's firm, SOS Security, couldn't guard the diamonds for another three days. Jarrett Adler, owner of SOS, had apologized, but they were short-staffed at the moment.

"No, the men will be here at seven a.m. and you're working hard enough. As a matter of fact, why don't you come in later? The security system is going to take a few hours and there's nothing for you to do until they're finished."

A shadow crossed his face. "Sure."

He probably hoped for overtime. Kara made a mental note to try to give him his monthly bonus early. "What about lunch? You've barely taken a break all morning."

His face dropped. "Not hungry. Besides, you wanted these boxes all moved today."

No lunch again. Dylan had that hungry look, though. Kara inwardly sighed.

Money was tight with nineteen-year-old Dylan. This was his only job. He should be in college. Her cousin had a sharp intelligence and quick learning ability, but Kara knew he saved every penny to help his mother.

Ever since she got cancer and moved from Nevada back here to Florida last year, Wanda Moore had become top priority in Dylan's young life. Kara suspected Bruce, Dylan's stepfather, beat him and her aunt. Dylan remained tight-lipped about it, but she'd seen him sport a few bruises.

Her father, Wanda's brother, gave his sister money for medical expenses and food, but each time he did, Bruce took the money and used it to gamble. Kara worried about her aunt and cousin all the time. Until Wanda willingly left Bruce, her family could do little.

Not for the first time she wondered what would have happened had her brother, Dylan's best friend, lived. Maybe Dylan wouldn't have had emotional problems and his father wouldn't have tossed his hands up in the air and divorced her aunt. Maybe ten years ago Dylan's mom wouldn't have married Bruce, who had a good job, but a violent temper. Maybe they wouldn't have moved to Nevada, where Dylan's stepfather's gambling addiction deepened.

Too many *maybes*. All she could do was offer Dylan that raise and hope it helped.

"All that work on an empty stomach isn't good. I need you energetic, kid." She reached for her phone. "How about sub sandwiches delivered? You deserve a break for all your help. Roast beef on whole wheat with mayo, lettuce and provolone sound good?"

"Cheddar." Dylan's face relaxed. "Kara, you don't have to…"

"But I will." She ordered online and waved her phone. "Done."

Shame flickered in his dark eyes. Kara went to him, put her hands on his thin shoulders. So thin.

"Dylan, you're the hardest worker I have on staff. Treating you to lunch once in a while is a job perk. You will get that raise, I promise, after the diamond sells."

How she wished she could do more, but she also knew his pride. Dylan wouldn't take charity. She considered calling Lacey Adler, her friend who ran a women's shelter, but she had to feel Dylan out on the prospect.

Dylan's phone rang. He answered. "Hey, Mom!"

His expression went from sunny to dark in seconds. Dylan shoved a hand through his hair. "No, Mom, wait, I'll come for you. Don't move. Don't worry, I'll be there in minutes. Mom... Mom...just wait."

He thumbed off the phone. "Kara, sorry, I have to take care of something."

Worried, she nodded. "Need help?"

"No." A line furrowed between his eyebrows. "I've got this."

When the order arrived, she kept his sandwich in the fridge, waiting for him. Two hours later, Dylan returned, sporting a fresh bruise on his cheek.

She found an ice pack and silently handed it to him. Dylan winced and put it against his face.

"Is your mom okay?" she asked gently.

His voice trembled. "She told my stepdad the insurance wouldn't cover chemo for breast chemo and found out he canceled the insurance four months ago. When she questioned him about it, he hit her. He didn't break anything. She'll be okay."

"Dylan, I can pay for her chemo. Please, let me help you and Aunt Wanda, I know people—"

"No! She's my responsibility. I have to get her out of there..."

He turned away, dropping the ice pack on the table. "Thanks."

Kara brought his sandwich from the refrigerator. "I saved this for you. You have to keep up your strength."

Sullen, not looking at her, he nodded his thanks as he devoured the sub. Dylan glanced at her. "Kara, there is something you can do. Can you follow me on my bike to Al's Body Shop after work? I need a tire change."

Kara winced. "I wish you wouldn't ride that bike, Dylan. Cars are safer…"

"My bike isn't any bike. It's a racing bike." His face lit up. Sandwich in hand, he gestured out back. "She's gorgeous and fast and the best thing I have in my life now, Kara. Every time I race her, I can leave the world behind."

Maybe the best way to reach him was through understanding the motorcycle he loved so much. "Tell me about racing. I don't know much about any kind of car or bike racing."

"Cars, that's a different world. When I race my bike on a track, I can go up to two hundred miles an hour. The turns are the trickiest. I have a suit and I bend into the curve, so low I can scrape my knee, so I wear knee sliders."

Kara's stomach roiled at the image he'd painted. Was the biker who crashed into her car twelve years ago going that fast? He'd died on impact. The police investigation said the biker ran a red light as he was escaping a crime scene, but it didn't matter. She had always blamed herself for taking out the car without permission.

She put a hand on his arm. "If your bike means that much to you, let's go now. Then take the rest of the day off."

He brightened. "Thanks!"

Kara understood all about leaving the world behind. She only hoped Dylan wouldn't lose touch with reality so much that he would keep refusing help for a situation that was growing increasingly worse by the day.

On his lunch break from the mechanic shop, Jace went home. He managed to down a slice of cold, leftover pizza and used one of his burner phones to message his boss. Got word the big job moved up to tomorrow night. Planning to knock off a local shop with more than six figures in jewels. Don't know more than that.

The phone rang. He answered with caution. "What?"

"Checking up to see how you're doing." Rafael Jones Rodriguez was his boss and a supervisory special agent in the FBI's southern Florida office.

"They're planning a huge job tomorrow night using the bikes." He blew out a breath. "Rafe, they're using teenagers on crotch rockets for their thefts. Biker named Snake, who did time for armed robbery, knows how to open safes and do quick smash-and-grabs. He and two other Devils ride on the back of the crotch rockets for a quick retreat before the cops arrive."

"They'll go down with the others when we do the raid. Time's not right yet. We want to nail the big boss—Marcus."

"Not these kids, Rafe. These are kids who fell in with the wrong crowd for the wrong thrills. Except for Dylan. Lance bought him a Ducati and this is how he has to pay him back. I hate this. Want to tell them to get the hell out before they land in prison." He thought of Dylan, a nice kid, and not the rough and cocky kids who enjoyed stealing for the thrill.

"Jace, we can offer the kids a deal after all the arrests, but the time isn't right. You have to keep on them. If you nab Lance, he'll lead us to Marcus. There's a plausible domestic terror threat on the table."

"How plausible?"

Rafe's voice tightened. "You hear about that train derailment in northern Florida? Found out today ten tons of ammonium nitrate went missing. Devil's Patrol members were in the same area not long before the derailment. Hell, they might have even caused it to seize the stuff. Chatter has it they plan to do something big."

His blood ran cold. Ammonium nitrate was a fertilizer

terrorists used to make bombs. That amount was enough to blow a city block. The Oklahoma City bomber used only two tons. It was regulated and hard to purchase, but now enough to blow up a city block had gone missing. If the DP planned a terrorist attack, maybe to cover their criminal activities, all they needed was to mix the nitrate with petroleum-based oil and add a blasting cap.

Pow. Major damage. Property destroyed. Innocents killed.

This assignment made him feel like the grime beneath his biker boots. He'd gotten into riding for the freedom and the friends who enjoyed motorcycles as much as he did.

But with this new threat, he felt a grim conviction to do whatever necessary to nail the bastards.

Rafe interrupted his thoughts. "Any leads on Marcus? Anything?"

He plopped onto the sagging sofa and rubbed his forehead. The studio apartment, necessary for his undercover gig, was decorated with used furniture, a far cry from his one-bedroom condo in a respectable community.

"All I've heard is Marcus is shifting his attention to something big that's personal and he needs quick cash. Lance is focusing on making one big score with these kids, and after, lying low. He's planning a trip to New York to sell the jewels from the last theft."

"What are your plans, Jace?"

"We have church tomorrow night," he said, indicating a meeting of the Devil's Patrol. "The kids will be there for Lance's orders to pull off this heist. Might get some intel at that point."

The gang liked him. Most of them, anyway. Called him Gator for killing a gator with his bowie knife and then grilling said gator at a BBQ. They liked that he could repair their bikes and trusted him up to a point. But still, he hadn't cracked open the inner circle with Big Mike and Lance, and had discovered only a little about the group of young thieves Lance recruited over the past three months to steal for him.

He thought for a moment. "There has to be another reason you called, Rafe. What's wrong?" His fingers tightened on the phone. Being deep undercover meant little contact with anyone from his normal world.

"Is it my mom? Stepdad? I haven't talked to them in months." Not that she'd worry about him. His mother hadn't bothered to check on him in a long time. All contact was made by Jace, and his mother was always too busy for dialogue. Naw, it was more one-sided, telling him her latest shopping spree and never asking how Jace was doing.

Still, he couldn't help but hope she cared a little...

"Far as I know, they're fine. But I got word of someone else." Rafe's voice lowered. "Your father was released from prison. He finally got parole. Soon as I found out, I contacted his parole officer. Your father wants to see you."

Jace closed his eyes. Swore. "Too late. He already did."

Now it was Rafe's turn to swear. "Jace, do you need to come in?"

"No. He didn't recognize me. At least I doubt he did. Hell, I barely recognized him. I haven't seen my old man in fifteen years. Not going to start socializing with him now."

"I know." Rafe's voice sounded soothing. "Sorry I couldn't get you a heads-up earlier."

"You mean in case he takes up with this chapter, or another one, of the DP? Damn." Jace rubbed a hand over his beard. Laughed. "He had to get paroled *now*, of all times? Couldn't they keep him locked up for a few more years?"

"Parole officer says he really did a one-eighty in prison. Taught other inmates auto and motorcycle repair."

"Yeah, he was always good at that. Taught me." The irony

wasn't lost on Jace. The same skillset had gained him respect and entry into the DP.

"He had to give an address to his parole officer. I'm keeping tabs on him, just in case he decides to return to his old haunts."

"Right. Where is he living now?"

A moment's hesitation. "Why do you want to know?"

"Where is he, Rafe?"

"Jace, you can't risk seeing him again. You'll blow your cover."

"Let me worry about that." Then, because he and Rafe were good friends and he didn't want him worrying, he added, "I have no intention of visiting. I didn't visit in prison, not going to start now. Now, where the hell is my old man?"

"He's in town. That's all I can tell you. That and he's changed. Let it go, Jace."

"Trust me, he's still the same asshole he always was."

"Need to tell you… I have a CI on the case as well, with instructions to keep an eye on your father in case he wants to rejoin the Devil's Patrol."

Interesting. "Who's the confidential informant?"

"You know I can't tell you."

He knew, but at least Rafe told him there was a CI. To protect an informant's identity, the FBI assigned the person classified numbers. As the CI's handler, only Rafe would know that number…and the person's true identity.

"Whoever it is, tell them to watch the old man. He's slick. Gotta go."

Glancing at the clock and realizing he needed to return to work, Jace stared at his cell phone and thumbed through the contacts until finding it.

Mom.

Seeing his old man had made the painful past rush back

in a flood. His father was right in that his mother, Al's ex-wife, had moved away. But she hadn't taken Jace with her. Nope, he'd been in the Army by then, in boot camp.

He hesitated. She might ask questions. Where Jace was, what he was doing. Maybe even worry about him. He only needed to reassure her he was on a big assignment and could take care of himself.

Jace hit the button. Deep inside, he had a tiny hope she might express concern. Maybe she might care.

This time.

"Hello?"

"Hey, Mom. It's me."

"Stephen? Is everything all right at school?"

Jace's throat tightened. "No, Mom, it's your other son. You know, the firstborn son. Jason."

"Jason. Oh, my. I thought you were Stephen and calling about your bank account again to borrow more money. That boy goes through his allowance for school like money grows on trees." A throaty laugh.

"I don't need money. I called to say hi," he said. "I thought you'd like to know… I mean, just in case if you don't hear from me… I'm working on this special assignment…"

"Oh, yes, that's right. You're home on leave now from the Army."

Jace closed his eyes. He hadn't been in the Army in years. He'd gone to college after, on his own dime and the government's. His mother knew he held a government job now. But it hadn't registered. "No, I'm working in Florida on something important…"

"Oh. Well, have fun. I have to go. The Maxwells are throwing a big party and I can't decide if I should wear the blue dress with my black heels or the black dress."

"Mom…"

She hung up. Gripping the phone so tight his palm hurt, Jace stared at the wall. Mom hadn't changed. Didn't give a damn. Didn't ask how her firstborn son and heir was doing, nope. For all she knew, he could be dead in a ditch and her biggest worry would remain what to wear to his freaking funeral.

The only real mother he got to know was Kara's mom, Claudia, who treated him like family. Welcomed him, fussed over him, made him feel accepted and cherished.

Strange how he loved his ex's mother and father more than his own dysfunctional family. He rubbed the back of his neck. Kara had always asked about his family. Even gently badgered him because she'd wanted to meet them. But he'd been too ashamed.

Add that to yet another reason they'd broken up.

Then there was dear old Dad…

For a minute he got lost in the past, back when he was a teenager and he'd wanted to be so much like his dad. Wanted his respect at any cost.

The wake-up call was a hard life lesson. Fast and furious. Following his old man to that biker bar, itching at fifteen to be just like him. Maybe have a beer, trade rough talk with the guys about girls.

Even though he'd barely kissed a girl. Too shy.

Jace closed his eyes, remembering sneaking into the club, seeing his old man and another biker have at it, the fists flying, the sharp explosion of gunfire…the metallic smell of blood slicking the floor, a wide-eyed gaze staring at the ceiling.

Soon after, his father went to prison and his mother divorced him.

Two years later, he enlisted and never looked back.

But he never forgot that day. It fueled him, gave him purpose all the times in his life when he wanted to quit.

Never be like your old man. Family wasn't anything to him anymore. He had no real family.

With a strangled curse, he threw his phone at the sofa. Screw family and screw the past.

He needed to get the information and get out from under this gang. Deliver justice by doing his job and keep the public safe from these rat bastards. That was more important than his terrible family.

Before someone ratted *him* out and he turned into a cold corpse lying out in the Everglades.

Chapter 4

After closing the shop, Kara followed Dylan's bright red motorcycle at a snail's pace to an industrial district. Warehouses crowded the streets, block after block. At the end of one road, he turned and entered a yard ringed by a chainlink fence with barbed wire atop it. The sign above the garage read Al's Body Shop. Oily smells of grease and gasoline filled the air, a far cry from the light floral scent filtering through her store. Kara parked near a row of motorcycles as Dylan wheeled his bike into the garage. Inside, a mechanic with shoulder-length dark hair, wearing a white sleeveless T-shirt and stained jeans, worked on a motorcycle. No one else was around.

She took a minute to admire the way the mechanic's muscles bunched as he worked. The back of his shirt was damp with sweat. Bad boys and mechanics were never her style, but this man exuded a base sexuality in his movements even she couldn't resist.

Now, if you were into repairing sedans instead of motorcycles... She almost laughed. Who was she kidding?

"Hey, Gator! Can you change out my tires?" Dylan asked, parking the bike near the mechanic.

"Give me a minute," the man grumbled.

Her nose wrinkled as she sidestepped tools lying on the

garage floor, her heels almost getting caught in a large socket wrench.

"Gator, can you change out the tires now? I need the bike for the big job tomorrow night…" His voice trailed off and he refused to look at Kara.

Alarm filled her. She'd heard from two other jewelers how someone had broken into their shops, taking only a few pieces, but the most expensive ones. The security cameras had been disabled with black spray paint, but one hadn't been covered enough in the last burglary and showed someone speeding off on a racing motorcycle.

Police suspected a gang of motorcycle thieves on fast bikes. In, out and away before law enforcement could arrive.

Surely, Dylan couldn't be involved in this gang?

She regarded Dylan with a severe look. "Dylan, if you need transportation for work, I can drive you."

"No, it's okay, you're busy and I won't bother you. You've already done enough. I'm going out with the guys for something. Bikers only." Still, he refused to look directly at her.

Kara's stomach roiled. Now she was certain Dylan was involved in something shady. Tempted to haul him away and lock him up until after tomorrow night, she started to speak when the mechanic finally sat up and turned toward them. She gasped.

Jace Beckett. Again.

She gave him a cool look that belied the tiny muscles in her stomach jumping. His hair was much longer, tied back in a ponytail that made him look even sexier than usual, and he sported a well-trimmed beard. Grease stained the front of his white sleeveless T-shirt. As far as appearances went, he'd done a total one-eighty from when he was her ex-boyfriend, with close-cropped hair and business suits, and preferred pushing papers.

Yet his blue gaze remained the same—warm, friendly and filled with sexual interest, which faded as he recognized her.

"Jace," she said tightly.

"Well, if it isn't the little lady from the Tiki Bar. Hello, Kara. Change your mind about that ride I promised?" he drawled, sounding and looking more like a cliché.

Fury filled her. Kara started to think of ways to berate him, tell him she was glad they broke up, when he narrowed his eyes at her, shook his head ever so slightly.

As if in warning.

Clamping down on her bottom lip, she glared instead. Impossible to know what was going on, but for now, in front of Dylan, she'd play along.

Dylan gave her a puzzled look. "Kara, you know Gator?"

"No. I don't know a Gator." She folded her arms across her chest. "But I do know Jace—"

"Brown," he said, interrupting her. "Jace Brown."

"Brown," she said slowly, totally confused.

Jace's gaze flicked to her. "I changed my name after my father got into some trouble."

Kara frowned, then turned to Dylan. "We used to…date."

Saying they dated hurt less than admitting their relationship had been a major failure.

Her cousin looked at Jace. "Wow."

Jace clapped Dylan on the back. "Don't worry, I won't hold your relationship with my ex against you."

Dylan cleared his throat. "Gator, I need this bike by tomorrow. Can you stop what you're doing and check it out, make sure it's in top-notch condition?" Dylan's face had a stubborn look she recognized.

Jace wiped his dirty hands on an equally dirty rag. "Dylan, maybe you should sit this one out. Bike may have some wear on it, and even if I keep it overnight it may need parts I don't have here…"

"No. Just check it over, 'kay? Text me when it's done."

Jace kept rubbing his hands with the rag. His deep blue gaze met Kara's. "So, how about it? I'm still available for a good time. I'll even go slow for you."

She scowled, then looked around the garage cluttered with equipment, cars and motorcycles. Dylan wandered off to examine a sleek yellow motorcycle with gleaming chrome.

Kara lowered her voice. "Can you afford it?"

His cheeky grin didn't annoy her as much as it had in the past. "I can afford the gas and the time, sweetheart. Just not tomorrow night."

"Jace, what happened to you? What do you mean, your father got into trouble?"

"Nothing for you to worry about."

"Is that why you changed so much? You had a great job with a good company in investments…"

Now, it was his turn to scowl. "Stop talking about my past. That's my business, okay?"

"But this place…" Her nose wrinkled. "Nothing wrong with being a mechanic, but you had a career with that firm, and seeing you like this… Do you need money?"

His eyes widened. "Kara, I'm fine for money."

She thought about the way they'd broken up, in a hurry, and he'd left for DC, while she had an important meeting with a client. Kara made a prompt decision.

"Are you busy tonight? Can we meet someplace and talk?"

He blinked, and a guarded look came over him.

"Why?"

"I need to talk to you. But not here, in front of him." She indicated her head.

"Earl's Place. I get off here at six and can meet you there at six thirty."

"Restaurant?"

Jace gave her one of his familiar, long, cool looks. "Bar. Beer and pretzels."

On his limited salary, probably more to his taste. "Fine. I don't have your cell. I deleted you from my contacts."

No emotion on his face. Jace rattled off a phone number, which she entered into her contacts, then she shot him off a brief message.

Tonight, Earl's Place. 6:30. Meet me.

Kara turned to Dylan. "Ready?"

"Yeah." The teenager shook his head. "Nice bike. How much, Jace?"

"It's been sold." Jace's gaze never left her. "Bikes like that are a lot of money, kid."

"Come on, Dylan. I'll drop you off. I can pick you up tomorrow and give you a ride here when your bike is ready."

"No need. I'll have one of the guys drop me off when Jace tells me the bike is finished."

Kara put a hand on his too-thin shoulder. "If you're sure, Dylan. But I wish you'd let me help you."

He shrugged off her hand. "I'm fine. Let's go. I know you have a lot of work."

Giving Jace another glance, seeing the indifference on his handsome face turn to worry, only raised more questions in her mind.

What was Jace involved with and how low had he sunk?

Jace threw down the towel, cussing up a blue streak. Kara, again! She looked as classy as ever in her yellow sleeveless dress—designer, of course—and those black high heels.

Long blond hair bound in a twist at the back. Elegant. She stood out in the dirty garage like a snowflake on a coal heap.

He'd fought every impulse to escort her out of the garage and tell her to get lost and never come back. What if one of the guys had seen her?

She needed to stay out of his life for good. But now, she was around Dylan. And she wanted to meet up with Jace tonight. About what?

The old feelings were still there for him. He hoped like hell Kara didn't want to rekindle their relationship. He'd asked her to marry him, slid a ring onto her finger with a one-carat diamond and a week later, they were finished.

They'd moved on. Why did she have to return to his life now, of all times? He needed to get rid of her.

Kara and Dylan. Bad combination. Did she realize the kid was into stealing from jewelry stores? Did she know he courted trouble and stood on the verge of arrest?

He focused on fixing the motorcycle he needed to repair before tomorrow. The smells of grease and oil lingered in the air, along with the delicate trace of Kara's perfume. Something light and floral. Not heavy. He remembered breathing it in as he'd nuzzled her neck with long, sweeping kisses that made her tremble in his arms…

His hand slipped on the wrench and he cursed another blue streak.

For an hour, he worked steadily on the bike until something made him glance up.

Big Mike stood at the garage entrance, silhouetted by the bright sunlight outside.

Not a social call, either. Jace could tell. Mike seldom visited the garage except when his own bike needed repairs.

This wasn't good. The garage floor seemed to quake beneath the tread of Big Mike's boots as the barrel-chested biker strode forward. He wasn't happy. And not about the condition of the bike Jace was working on right now.

Jace set down the socket wrench, trying to ignore the little hairs on his arms and the back of his neck saluting the air. Mike stood six feet, four inches tall and outweighed Jace by at least one hundred pounds.

He can turn me into dog food. Show no fear.

Too much had been invested in this assignment. He was closer to nailing the guy at the top of the food chain. Couldn't blow it now.

"What's up, big dog?" he asked Mike.

The man scowled. "I saw you talking with Diesel earlier. He just got released. How the hell do you know him?"

A bead of sweat trickled down Jace's back, nudged itself into the waistband of his jeans. He shrugged. "Fellow biker, just chatting. Guy told me he was imprisoned. He wanted to know a cheap place to rent."

Not a lie, but not the full truth, either.

My own father didn't know me. Thank You, sweet Lord.

At Big Mike's silence, he broke his own rule to never offer more information than necessary. The biker's scowl hadn't lessened.

"Diesel told me he used to go on runs with the DP. I think he was looking for work. He told me his name was Al and the garage was named after him. You think I should avoid the guy?"

He made his voice flattering and subservient, eager as a puppy wanting to please his owner for treats. *Here's a good boy.*

Big Mike's expression didn't change. "Stay away from Diesel."

Jace saluted him with the wrench. "No problem."

My pleasure, dickwad. I have no intention of seeing dear old Dad again.

As Jace squatted down to the floor again, the other man added, "There's something about you I don't trust. You smell all wrong, Gator. Like trouble. Big trouble. You're not telling us everything."

"Sure I am, man." Jace kept his voice steady. "What do I have to hide?"

"I've been watching you," Big Mike said, squatting down and coming inches from Jace's face. "And I gotta say, I don't think you're who you say you are. You act funny."

Think of a way to defuse the situation. "Funny ha ha?"

"Don't mess around with me, Gator." Big Mike narrowed his eyes. "You've been acting weird. Asking too many questions. I don't like how you're getting close to Lance. Not when you're acting as if you have something to hide."

Jace felt real alarm. He had to think fast. "Yeah, I get it. You're right. I do have something to hide."

Big Mike stood and stared him down. Jace stared back and stood, flexing his arms. "The something I have to hide is that girl you saw at the Tiki Bar two months ago. Her name's Kara. I finally got her interested again. I don't want Lance or anyone sniffing around her, disrupting my plans to get laid." He narrowed his eyes. "Got it?"

"Kara," the biker said slowly.

Jace whipped out his cell, showed Mike the screen and Kara's text asking him to meet at the bar. "I've got her interested and it's just a matter of sweet-talking until I score again. She was a real sweet piece and I'm in the mood for quick loving. So back off."

He hated making Kara sound like a cheap thrill, but he had to stick to his cover.

Big Mike studied the text as if trying to puzzle out a passage from *War and Peace* in the original Russian. "A girl." He shook his head and handed Jace back the phone. "Gator, you have to stop thinking with your little brain because it will get you in trouble."

He offered a full-wattage grin as he pocketed the phone. "Nah. I've handled her before and the sex was amazing. That's it."

"It had better be. Your first loyalty is to us and not a woman. Get it?"

As he nodded, the other biker gave him a long look. "Just make sure you keep your business in her and she stays out of our business."

"No problem."

Big Mike's cell rang. He answered, frowned. "No, I don't think we have that ready… Okay, okay, let me check. Call you right back."

The biker carried his cell phone over to the shelves. He started searching and cursed. Seldom had Jace seen the steely-tempered biker so rattled. "Dammit, it has to be here some-place."

After setting down his phone, the man rummaged through the mess on the table. "Gator, you have to clean up this crap. I can't find anything. Where the hell is the stuff I ordered last week?"

Jace waved his wrench. "Outside. Got a huge shipment earlier, and the boxes still have to be unpacked. Planned to tackle them soon as I get this baby fixed. There's a few of them. Help yourself to looking."

Maybe if he got lucky, Mike would walk outside and he'd overhear some good intel.

His luck held. Big Mike not only walked out to inspect the new shipment, he also left his cell phone on the table. Guy was truly rattled.

After sprinting over to the table, keeping one eye on the back door Mike had walked through, Jace glanced at his phone. Using his own phone's stylus to avoid leaving prints, he quickly scrolled through Mike's recent texts. Someone named PrisonerXYZ told Mike to stand by.

No time to investigate further. Jace left the phone as it was and pocketed the stylus. He bolted back to the bike and returned to fixing it. A minute later, Mike returned, grabbed his phone. Jace glanced up.

"Problem?" Jace asked.

"None of your business."

As Big Mike lumbered off, Jace let out a long sigh of relief, but he knew he couldn't let his guard down. He was in deep with this gang, and he knew that any slipup could cost him his life. He was going to have to be more careful than ever.

Especially with Kara.

The job Dylan and the other kids had planned for tomorrow night sounded like Kara's store. He'd overheard Dylan talking about how his employer planned to upgrade security tomorrow, so they had to move tonight. But, hell, he never imagined Dylan worked for Kara.

He needed to warn her, subtly, to stay home tomorrow night, so if they did knock it off, she'd be safe.

For her sake, and his, he hoped he'd heard wrong about the gang's plans to burglarize Kara's shop. Because if Dylan and his pals dared to rip off Kara, she wouldn't take it lightly. He knew his ex and her courage and determination.

He had to dissuade her from being in the vicinity tomorrow night. She would come storming after Dylan with a vengeance, not hesitating to go the clubhouse and confront Dylan in person.

And run straight into danger, risking more than losing her jewelry.

She could lose her life.

Chapter 5

Earl's Place was a dark, rectangular building with a flickering red neon sign that had seen better days.

As she entered the parking lot, two motorcycles drew up. Most of the spaces were taken up by motorcycles, from huge Harleys to smaller ones, like the racing bike Dylan owned. Music filtered out of the door as two bikers opened it.

She drove around to find a space in the back, saw an outdoor area with a makeshift bar surrounded by leather sofas and bikers lounging on them. One biker had a hound dog stretched out on the sofa. The dog stretched and yawned, making her smile. The vibe was friendly, and her shoulders lost some of their rigid tension. The music sounded lively, lyrical, and she caught the sound of an acoustic guitar.

She hoped Jace was inside. The sooner she got this over with, the better.

Kara took a deep breath and entered the bar. She stood at the entrance, trying to adjust to the darkness. A string of Christmas lights hung from the back of the liquor shelves, adding a festive touch. She studied the unique decorations on the wall—motorcycle parts, an antique bicycle wheel, even a plastic doll dressed in leather.

No one turned to stare at her. The patrons were too busy talking or listening to the band in the back of the bar. Standing in the dim light to adjust to her surroundings, she saw Jace at the bar. An empty stool was beside him.

Jace waved a beer bottle at her. She joined him, glancing at the crowded bar.

"Have a seat, babe."

The familiar, loving nickname from the past caused butterflies in her stomach, the same way as it used to do when he uttered it. A memory fluttered in her mind—that time they made love as soon as she'd walked through the condo door. He couldn't wait to kiss her, breathe her in as if she was oxygen and he was gasping for air.

"Babe, you're the only sweetness in my life right now," he'd said roughly, pulling to her to him. "I am having a bitch of a time with my latest assignment. You're my reason for getting through each day."

She had given him everything he'd needed, and fulfilled her own needs as well, for she had spent every waking moment anticipating seeing him again…

A lump formed in her throat. Kara swallowed past it. "Jace." Her tone was formal and stiff, belying the feelings inside her. "I was hoping for a table with a little more privacy. A table where we can talk without being overheard."

His smile dropped as a guarded look came over him. "Sure."

He dropped a few bills on the counter, then beckoned to a bartender. "Sam, I'm headed to the booth in the corner."

As they started for the empty booth far away from the band, he added, "Sam owns the place. Great guy."

"The sign says Earl's Place."

"Earl's his hound dog. Earl runs everything." Jace grinned.

As they sat, she wondered how to deal with him. Conversation had never been difficult with Jace. She'd always felt free to discuss anything with him. He'd been an honest, ethical man with a courteous manner and generous attitude, treating her as if she was priceless. She had truly loved him and thought he loved her with the same passion.

Kara set down her purse and gazed at him. "Any reason why you changed your last name?"

A slight lift of those broad shoulders. "Needed to escape from the past. Thanks for keeping that on the DL from Dylan, by the way. My brothers in the club don't know, either, and I'd like to keep it that way. Fresh start, so to speak."

Sensing a story there, she wanted to know more. "No worries on keeping it on the down-low, Jace, but I'm curious. What have you been doing since we broke up? Other than joining a notorious biker gang and working as a mechanic. Any new hobbies, like goat yoga? Gardening? Scrapbooking?"

His mouth quirked and amusement danced in his blue eyes. "I forgot your delightful sense of sarcastic humor. Nope. My job and the guys in the club keep me busy."

"Too busy to date?" Kara bit her lip. Hadn't meant to let that out, but she itched to know.

He blinked. "Yeah, I've dated, but no one now. Some women who wanted more than I did."

"Situationships," she said, guessing. "Those relationships that are more than friends with benefits, but one-sided."

"Situationship." He grinned and she gave a little laugh. "Guess you've been in one or two as well."

"Caught me." Her smile dropped. Her "situationships" weren't merely with guys who liked having sex with her, and were more emotionally committed than her. Kara enjoyed their company, but something kept holding her back from further commitment.

Not that she'd admit to Jace it was memories of how good they'd had it that put the brakes on moving ahead with another man.

He gave her a long, thoughtful look. "They always wanted more and I didn't, so I had to break it off gently. No hurt feelings."

Tempted to ask why he didn't want more, she bit her lip. Too tempting to find out if Jace had felt the same way she did—unable to move forward, still caught in the past and how they had loved each other.

"What about you, Kara? Store doing well? Dylan says he enjoys working for you and you've cultivated quite the reputation in town for estate sales."

A waitress in black pants and a form-fitting black T-shirt appeared. "What do you want, Jace? Sam told me to take extra special care with you as thanks for fixing his bike last week."

He ordered a beer and glanced at her. "Another beer. And get her whatever she's having. Gin and tonic, Kara?"

"Just the tonic," Kara replied. "I never drink and drive."

As the waitress walked off, he blinked. "I forgot about that. You always were so careful on the road. More than the average person."

As she relaxed with the praise, her ego deflated as he added, "Driving like you were eighty-three instead of twenty-three. I swear it was a miracle you got to work in less than eight hours."

Kara gritted her teeth. "I didn't come here to be insulted, Jace."

He leaned back against the wall. "Why did you come here?"

She glanced around. Satisfied no one was watching them, Kara dug the last reminder of their relationship out of her purse. "To give you this."

Jace's jaw dropped at sight of the diamond ring on the table. He took it, the light from the little lamp at the table winking in the stone. Emotion clogged her throat as she remembered the day he'd proposed at the beach, on one knee, the lacy waves swirling at their feet.

"What the hell…"

"I never did return it to you, obviously." She struggled for a reason why, and settled on the truth. "I really didn't want to see you again. But I figure you could use it now."

"Use it? You know something I don't? Am I getting married to someone else?"

The thought of him marrying someone else made her heart lurch. Kara had always envisioned their wedding day—Jace standing at the altar, looking resplendent in a silk tuxedo and a wide smile as she swept down the aisle toward him, clad in her mother's wedding dress.

The dream died, but still haunted her once in a while. When it did, she usually threw herself even more into work.

"No. Your life is your business. I thought…I just thought…" Kara bit her lip and finally looked at his face. "It cost a lot of money and you can pawn it."

He stared at her for a full moment and then began to laugh. "You think I need money. Because I'm working in a garage."

"You had an amazing job on the ground floor with a well-known investment firm, Jace. You could have fast-tracked to real financial success… You were never the outlaw biker type. What happened?"

He scowled, his expression turning stormy beneath the well-trimmed beard. "Stop. Stop it. My past is my past. I have my reasons for what I'm doing and they're none of your business."

Jace reached out, took her hand. His fingers were calloused, but warm, and the touch sent an anticipatory shiver down her spine. Just like in the past, when he'd hold her hand and she'd gone warm inside from the contact.

Gently, he turned over her palm and placed the ring into it, and closed her fingers.

"When I gave you the engagement ring, I told you it was yours. Keep it."

Jace sat back, his expression inscrutable.

The transformation was too great to ignore, but he'd made it clear she had no right to ask questions. Kara placed the ring back into her purse. "I apologize if I insulted you. You're right. It is your life and I have no part in it anymore. I just…"

"You just what, Kara? You didn't come here merely to drop off an engagement ring. Why are…"

The arrival of their drinks cut him off. Jace nodded his thanks at the waitress, raised his bottle.

"To the past and what we had once."

Kara didn't lift her glass. "I can't toast that, Jace. It's too painful."

"And you want to be here, with me, because you like pain? You could have called and told me over the phone, Kara, instead of ripping the scab off the wound."

His anger was justified. Kara wrapped her hands around her glass. "No. I didn't intend to insult you. I never wanted… Please believe me, I just thought you should have it back…"

So much for good intentions. After priding herself on being good at reading people, she'd totally underestimated him. This. What they'd had between us.

Kara's voice broke. "I'm sorry, Jace. I'm sorry for what happened with us and if I hurt you."

Anger faded from his expression. "It's not your fault."

"It takes two to break up, Jace. It wasn't you. Or me. It was both of us."

Too upset to continue, she sipped the tonic water the waitress had brought over, the cool liquid sliding down her tight throat.

He sighed. "I'm sorry we had to break up, too, Kara. And if I did anything to hurt you as well."

"What happened to us, Jace?"

Anger died on his face. He rubbed his beard. "I don't know. Things change, Kara. Or don't."

"It was the motorcycles, wasn't it? They meant more to you than me and I resented you for it."

His expression became guarded. "They didn't mean more to me, Kara. But your demands that I sell my bike and stop riding were unreasonable. You knew how much I enjoy my motorcycle."

"They're dangerous." She didn't want to argue but had to press the point. "Jace, I worried constantly about you when you took it out. If you'd skid from an oil slick on the road, or someone would turn in front of you because they didn't see you…"

She couldn't voice the real fear still lurking deep inside. *If you get into an accident and get killed like my little brother did.*

He took a long gulp of beer, set down the bottle. "Kara, I told you. I'm careful. Always careful. I never set out to ride in the rain or bad weather. I gave up some runs so we could be together, and do other things. I asked you to go with me, understand this was something I loved, a lifestyle that was only part of my life, one you knew about when we first met, but you refused."

Kara sighed. "I never understood your love for motorcycles."

His gaze grew dreamy, and distant. "I tried to tell you what it was like. It's more than the freedom of riding. It's the sound of a V-twin engine blowing out that classic Harley rumble for everyone to hear. Feeling the bike surge beneath you, pure power. The outdoors is clean and fresh and in your face."

Kara had to smile. "And the bugs in your teeth."

He grinned. "Which is why my helmet has a visor. But that's a small inconvenience compared to the feel of a bike beneath you, and everything opening up in a way you can't feel when you're stuck in a car. Taking the turns on a long country road, the ultimate feel of being outside, like you're flying."

For a moment, she felt wistful, wishing she could join him in this bliss he described. Then she recalled the horror of her accident, the screams and the stillness…

"Your bike seemed more important than I did, Jace."

He shook his head. "No, it wasn't. But you kept hoping I'd give it up. It was like you hoped I would change to suit your needs."

"I didn't want you to change. Only give up the bike. Everything else was fine."

The deep timbre of his laugh had once enchanted her. Now, it carried a note of bitterness.

"Give up the bike. If that isn't change, what is? You've got a strange idea of change, Kara."

Her fingers curled around the cold glass. "You know how I felt about your rides, Jace. You spent more time with your bike than me."

Blue frost. His eyes became colder than a winter's day in Michigan. Kara felt the chill down to her manicured toenails.

"I spent time on weekends on runs because you were so busy with your social calendar. This gala for Mothers Against Drunk Driving. That gala for that charity you insisted on chairing. All those charity balls and charity work. It got to the point where I had to pencil myself into your schedule, dammit."

She struggled with her rising temper. Jace had no clue she'd thrown herself into charity work to make up for what happened to her brother. Teens Advocating Safe Roads, TASR, was the principal charity she supported. When the board of directors asked her to join, she eagerly responded and threw herself into fundraising work in what little spare time she had.

It meant less time for Jace, but the work eased her guilty conscience—a conscience that couldn't talk about the accident to anyone but her therapist. Jace had no clue about her past.

Maybe if I had joined TASR when I was seventeen, Conner would still be alive and so would that biker.

"It wasn't only the bike, Jace. It was the secrets you kept. You were always honest and open with me about everything except your family. You kept being evasive when I wanted to meet them…"

His gaze darted away. "I told you, my dad was dead and my mother moved away."

"To where? The Artic? I would have gladly hopped on a plane to meet her, but you kept shutting me down."

Now, he did look at her. "You shut me down as well, Kara. That time when I joked with you over dinner about us being only children? I don't know why your mother got up from the table, or why you changed the subject. What gives?"

Guilt filled her. She never had the strength to admit to Jace what happened with Conner. Sometimes her family found it easier to pretend he never existed, rather than that he would never return to them.

Once more, she evaded the question and changed the topic.

"There were problems we couldn't seem to resolve, Jace. I was into my society functions, but I gave up some of my functions to be with you. I would have done more, but you made it clear your bike was too important."

"It wasn't but, dammit, you never even wanted to try riding with me. Not even to the grocery store. You shied away from my bike as if it were poison." He threw back his head and stared at the ceiling, where photos of motorcycles had been plastered there among the tiles.

"You never understood the freedom, the joy I got in riding. You never wanted to understand. You only condemned my love of motorcycles as if I were a member of a criminal gang."

She gave him a pointed look. "And now?"

Jace shook his head. "What if I asked you to give up your estate-sale business? Or your love of seafood? Or how much you enjoy the ballet?"

"The ballet never killed anyone," she blurted. "And you know my business isn't my life. I had to make it into my life after we broke up because everything became so empty."

Oh, dear. She hadn't meant to confess that. Give him a nugget of power over her, let him know how deeply she'd been hurt by their separation.

But instead of him gloating or looking as if she'd empowered him, Jace's expression filled with regret.

"Maybe if we'd had this discussion earlier, before we broke up, things would have been different."

"We can't return to what we were, what we had. In any case, you've changed for good, Jace. Now look at you." She glanced around the bar. "You've changed. Gave up a promising career path to be a biker. I don't understand you. You didn't flirt with the lifestyle. You married it."

He wasn't paying attention to her, his sharp gaze centered on the bar's entrance. Suddenly, he reached over, clasped her hand and raised his voice. "Kara, sweetheart, you're killing me. All I want is one date. Is that too much to ask? You agreed to meet me here, giving me hope. Give me a chance. I'll make it a night to remember like we once had."

Kara reeled back but did not tug her hand away. Jace made

no sense. One minute they were having a conversation about breaking up and now, he acted smitten with her...

Her gaze flicked over to a few rough-looking bikers who'd entered the bar and headed for the counter. Even in the smoky darkness, she could clearly see them study Jace.

His friends. She recognized them from the parking lot. Utterly disgusted, she started to pull away when Jace shot her a warning look. "Don't," he said quietly. "Play along with me. Please."

She didn't understand, and wanted to get up and head outside, erasing him forever from her life. But something in his eyes nudged her into trusting him.

You owe me for this, Jace.

Kara leaned forward as if absorbed in his every move, every nuance of his soft expression. "A night to remember sounds like a night I can't pass up. Very well. But you'd better make it worth my while, because I'm a busy woman."

"I'll keep you busy all night if you clear your schedule for me," he said in a teasing tone.

A small smile touched her mouth. How well she remembered their times together like this, when they'd both been absorbed in their work and would meet for a quick drink at a favorite waterfront restaurant bar and flirt as if never seeing each other before.

It kept the magic of their romance alive.

It wasn't enough to keep their relationship alive.

"Let me know if you can make it."

He winked at her, and then, reflecting the Jace she remembered well, he lifted her hand to his mouth and kissed it. His lips were firm, warm, and a shiver raced through her. How much she'd enjoyed his kisses and missed their long, intense lovemaking.

Focus, Kara. Giving him a smile, she tugged away her

hand, slipped her cross-body purse over one shoulder and slid out of the booth. Her heels clicked on the ancient wooden floor as she headed for the exit, aware of Jace's new friends eyeing her as she strode forward. Staring at the door, her heart thumping as hard as the beat of the drums from the band, she gathered all her courage and confidence.

Now, she knew what it felt like to be a deer studied by hungry wolves. She reached the door, and a man standing nearby opened it for her. Kara thanked him with a smile and slid out into the dark night.

Not relaxing until she was behind the wheel, she barely managed to start her sedan. Kara inhaled a deep breath again. Good thoughts. *Remember the first time you met Jace at that cocktail mixer, and the light in his eyes as you talked about how much you adored traveling in Rome and Greece, and meeting different people and learning about different cultures?*

Deep breaths.

Finally, she managed to start the car. Kara drove quickly out of the crowded parking lot.

At a red light, she drew in another deep breath. That had to be the strangest conversation she'd had with Jace. What was he involved in with these bikers?

Her phone pinged a message. Kara glanced at it. Jace.

Hey, sweetheart, I promise you will have a great time with me. Give me a chance.

Frowning, she set down the phone. Not worth answering.

I don't know what kind of mind game you're playing Jace, but I'm not interested.

Yet she couldn't help but wonder if something else was going on here. Something odd and definitely more dangerous.

Chapter 6

The next morning, Kara couldn't shake the feeling something bad would soon happen. The meeting last night with Jace had brought up all kinds of mixed feelings. Regret that they had broken it off badly. Wistfulness for what they'd lost. Anger he'd changed into a motorcycle fanatic and joined a gang.

Most disturbing was the desire he still managed to kindle inside her, the feeling of being alive and excited about life again.

Forget Jace. She had bigger worries.

A twinge of guilt shot through her. Although it was Saturday, she had asked Dylan to work a couple of hours, promising overtime. Dylan had left his phone lying on the counter when he went out back to toss out boxes. Kara had scrolled through it. Worry propelled her, but still, it was wrong. Even if she did it for the right reasons—to protect Dylan.

Nothing suspicious. Dylan was careful, with messages written in popular teen text lingo she couldn't decipher. Still, she found a text regarding a party at a clubhouse. Kara made a mental note of the clubhouse address and replaced his phone.

A couple of hours later, Dylan was gone, using the excuse he needed to leave early to check on his mother. Kara finished locking up her store, checking the front and back doors twice. Gripping the keys so hard they left marks in her palm, she hesitated walking to her car, which was parked out front.

Maybe I should stay here tonight. I've got plenty of paperwork.

She'd locked up the Vandermeers' jewelry in the store safe and it was secure. As a precaution, she'd locked up some of the other jewelry as well.

The rest she wore. Sunlight glinted on the ruby teardrop around her neck, the six rings on her fingers and the pearl-drop earrings with rubies snug against her earlobes.

Kara never took home her store inventory. But she couldn't ignore the niggling feeling she needed to split her stock.

Her home security system wasn't as efficient as the store's, but still, her house wasn't as visible.

Jace knew.

Well, who cares about him? He's changed.

Not that she cared. No, the tiny sting of hurt upon seeing him wasn't regret. They were finished. Over. In retrospect, she'd made a good decision.

Jace would never know her terror with regard to motorcycles. Judging from how he acted now, hanging with a dangerous biker gang, bikes did mean more to him than anything else.

Kara drove slowly away from her shop downtown, toward her home. As she pulled into the driveway of her house, something in her chest eased.

The three-bedroom, two-bath modest ranch house blended with the other homes on the street. Here was her sanctuary. Few people knew she lived here. She'd searched for a home in a good neighborhood just before she and Jace broke up. The community was a far cry from her parents' house in a waterfront country-club community.

The key slid smoothly into the lock as she opened the front door. Tierra Woods was a nongated community, where all the homes didn't look as if they were stamped from a cookie cutter. Most of her neighbors were strictly middle-class with families, a few single professionals and retirees, with a mix of Black and Latino households. They all looked out for each other.

She'd bought here on Jace's advice just after their painful breakup.

"I promised you I'd help you find a good home in a great neighborhood and I don't back away from my promises," he'd said. "I want you to be safe, Kara. Even though we're no longer together," he'd said, his blue eyes serious.

Jace had heard it through the computer department at his work that it was an up-and-coming neighborhood.

"Little crime in that area. Lots of cops," he'd told her.

Kara loved it. After she'd moved in, neighbors had greeted her with food, offers of help to fix the broken porch railing and knowledge of reliable electricians, plumbers and contractors.

She'd barely walked inside, keyed the alarm code and set down her purse when the doorbell rang. She glanced at her phone. The security camera showed Maria Michaels, her neighbor from across the street and a good friend. Her husband, Hank, worked at the city's police department as a detective.

"Maria, come on in." Kara opened the door wide.

Maria waved a hand. "Dinner's in the oven. I only have a minute. Wanted to remind you about the potluck party tomorrow."

"Ah, sorry. I have plans. Rain check."

Maria's bright, inquisitive gaze traveled over Kara's body.

"Nice bling you're wearing, sweetie. You going to another one of those hoity-toity black-tie galas? A little much, huh?"

Her hand dropped to the necklace. "Safekeeping. I don't have the security system on the new shop yet."

"Better lock them up. My Larry would love those. He keeps raiding my jewelry box for ways to decorate his new train."

The thought of her friend's toddler gluing nearly six figures in jewels on a plastic toy train made her smile. "No worries. They'll be safe from his sticky little hands. Have a good night."

As she started to close the door, Maria stopped her, her expression serious now. "The potluck isn't the real reason I came over. I wanted to let you know in person instead of calling. There was a guy riding up and down the street earlier. Cute guy, dressed in black leather, on a motorcycle."

Her heart dropped to her chest. "Was the motorcycle red and the guy had long, dark hair?"

Maria seemed to consider. "Yeah. He stopped in front of your house for a couple of minutes, pulled off his helmet. I saw his face for a minute—he was cute, and I thought for a minute maybe he was your new boyfriend."

Ex-boyfriend. Her heart sank. Jace had gone to her house. But why?

"When was this?"

"Around one or two." Her friend studied her. "You're pale, hon. You okay?"

No, but I will be. She'd trusted her instincts in the past, ever since the accident, and wasn't about to stop now. Since Jace knew where she lived…maybe he'd been sent to scout out her home to ensure she was home so he could break into her shop.

Had he sunk that far? It was so unlike him, but again, so was the long hair and the beard.

"Did he say anything?"

"No, he drove off before I could ask him what he wanted."

"It's okay. I think I know who he is, but thank you for letting me know. His name is Jace and he's an old boyfriend."

"Maybe you should turn him into a new boyfriend." Maria winked. "As far as anyone hanging around your house, no worries. You know we always look out for you and Hank thinks of you like a sister. Need me to do a little digging on this Jace for you?"

Maria did some government contract work with computers, Kara remembered. She was supposed to be a cyber whiz.

"No. It's okay. He's harmless."

I hope he is.

"You need us, any time of day or night, call." Maria gave her a quick hug and then walked away as Kara closed and locked the door.

Kara wondered why Jace was casing her home. Why now?

Filled with worry about the jewels she'd purchased, Kara headed into the bedroom, removed the jewelry and locked all of it in the safe in her bedroom closet. The safe had an alarm rigged to it.

She slipped out of her business suit and took a quick shower, rinsing off the day's tension. After dressing in a pale peach sweater, jeans and sneakers, she fished through the refrigerator and settled on a quick leftover salad.

Kara kept glancing at the kitchen clock as she ate at the counter. When she finished, she dumped the dishes into the sink and called her parents. The brief call reassured them she was fine, only tired.

The roar of a motorcycle outside made her jump. Kara pushed back from the table and ran to the window, peeking outside. Dread and a trill of delight rushed down her spine as a tall man dismounted from the bike parked on her driveway. The late-afternoon sunshine picked out gold streaks among the dark brown strands of long hair spilling down to the collar of his brown leather jacket.

Jace.

At least he had the courtesy to show up instead of stalking her neighborhood.

She flung the door open as he sauntered up the walkway. "You'd better have a terrific reason for coming here. This can't be a social call."

"Maybe it is a social call."

His expression gave away nothing. Jace always did play it close to the vest. Kara almost didn't let him enter, but out of a sense of curiosity, she stepped back and closed the door behind him. Jace strode into the living room as if he belonged here.

"Why are you here?"

He looked incongruous standing there, larger than life, as out of place as the statue of *David* displayed in a garbage dump. The delicate silk-covered chair by the window looked too fragile to support his muscled weight, while his biker boots would leave marks if he propped them up on her glass coffee table.

He looked around the room. "Place looks nice."

"It's an investment in a home in a nice neighborhood. I'm thinking of my future, something I once thought you did as well."

Those wide shoulders lifted as he raked a hand through his long hair, making the curls messier and somewhat endearing. Do not go there, she cautioned herself.

"Got bored with planning a future."

Jace glanced around, his blue gaze sharpening as he took

in the artwork on the walls, the inlaid bookshelves filled with well-loved paperbacks, not leather-bound antiques.

He strode over, past the twin mirrors framing the inlaid fireplace and the brass lamps set upon matching tables, and removed a book from the shelf. Kara inwardly fumed as he thumbed through the pages of a well-known thriller novel.

Jace arched a dark eyebrow. "Kind of plebeian for someone with your breeding."

She snatched the book back and set it on the table. "I enjoy reading all genres. Unlike you and those foul-mouthed knuckle-draggers whose company you're frequenting. I imagine your reading choices are limited these days to beer-bottle labels."

Something flickered in his gaze. Kara felt a tug of remorse for sharp words. This wasn't her. Not him.

"Touché. Guess you have me pinned down."

"I'm sorry. That was nasty and that's not me. What happened to us, Jace?" she asked quietly.

His chest rose and fell, as if he'd inhaled her words. "We knew each other really well. Maybe too well."

"When did we become cruel instead of being each other's everything?"

For a moment, his expression turned haunted. "People change."

"Or don't." Kara thought of all the reasons she'd broken it off with him. "It's obvious you still adore that machine in my driveway."

Now, he did look at her, his blue gaze narrowing. "I told you riding bikes wasn't something I was willing to give up. Not for you, or anyone."

"Don't put this on me, Jace. Keep denying it, but we both know your motorcycle meant more than I did."

Jace went over to the windows, jerked the drapes shut.

His jaw tensed, as if he was trying to keep back words he wanted to spill out.

"It never did, Kara. You were unreasonable. I never much liked your habit of taking an Uber to the grocery store, but I never asked you to give it up. Yet you insisted I give up my bike."

"Motorcycles are dangerous!"

"And I told you, I'm careful. I was willing to give up time with my bike, but you sure as hell weren't willing to compromise so we could spend more time together."

Guilt rippled through her. "You knew how important my work was."

"I felt like you were penciling me into your schedule just so we could have dinner once a week, and even then you canceled."

"And you roared off on your bike even when I tried to make time for you. God only knows where you went. You never told me. For all I know, you went to see your family— the family you refused for me to meet. Even after you asked me to marry you, you changed the subject when I asked about meeting your parents."

"Don't go there, Kara," he said in a low voice. "You know this wasn't about my bike, or my family."

She bit her lip. "This is pointless. Answer my question. Why are you here?"

"Came to make sure you were home and going to stay home and not anyplace near Cannon Avenue tonight."

The blunt answer set her back on her sneakered soles. "Why should you care what I do tonight?"

Especially on the same street as my store?

He raked a hand through his messy hair again. "Things are…going down tonight, Kara, and it could get intense in that area. Big party with a lot of people you don't like. That's all I can say."

Lifting her chin, she glared at him. "You and your biker buddies planning a party on Cannon? Or something that would break the law?"

Jace drew in a breath. "Listen to me, Kara. For once, please, listen to me and do what I say. Stay inside tonight, for your own sake."

"Tell me what's going on."

"I can't."

He looked so conflicted she almost felt sorry for him.

She softened her voice. "Jace, please, what's wrong? I know you, even if you have changed. You're worried about me. Why?"

Those blue eyes, as deep as the ocean and just as concealing, studied her. "Will you do as I ask?"

Kara folded her arms. "Not unless you level with me."

Jace's gaze flickered. Then he snapped to military-straight attention and looked around. He spotted her cell phone on the coffee table and pocketed it.

For a moment in pure disbelief, she stared. "You're stealing my cell!"

"Yeah. Just for tonight. I'll return it tomorrow morning, when I find you here, safe and sound."

"You can't do that!"

"Just did."

"What if I have an emergency?"

He pointed to the sophisticated alarm system blinking on the hallway wall. "That's a Fontaine special. Know them well. Press a button and first responders will be here in a few minutes. If that fails, you can run across the street to the neighbor who kept watering her lawn every time I passed by this afternoon. I'm sure she'll let you use her phone."

Jace headed for the door, then turned slightly and spoke over his shoulder. "I'm sorry for the way we broke up, Kara. I really am. But I do still have your best interest in mind. I wish you would trust me in this."

She rubbed her temple as she followed him to the door. "I want to, Jace. But...my phone!"

Turning, he reached up and ran a thumb over her cheek, evoking a shiver of recognition. Jace always did that to calm her worst fears. "It's for the best, babe."

When the bike growled away, Kara locked all her doors and windows.

Then she set the alarm on her house, and headed to bed to take a long nap. Jace had never given her bad advice before. Despite his nefarious acquaintances, he seemed on the level. His old protective streak still ran strong.

Maybe she should stay home tonight to avoid trouble. Or not.

She dressed in green sleep pants and a bright pink T-shirt, and climbed into bed. A smile lit her face as she touched the cell phone on her nightstand.

Jace hadn't stolen her phone with the address of the biker clubhouse. No, he'd swiped her business phone, one she only used to advertise her business on social media and for soliciting clients.

If Jace's criminal pals planned to steal from her, she knew where to find them.

Chapter 7

He risked a lot meeting with his team leader in person, but Jace needed an update, fast.

The meeting spot was too close to the apartment complex where he currently lived, but he couldn't risk riding his bike. Too conspicuous. Instead, he changed into worn jeans and a shirt with a baseball team logo on it, then stuffed his long hair into a baseball cap. For good measure, he carried a baseball glove. Now, as he walked on the sidewalk toward a local park, he looked like an average guy on his way to a game with friends.

The sun sank behind fluffy clouds, turning them gold and pink as he entered the field. Jace punched the glove as if eager for a game, skirted the bleachers that contained a few people watching a game in progress. Stadium lights buzzed into life, illuminating the darkening field.

Rafael Jones Rodriguez lingered by the chain-link fence near the bleachers, eating a chocolate bar and studying the game as if it held all the answers in the world. Rafe, who was about the same height and build as Jace, had the same dark hair, but any resemblance ended there. With his striking good looks and dark eyes, Rafe was a lady-killer. Gray feathered his temples, making him look older than his thirty-five years. Rafe had seen a lot of action in his career with the FBI, and sometimes Jace wondered what secrets he held.

They'd been good friends growing up together. Jace's mother worked for Rafe's family, cleaning their house, and Rafe had taken Jace under his wing, teaching him Spanish, sticking up for him when other kids bullied him and Jace wanted to fight. They'd lost track of each other when Rafe graduated, but after the breakup with Kara, when Jace felt lost, he'd contacted Rafe to get advice about moving on.

Rafe told him to apply to the Bureau. He needed good men on his team like Jace.

A pink scar snaked down his neck, vanishing into the collar of his red polo shirt. Rafe had gotten the scar during an op that went south about a year ago. Two agents on his team were killed and Rafe spent six weeks in the hospital, fighting for his life. Since then, Rafe had returned to duty, but seemed more guarded than ever.

But they'd caught the bad guys. Guy put his own life on the line for his team, no questions asked. But he also didn't put up with any BS from them, either.

Rafe didn't glance up as Jace approached. "I take it you walked here and didn't ride."

"Yep. You?"

Rafe made a quick gesture with his hand. Jace glanced around and saw a gleaming Harley parked in the space closest to the field. "Sweet. New? What happened to the Triumph?"

"Sold it. Bitch to start ever since the surgery. Needed an electric start, so bought the Harley."

"Good game?" Jace asked.

"Not bad. Horner's Plumbing and Hardware could use a better outfielder, but they're beating Davidson's Medical Supplies." Rafe took another bite. "I love baseball. Even amateurs."

For a minute they stood in silence, watching the players. Jace punched his glove.

"I have a number. Overheard Lance needs two hundred thousand for Marcus."

Rafe didn't look at him. "That number will buy a lot of weapons. Or something bigger the DP plans."

Nodding, Jace felt his stomach lurch as he remembered the violent rhetoric tossed about the clubhouse recently. "Lance said Marcus wants to make a statement, loud and clear."

"A statement," Rafe mused. "Same chatter we've been monitoring. We still don't have a target. But whatever is going down is big unless it's all talk and bluster, and nothing solid."

"The target is local and he plans to make the execution of his plans public for all to see. That much I know. But Lance needs to score big on tonight's smash-and-grab to pay for it. He has a buyer in Miami who will pay cash, untraceable bills, for the jewels, soon as he returns from New York."

Rafe finished his candy bar. "What about Marcus? Anything on him, anything at all?"

"Something that might come in handy." He told him about finding PrisonerXYZ's text on Big Mike's cell. "The message was cryptic. I didn't have time to investigate further. Big Mike is already suspicious of me."

"I'll check it out. You watch yourself. Anything else?"

"Lance won't even blink without direction from Marcus." Jace squinted at the baseball field, where someone had just hit a home run. "I did get something on him. Marcus did time and got out two years ago. Went underground after to run the DP. No more riding in the open. Big Mike said Marcus found something in prison and it wasn't the good Lord."

Rafe's gaze darted to him. "He found purpose?"

"That's what I think. Lance shut Big Mike up pretty quick after he spilled that. I don't think Mike was supposed to blather about Marcus's prison time."

"State prison in Florida? Any idea of the charges?"

Jace rubbed his neck. "Tried to open up a convo about it without being obvious. I mentioned my record and doing time in jail and how bad it was, and Mike just laughed and said Marcus did the big time, not like me."

"Federal charges," Rafe mused. "That doesn't give us a lot, but I'll have Darkling run records, see if anything pops up."

"Maybe this PrisonerXYZ is Marcus."

"Possibly."

"Marcus has been eyeing this target for a long time, maybe even years. He's cautious, but elated, I keep hearing. When it all goes down, he will be vindicated. It may be public, Rafe, but it's sounding personal. Lance said something about blowing everything sky high to the heavens."

"When will it go down?"

"Lance is headed on a red-eye to New York, selling the jewels from the last heist while the others make sure the new theft goes down tonight. Risky, but he needs quick cash. He's using the kids again on the crotch rockets to make a quick exit."

Rafe's eyes never left the game. "Keep at it. Let me know the minute you find anything useful about Marcus. Lance is at the bottom of the food chain, but even minnows can prove useful."

"Lance doesn't talk much. Not forthcoming with info, but I think with a few beers, his tongue will loosen more. He trusts me."

"Good. Whatever you do, keep your cover. You're the best chance we have of cracking this and helping us nail down who Marcus really is."

"You let me know through Darkling soon as that target's nailed down." Jace nodded at the game. "Think I'll bat a few balls around."

Rafe glanced at him. "Think you were followed?"

"Nope. Just need to work off some steam."

Rafe caught his arm. "Jace, I wanted you on this case. Asked for you personally. You're good, smart and this will get you promoted. I want that for you as much as you want it. But you're not alone. You get in a jam, let me know. I won't lose you…like the other guys on my team. Got it?"

Throat tightening, Jace nodded as he remembered the two agents killed in the line of duty. Good men, both of them, leaving behind wives and kids. Rafe had taken it personally.

"I won't let you down. I'm no Rambo. We're a team."

"Better than they are." Rafe nodded to the outfield, where a man missed a ball and someone yelled at him.

Jace flashed a brief grin. "Better believe it."

He headed to the field, his blood running hot as Rafe remained by the fence, watching the action.

By the time Jace retrieved a bat and a ball, Rafe had vanished.

The Devil's Patrol clubhouse, nicknamed the Devil's Den, was a somewhat dilapidated two-story wood building that once housed a family. They got evicted and the club bought the property under a corporate name.

Jace trudged up the outside steps to the second floor and used his key to open the outside door leading to the rooms used by bikers to either crash after a long night of partying, or indulge in other activities, such as bringing their old ladies up here for a quick bout of sex. Lance had given him one of the bedrooms for his own use, as a reward for all the business Jace was bringing into the garage with his repair skills.

He unlocked the bedroom door, and then closed it, leaning against it to survey his "reward." The room was as small as a walk-in closet, but clean, with a window overlooking the wooded backyard, where rusty car parts grew more rapidly than weeds. There was a table, chair and gooseneck lamp, and a rickety wood dresser with drawers that creaked. Ignoring the sounds of loud music and laughter drifting from downstairs, he sat at the chair and dug out his cell phone.

On his cell, Jace scrolled through emails and read one from his contact at the FBI who was working the cyber side of this case, a skilled agent whose code name for this case was Maria Angelo. Her nickname at the Bureau was Darkling. Darkling was a tech expert, and she played the part of an average mom living in an average suburb.

Not just an average suburb. He grinned as he thought of exactly where Maria lived. Neighborhood filled with cops.

Darkling didn't have much, but she warned him the social-media chatter had picked up a bit, warning about the DP having a personal vendetta. It could be anything.

Jace stuffed the phone into his jeans pocket and fell onto the bed, utterly exhausted.

The big mattress sported clean sheets—his—and a soft pillow, and a few minutes later, he fell asleep. The edges of a dream teased his subconscious. Kara, her long blond hair spilling past her shoulders, a shy smile teasing her carnation-pink mouth, her big blue eyes soft with emotion. An azure blue ball gown clung to her slim curves, billowing in the wind. Damn, he adored her in that color, as if she was Venus rising from the depths of a clear blue ocean with a cerulean sky overhead. Her arms were outstretched, beckoning to him. But as he took a step forward, her shy smile turned into a terrified scream, her eyes wide with shock as something pulled her backward, something smelling of hot metal and death…

Jace awoke with a strangled sound and sat up. Only a dream. But the light outside the grimy window had vanished, showing a silver nickel of moonlight beaming in the sky, peppered by dozens of stars.

Something he'd forgotten—damn, he'd been working so hard lately living this double life as a biker and trying to keep up with tracking information on the gang…

Kara. His brain cells kicked into gear and he rubbed the back of his head. She'd better not show up at her store tonight. The cell phone he'd swiped was a message to her that he meant business.

With a muffled curse, he rubbed the sleep out of his eyes and accessed the staircase leading downstairs. *Stay sharp. Don't let your guard drop for a nanosecond.*

As he entered the clubhouse living room, finger-combing his long hair, he surveyed the scene. About one dozen bikers draped in chairs or at the pool table, indulging in a game. Three young people, barely out of their teens, sat near Lance on the sofa, Dylan included. They were doing their best job of looking tough.

But Dylan's mask slipped a minute. Too obvious. The kid was scared and showing it. Lance, who could smell fear like a bloodhound on the trail of a fleeing fox, narrowed his eyes at Dylan.

"What's wrong with you?" Lance demanded.

Dylan's Adam's apple bobbed up and down. "Nothing."

Jace crossed the room to hose down the tension. "Hey, Dylan, how's the bike running now? I know you're worried she won't be fast, but I put a lot of work into her, so relax, kid. I got you covered."

Was that the faintest shade of relief on the kid's face? Even if not, Lance's muscled shoulders relaxed. Jace felt a surge of his own relief. He liked the kid, who had looked up to him as a mentor. Dylan had even asked Jace to show him the basics of bike repair.

He hoped like hell that the kid would gain common sense and get away from this crowd, but suspected he owed Lance. A lot.

"Good job, Gator. Dylan's gonna need speed tonight." He glanced at Jace. "Appreciate you staying late to work on all the bikes."

Bile rose in his throat. He swallowed past it, thinking of the letters flashing in the air. Aiding and abetting in a felony.

If he had his preferences, he would have dismantled every single crotch rocket Lance brought to the shop for him to work on today.

But the big fish still remained out there, waiting to be hooked. Bringing in Lance and the other bikers wasn't the goal. Lance reported to someone heading this ring of jewel thieves. The same someone orchestrating the as-yet unknown domestic-terrorist event that would light up the night with horrific violence.

Jace grabbed a beer from the fridge. Lance thumbed at a teenager named Cody to leave and gestured for Jace to take his place on the sofa. Jace sat, yawning, and stretched out his arms, nodding his thanks. He took a long swig, relishing the beer sliding down his throat.

Remaining quiet, pretending to be absorbed in his beer, he listened to Lance dole out instructions to the kids, including Dylan. They were doing the job at 1:00 a.m. Definitely knocking over Kara's store. He hoped the hell she would stay home with a pizza and watch *Antiques Roadshow* or one of those rom-coms she'd always tried to get him to watch.

"About tonight. Sweet job. Dylan's employer has about half a mil in jewelry stashed in her store, and a puny alarm system."

Lance stood, paced over to the wooden bar near the pool table and gestured for Jace to follow. Clutching his beer, he joined the gang leader. Lance was tense, more wired than usual, and not even the three beers he'd consumed had taken the edge off.

"Gator, remember I'm leaving tonight for New York. Sales trip." Lance popped open another beer and swigged it.

Jace knew the New York trip was urgent because Lance's European contact to sell the stolen jewels had been arrested by Interpol. The Bureau had worked with Interpol to cut off Lance's source at the knees, nudging him closer to home.

"I'll be gone about a week. While I'm gone, Big Mike is in charge. I'm appointing you in charge of watching over Dylan."

Jace nearly choked on the beer he'd intended to swallow. "Why me?"

As a newer member, he was not trusted as much as others. Big Mike had been with Lance since Lance became club president five years ago.

"The kid is skittish and I don't want him messing up tonight. Too important. I want you watching him pull off tonight's job. Let me or Mike know if they're running scared." Lance's beady brown gaze narrowed as he studied Dylan in the corner, playing a video game on his phone. "Dylan's trying to prove himself, and I don't fully trust him, and if he screws up tonight, he's out."

A cold chill raced down Jace's spine. Out, as in not booted from the club, but out as in lying cold in a ditch by US 27, where only the gators would find him.

"If you don't trust him, don't send him."

Lance frowned. "He knows the store and has the alarm codes. He's the one who alerted us to the new alarm system being installed tomorrow. We need his wheels. He's fast and I need speed for this job. Dylan will disarm the alarm system and wait outside the store with you and the other two kids. Snake will crack the safe, Big Mike and Maverick will grab the goods. You'll be on a separate bike and if there's trouble, you're the diversion."

Meaning the cops. Lance planned to sacrifice him to the

police, after he led authorities on a chase through down-town streets.

Lance gave him a long, cool look. "Don't disappoint me."

"I won't."

"Good. You like it here, having a place to crash?"

As far as couch surfing went, he could do better. Like at a flea-bitten motel with enough bedbugs to start their own country.

Jace nodded.

"Room's yours for as long as you need it." He gave him a sly look. "How's it going with that good-looking broad at the Tiki Bar? She call you yet? Saw her with you at Earl's."

"Got a date with her tomorrow night," he lied.

The interest on Lance's face increased. "Told the guys she wanted you. Give her a tour of the clubhouse and then use the room upstairs. Maybe you can warm her up for me if you don't want her as your old lady."

Scoring with Kara was the guy's real goal, Jace realized. Cold sweat trickled down his back.

"Wait until tomorrow night, after Mike moves the jewels out. Let me know how you make out."

Lance continued to make sexual suggestions about Kara that made Jace's blood boil. But he managed to stay calm, and grin.

Lance glanced around. "Your job tonight is keeping Dylan in line. If I hear Dylan screwed up this job, I'm blaming you."

The gang leader's next words were a grim warning.

"Your new address will be out in the Everglades with the real gators. Permanently."

Chapter 8

Jace knew he had to let the theft play out.

Shortly after 1:00 a.m., Jace waited in the shadows a block away from the target on a crotch rocket borrowed from the garage, one he'd fixed in a hurry after Lance gave the directive. He scanned the area. No cops. The night was quiet, not even the hint of a security guard patrolling this section of town.

No traffic, either, which made the store a perfect target.

Kara's store. How he wished she'd moved someplace. Anyplace. Alaska would be fine.

Balancing himself on the bike, he gritted his teeth, watching the store while listening for traffic, for an alarm, for a poor innocent bystander chancing upon the scene. Lance had given orders. Jace was a diversion if anyone spotted them leaving the scene. He'd given Jace a semiautomatic pistol and ordered him to eradicate any witnesses.

Jace agreed, but he was here to make damn sure no one got hurt.

Stars blanketed the dark night, but a few clouds scudded over the lemon wedge of moon. The air was crisp and cool for southern Florida. He tugged at the hoodie of his black jacket, flexed his fingers. Tucked into a holster in the back of his jeans was the gun he didn't intend to use, except to fire into the air overhead if necessary.

Lance never asked if I had good aim.

Engines running, three crotch rockets with riders sat outside Kara's store, including Dylan. Kid was nervous as hell, bouncing up and down on the seat, revving the engine. The two others joked in low voices while the bikers were inside, helping themselves to the jewelry. Finally, the trio emerged, carrying backpacks. They jumped on the waiting bikes and roared off.

As instructed, Jace remained behind for a moment. He knew Lance set him up to take the fall for the burglary if cops showed up. He was the newbie.

Craning his neck, he saw a late-model sedan pull up near the store. Jace cursed. He knew that car. Kara.

Jace gunned the engine and took off after the others, weaving in and out of traffic as they reached downtown, hoping if Kara was foolish to give chase, she'd follow him and not the others. Diversion, all right.

Taking a turn, he leaned into it, using his right foot to balance as he glanced at the rearview mirrors. No one following.

After a few minutes, satisfied that Kara hadn't given chase, he headed for the clubhouse. He stopped in front of the garage attached to the building, opened the door and parked the bike inside. Breathing easy, he sauntered into the clubhouse.

Club members were scarce tonight, knowing something was going down. Only the three kids, Dylan included, Big Mike, Snake and Maverick gathered in the living room around the scratched dining table. They all glanced up. Light glinted off the barrel of the Glock that Big Mike pointed at him.

Jace held up his hands. "Relax. It's me."

Big Mike lowered the gun. "Lock the door."

Jace locked the door, then removed the pistol and placed it on the table. "No one followed me. Made sure of it."

"Better not have." Big Mike holstered the Glock. "Okay, guys, dump it."

Three backpacks were tipped over, the contents clattering as they hit the wooden table.

Jace stared at the glittering array. Had to be more than six figures in bling. Rubies, sapphires, designer watches and the big prize—a diamond necklace.

Big Mike held up the necklace, grinning. "This will fetch at least two hundred grand."

He anticipated Kara's reaction. Fury. Frustration. And laced through those emotions would be determination to find the thieves. His ex wouldn't be satisfied with a police report or letting authorities handle this.

His gaze flickered to Dylan. Guilt was carved all over the teenager's expression, which became neutral as he realized Jace was studying him.

Jace turned his attention to the jewels. "Nice," he drawled. "But you can't hide them here. Place isn't secure enough. Where are you gonna move them?"

Big Mike frowned. "Marcus is coming for them tomorrow."

Keeping his expression calm to hide his excitement, he nodded. "I get it. Too hot to move until tomorrow."

Maverick, a former tech worker, whistled. "Sweet. That will buy a lot of software."

Big Mike frowned. "This is all for Marcus, dolt. Not us. We'll get our take later."

The biker scooped up the jewels, stuffed them into a small black bag and walked behind the bar. He uncovered a safe hidden behind a loose panel on the wall. He unlocked the safe, placed the bag inside and spun the dial to secure it.

Jace headed for the fridge and popped open a cold one,

needing it. He rolled the bottle over his forehead, relishing the coolness, and then took a long drink.

Snake, who had opened the safe and stolen the jewels, stretched. "I need to score some action. Mike, let's get out of here."

"No can do. Someone has to watch the store."

"Gator's here. Let him do it," Snake told him.

"Yeah, but Gator needs sex, too." Maverick winked.

"I'm getting plenty of that tomorrow night," Jace quipped. "Gonna wait for the good stuff. You guys go."

Eyes narrowing, Mike seemed to consider. "Gator, you watch the store. I swear, if I come back and anything's wrong…"

Jace picked up the handgun. "I won't let anything happen."

When they left, Jace went upstairs and texted Rafe that the deed was done.

He returned downstairs to check on the two teenagers who drove the crotch rockets. Seated on the big orange sofa in the game room, they were playing a loud video game on a big-screen television.

Dylan wasn't with him. He was sitting on the sofa in the other room by the window, staring at his phone and looking miserable. Jace joined him.

"Seat taken?" he asked.

Dylan looked up, a little too pale. A little too shaken. "No."

"Everything a-okay?"

A shrug. "My mom's gotten worse. I told her I'd be out all night. She still worries."

His mother's cancer had advanced, from what Jace had overheard. Must tread carefully here, because Dylan looked as skittish as a new colt.

"Chemo can be a real bitch." The casual statement belied

his true emotions. He felt for the kid, who had been dealt a raw hand in life.

"The chemo isn't too bad. It's the money." Dylan bit his lip, his brown eyes filled with worry. "Insurance isn't paying anymore."

Jace wished he had enough money to help the kid out. He knew his pain. He had some savings, but it would look suspicious if he gave Dylan money, might blow his cover as a down-and-out mechanic.

"There are ways. Start a GoFundMe," he suggested.

Dylan's expression turned moody. "Yeah, whatever. Lance promised me a cut from tonight's job. A small one because I still owe him a lot for the bike."

Not for the first time, Jace inwardly cursed the gang leader. Dylan was a decent kid. Lance had ensnared him into the gang by buying him a sleek blue racing bike that cost nearly fifty thousand dollars. No way could Dylan afford the motorcycle.

Lance promised Dylan he could pay it off in small installments.

Lance had not told Dylan the installments would include using the bike to steal for him.

"What about selling the bike?" Jace asked. "It's worth a lot of money. I can find you a less expensive one."

Never had he seen the teen more miserable. "I don't own the title. Lance is on the title as well. Can't sell unless he signs off and he won't…"

His voice trailed off. Dylan looked like a fly trapped by a hungry spider, resigned to a fate of being utterly consumed by the spider. The kid looked around, dropped his voice.

"Can I trust you, Jace?"

He nodded, not wanting to push it.

"Trust you not to tell the others?"

"What's wrong? You can, Dylan."

"I feel horrible about tonight… The woman we stole the jewels from tonight—she's my cousin, Kara."

Jace pretended to be surprised. "Kara? Your cousin, the woman I used to date?"

Dylan hung his head. "It's my fault Lance targeted her. He knew I worked for her, heard me talking about that diamond necklace. I don't think he knows we're related, though."

Dylan rubbed his face. "I feel so bad. She's been terrific, giving me a job, cutting me a break and now, I went and stole from her."

"Keep your voice down," Jace warned, glancing around. "I understand. You didn't have much choice, Dylan."

Dylan picked up his cell phone. "Kara's more than my cousin. She's a friend. She understands me. She knows I love video games and she plays them on her phone, too. I even gave her the link to one that Big Mike sent me. Kara loves movies about royalty and kings and queens."

He showed Jace the game he'd downloaded about a prince trying to rescue a princess from a dragon and a burning tower.

"Kara's cool. She's always giving me a monthly bonus, trying to help."

He handed Dylan back his cell. The kid looked miserable.

"I took photos of the inside of the store, told Lance about the layout of the shop. Lance said she'd be covered by insurance. It doesn't matter. I still stole from her."

A conscience was a welcome sign. Guilt. Dylan wasn't like the other kids, who didn't care about the consequences for the people they robbed.

"Something will work out. Believe me, it will."

More than that, he couldn't say.

Dylan didn't answer, only stared at his boots, looking morose. Jace sighed. "Why don't you join your friends? Sounds like they're having fun."

The teenager scoffed. "All they care about. They live for the thrill. They're not my friends. I haven't had a real friend since my best friend, Conner, died when we lived in the old neighborhood. Sometimes I think Kara hired me because of what happened to Conner."

Interest pricking, Jace studied him. "Why would she care?"

But Dylan shook his head. "Long story. Jace, I have to get out of this. I have to find a way out. My mom doesn't need to worry about me anymore. The stress can make the cancer worse."

If Lance will let you go. A chill raced down his spine. "Worry about that tomorrow. Go have some fun."

He shoved at Dylan. "Go on, kid."

The tension in his chest eased a little as Dylan went into the other room. Dylan was right. He had to get out of this gang. But he was a material witness and Jace knew Big Mike and Lance wouldn't let him go so easily. The gang was like a roach motel—once you checked in, there was no leaving.

And Lance is the head roach, who makes promises to a desperate teenager who only wants money so his mom can get chemo. Disgusted, Jace stood and went over to the window.

He went still.

Someone was outside, listening.

Jace slipped out the back door. With extreme stealth, he hugged the building, staying in the shadows until coming to the window over the sofa where he and Dylan had talked.

Though darkness shrouded the figure trying to peer past the partly closed curtains, he needed no light. He knew the slim curvature, every inch of the athletic frame he'd once held in his arms and made love to each night.

Kara.

Chapter 9

If blood could boil, hers was volcanic right now. Kara stood outside the white concrete, dilapidated building, trying to see inside. She'd gone to her shop, only to see four fast racing bikes speeding away on Cannon Avenue.

Inside the store, she found smashed glass display cases with missing watches and rings. But the safe yawned open, an empty cavity.

The Vandermeer jewels. All gone.

One of the bikes racing away was Dylan's. The bike he adored and was paying off. He could pay it off a lot sooner now with the money he'd get from selling the stolen jewels.

She'd come here to the clubhouse, driven by fury, wanting to snatch Dylan away from here. Get him to confess what he'd done, get him away before the police nailed him.

This is what you get for trust. You felt bad for him, gave him a job and he stole from you.

She inched away from the window. How could Jace hang out with such a group of criminals? Kara partly understood Dylan's reasons. He was desperate. How she wished she'd seen the signs earlier, had gotten him to open up to her. But she was too busy with her inventory, her sales.

You let your little brother down and now you are letting your cousin down.

As she headed toward the parking lot to call the police, two rough hands seized her by the waist, spun her around. Next thing, she was tossed to the ground, her cheek pressed against the cold, hard dirt.

She smelled spicy cologne, and it reminded her of those nights in Jace's arms. Panic took hold and she struggled.

"Stop it," a low voice hissed.

Jace. He grabbed her arms, immobilizing her as he pinned her, trapping her against his big, muscled body. Terror scrambled her thoughts. As she tried to scream, he clapped a hand over her mouth.

Then Jace spoke in a low, urgent whisper into her ear.

"I'm going to help you, Kara, but you have to trust I won't hurt you. Please."

She relaxed slightly but trembled inside with fury and anger at herself as well for dropping her guard.

"I'm going to remove my hand from your mouth now if you promise not to scream. Nod if you agree to what I say."

Kara managed a nod, but as he removed his hand, she bit hard, tasting blood. He released a low curse, but sat back on his haunches, regarding her as she scrambled up against the wall.

"You son of a bitch, how dare you—"

"Keep your voice down. What the hell am I going to do with you? Do you know how dangerous and risky it is, sneaking around here, especially tonight?"

"You'd better release me and let me go, Jace."

"So you can run straight to the cops? No." He rubbed a hand over his face. "Come with me. Upstairs. Let's get you out of sight before anyone else spots you."

As he led her around the building to the steps leading to the second floor, she began to shake. "No. Don't do this. Let me go."

He tweaked her nose the way he once did. It was a little reassuring, a reminder of their shared past. She drew in a breath. Jace might have broken her heart, but he'd never hurt her physically, or let anything happen to her.

Feeling as if they'd walked into a den filled with hungry lions and she was a tasty gazelle, Kara let him herd her up the stairs, then he unlocked the outside door. As he closed the door, she squinted in the dim hallway light.

He led her down the hallway to a bedroom. Jace led her inside and then closed and locked the door. She looked around, hugging herself, and sat on the bed, wondering.

What now?

"Jace, why are you living here? What's going on?"

Real fear spiraled through her as he stood listening at the door. Jace didn't respond, only glanced at her and put a finger to his lips.

"Stay here. I need to erase that security feed of you sneaking around outside."

As he went downstairs, Kara sat on the bed, her hands folded into her lap. She'd followed Jace here, hoping he wasn't involved in this. But she'd seen the bikes speeding away. Never had she thought Jace would turn to crime.

She thought she knew him. He'd changed.

Jace finally returned. The bed creaked beneath his weight as he joined her.

"Did you erase the tapes?" she asked.

"Couldn't. I broke the receiver instead. Now, they can't retrieve the footage."

His voice was low and urgent in her ear. "What the hell are you doing here?"

"Don't deny it, Jace. You and your friends broke into my store and stole from me tonight."

He made a dismissive gesture. "That's not important

now, Kara. You need to follow along with me if you want to stay safe."

Anger bubbled up. "I don't think…"

A voice yelled from downstairs. "Gator, where the hell you at?"

Jace released a low curse. "Mike's back. I knew he didn't trust me. If he sees you…"

Her heart raced. She thought only about following Dylan back to the clubhouse, and trying to get him out of here. Not about her own safety. She'd been too furious and upset.

Stairs creaked. Her pulse raced. "You have to get me out of here."

"Too late. I know it's tough, but trust me in this." He brushed a strand of hair from her face. "I hate doing this, but I don't have a choice, not if you want to live. If Mike knows you're here tonight… You have to trust I won't hurt you. Ever."

She wanted to run. But Jace was right. He had never put her into any situation where she felt endangered.

Jace always ensured her safety. Made her feel protected. Even though his lifestyle changed and he'd turned to stealing, she had no reason to believe he'd lie to her. Not about this.

Jace locked his gaze to hers. "You and I may have to pretend we're up here, having hot sex."

Heat flooded her face, as if her internal thermostat shot up to boiling. Jace removed his shirt and unbuckled his jeans, then shrugged out of them. Her heart nearly stopped.

Not waiting for her, Jace kneeled at her feet and removed her sneakers, then slid off her socks. Kara's heartbeat thrummed the way it used to before they made love.

This wasn't lovemaking. This was survival.

In his black boxers, his shoulder-length hair curling at the ends, he looked sexy as hell. If she wasn't so scared, she'd be turned on.

Who was fooling whom? She was turned on despite the gravity of their predicament.

Kara unbuttoned the striped shirt and threw it aside. Then she tugged off her jeans and they landed next to the shirt. In her red lace bra and matching panties, she sat on the bed, studying him. A pulse beat madly at the base of his throat. Jace swallowed hard.

"Damn," he said hoarsely. "You're so beautiful."

Kara gave him a little smile, similar to the ones she used to bestow on him when times were good and she thought they had something.

Something lasting.

Jace joined her on the bed. He pointed to her mouth. Kara framed his face with her hands and kissed him the way she once did. His beard tickled, scraped her face, but the sensation made her nerve endings flare with awareness. He tasted like the slow burn of whiskey and the hot promise of sex.

It was a long, deep kiss and he responded in turn, kissing her back as they rolled on the bed. His hands roamed over her body, the way they once did when they made love.

Her eyes closed as she surrendered to the sensations. In Jace's arms, loving him once more, rekindling the fire that consumed them both...

A snicking sound at the door and a doorknob turning. Jace ignored it, rolled her over to her back and kept kissing her. Kara closed her eyes again, this time from terror and not pleasure.

"God dammit, Gator, you weren't supposed to bring a woman here tonight. What the hell?"

Jace sat up. Kara shrank back, desperately groping for the bedsheet to cover herself.

"Couldn't wait. You're not the only one wanting to score. Go away," Jace muttered.

She didn't like the speculative gleam in the big man's eyes. "Make sure she stays upstairs and doesn't go downstairs. I'm headed out, be back in a couple of hours."

Jace flapped a hand at the door, indicating the other biker needed to leave.

A low chuckle, followed by sexual suggestions and then footsteps out to the hallway. The door closed.

Jace sprang up, sharp and alert. He put a finger to his lips and silently walked to the door. Listened.

She could barely breathe. Kara waited, hoping he knew what he was doing.

As the sound of a motorcycle roared, Jace walked to the window and lifted the faded green curtain with the back of one hand. Kara joined him. Inky blackness outside, cut by the red glow of a bike's taillights.

Anxiety filled her as he turned back. She didn't care for the predatory look in his eyes.

"Now what?" she asked.

For the first time since beginning his career with the government, Jace wished he'd never worked for the FBI. Maybe he should have been a mechanic. Working on bikes and cars all day, able to leave his work in the garage when he got home. Maybe by now, he'd be married to a sweet girl and have a kid or two on the way.

Not this dread and lingering fear working undercover, knowing Kara's life was in danger. Hell, he didn't care about himself. He could handle things. Always had, even growing up when his old man gave him the occasional beating. Jace took it on the chin and moved on. But when someone else was involved, that's when his sure footing slipped.

He couldn't afford to slip up on this case. Mike might not be forgiving, and could be setting him up for something.

"Get dressed," he told her.

When he finished dressing, she watched him with big eyes, her fear smelling like warm floral perfume and perspiration.

Not taking chances, he went to the closed door of the bedroom.

Downstairs, the kids were still drinking and playing video games.

He allowed himself a moment of relief, but not before adjusting himself. Damn, if they still didn't share the same chemistry as before. Maybe his mind never wanted to see her again, but his body sure as hell reacted as it once did whenever they'd started to get naked with each other.

"I'm taking you home now." He kept his voice neutral.

"The jewelry, Jace. The jewelry is here. My jewelry." Her voice rose above a whisper. "Jace…"

"Do as I say, Kara. You walked into this problem and you're following my orders unless you want to end up carved up like a turkey when Big Mike returns."

She paled. Gulped. Nodded.

"Good girl."

"You still have my phone?" she asked.

"It's in my apartment, locked up."

A brief smile touched her mouth. "Oh?"

Kara reached into her jeans pocket and withdrew another slim cell phone. He stared at it.

"How did you…oh. New phone?"

"I have more than one phone, Jace. I do run my own business."

He liked her smirk, since it was far better than her look of fear.

Jace shook his head. "And here I thought I was keeping you safe."

The sounds downstairs had ceased. Even the violent video games no longer blasted from the television, though someone had switched to an action movie that sounded equally loud.

The kids were settling in for the night, probably would crash here. Dylan as well.

He had to get Kara the hell out of here. Jace couldn't trust Mike. All Mike needed to do was find out Kara's real identity as owner of the stolen jewels and her life would end. Badly. Lance had too much invested in this operation to spare her.

They went down the hallway. Jace opened the outside door quietly.

As they reached the bottom step, he led her toward the garage.

"I'm taking you home."

"On your motorcycle? Not a chance."

Jace swore loudly. Always his motorcycle, the big bad beast she feared.

"You have no choice, babe. Let's go."

"I'll walk to my car."

"Where did you park?" he asked Kara.

"I left my car on the next street near some houses."

He gave an approving nod. "Smart. I'll take you there on my bike. It'll save us time."

"I'll walk there."

"Not alone. Not in this area this time of night. Too risky."

Not taking chances with her safety and no way could he risk her driving to the police station instead of going home.

Jace started to curse as she took off at a fast clip. She'd always enjoyed jogging, and they had done early morning runs together, mainly because Jace didn't like her running alone. The trail they used was safe enough, but still…

Would he ever stop worrying about her?

He retrieved his bike, started the engine and followed her. He made it to the end of the street and the busy intersection off the main road as she turned the corner. Kara fumbled for her keys and slid behind the wheel, then turned on the engine.

She rolled down the window, peering at him. "You can go now, Jace."

"No way. I'm following you home."

Kara made a strangled sound but pulled out. He followed her at a close distance. If she detoured to the police station, he was toast.

But she headed for her home. Kara pulled into the driveway, and parked, engine still running. He parked behind her, peered down into the driver's side window.

She was on her cell phone. If she was calling the cops...

After rolling down the window, she made a frantic gesture and cupped the phone. "It's Dylan. He called me. He's scared, Jace. Really scared. He said he saw something...he wasn't supposed to see."

All his senses went on alert.

"What?"

"Some man named Marcus. He saw him in the clubhouse with Mike."

Jace went still, a thousand scenarios playing in his mind. Savage joy that there was a witness he could use to identify Marcus. Worry about Dylan himself, for few bikers knew Marcus's real identity. "Tell him to stay put. I'm coming back for him."

Kara talked to Dylan and gasped. "Okay, okay. I'll be there. I promise." She hung up.

Jace's heart raced. This wasn't good. What the hell did Mike have planned?

"I'll get him. You stay here."

"He wants to see me. He doesn't trust anyone else, Jace."

Great. The kid had a guilty conscience now? Couldn't he have waited? Dylan knew who Marcus was, and that wasn't good for the kid.

Exasperated, he pulled off his helmet. "Fine. Leave the car. Get on. But let's hurry."

Kara leaned away. Huge blue eyes stared at him.

The real terror in her voice made him pause. Squint at her. "Babe, why are you so scared of my bike?"

"Please, Jace, I can't do this."

Exasperated, he looked at her. Really looked. It wasn't scorn on her face, or disgust for the lifestyle she thought he'd embraced. No, it was simple fear.

Real fear, the paralyzing kind. Fear for Dylan.

Panic flared in her eyes, the pupils indicating Kara was ready for flight-or-fight. He couldn't risk either.

"Take your car. But you have to hurry."

When they arrived back, Kara parked a block away. Jace parked next to her.

At the clubhouse, he paused outside the door. It was quiet. Too quiet.

Not even insects hummed, as if creatures of the night sensed something dreadful.

He unlocked the clubhouse door and went inside, motioning for Kara to remain outside.

Someone had turned off the television. The kids finally fell asleep. Jace removed his Glock from the back holster and chambered a round.

Ominous stillness. No snoring, no sounds of anyone turning over in their sleep, or someone padding to the bathroom and flushing the toilet. Even during the night, people made noise.

Gun cupped in his hand, he advanced into the clubhouse.

Now, the tingling down his spine increased, as he smelled something in the air other than the sour stench of beer, stale cigarette smoke and fried food.

The coppery slickness of blood.

A single light that illuminated the bar remained on, cutting through the darkness. Jace rounded the corner, his gun held out. Nothing. No one. His gaze roamed the room. All seemed normal.

He glanced at the next room, where the young bikers had been playing video games. The three kids, including Dylan.

They'd been celebrating a daring heist of six figures in jewels. And Dylan had seen Marcus. Dylan knew the man's identity.

As he entered the room, he knew instantly there was nothing to celebrate.

Two of the bikers sat on the sofa, heads flung back. He instantly saw the wounds on their bodies. Stabbed to death. Quiet and lethal.

Dylan was missing. Where the hell was the kid?

His heart thudded loudly. Careful not to leave evidence, he searched the room for another body. Nothing. Jace backed out of the room and headed for the safe tucked behind the bar. No need to remember the combination. The metal door was opened, showing the safe's interior—a stack of one-hundred-dollar bills, drugs and some passports.

The stolen jewels were missing.

Squatting down, he studied the safe. The door had a combination lock only Mike and Lance knew, but anyone who watched Mike could have memorized it.

Jace uttered a low curse and stood. It had to be one of the guys who'd participated in tonight's theft. Or Dylan.

He rounded the bar as Kara entered the clubhouse and started for the game room.

"Dylan? I'm here, baby."

Cursing, Jace sprinted after her.

Too late. She saw.

Immobilized, she stood at the room's doorway, her body wrought with tense fear. A whimper escaped her. Suddenly, she seemed to be boneless, staggering back as her knees buckled.

Jace caught her in his arms. "Easy," he soothed.

"Dylan…oh, dear heavens, Jace. Where's Dylan? He couldn't have done this!"

He turned her around, put a finger to his mouth. Wide-eyed and trembling, she swallowed hard and gave a brief nod of understanding.

Wasting no time, he hustled her outside.

He wiped his prints off every surface he'd touched. So careful he'd been not to leave evidence of his presence for the local cops to find that wiping off the prints didn't take long. Upon returning upstairs, he did the same to the room, the doorknobs and the common bathroom.

By the time they left, hurrying out of the parking lot, dawn had broken on the horizon. Fiery orange and deep violet streaked the sky, a wash of nature's watercolor art. Warm air tinged with a hint of thick humidity greeted them. It was still quiet, but sounds of the world waking up filtered through; traffic on the nearby roadway, dogs barking in the distance and birds singing a sweet melody.

It was a sharp contrast to the brutal ugliness they'd left inside the clubhouse. Jase's heart pounded as he thought of how he'd been upstairs with Kara. They could have been dead as well if they had stayed.

Or more than likely, whoever did this knew he was upstairs and wanted him to take the fall for the murders.

She shook her head. "Jace, we have to call the police! Those poor kids… What is going on here? Who would kill them?"

He whirled, gripped her shoulders. "No cops. We can't risk it."

As she stared at him with huge eyes, he softened his tone. "Please, Kara. I know you haven't given me reason to lately, but please, trust me."

Her shoulders rose and fell. "Do I have a choice? Where's Dylan? We have to find him."

"That's one reason I don't want the local authorities alerted yet."

Kara stopped in her tracks. "You mean…he could have done this?"

"Anything is possible."

"No! Not Dylan. He's a good kid who got mixed up with the wrong crowd. Jace, he's not a cold-blooded killer!"

I want to believe you. But it isn't looking good for him, Kara.

He herded her toward the street where he'd parked his motorcycle and she had parked her car. "Let's go."

"Where?"

"I'm following you back to your house, where you're going to pack a few things and then I'm taking you someplace where no one can find you. And if they do, you'll be protected."

Kara began to shake. Jace put his hands on her trembling shoulders. "Bend over and breathe deep. That's my girl."

Droplets splashed on the concrete like raindrops, yet it was a clear night studded with starlight. Kara was silently sobbing, her tears staining the ground.

"We used to call nights like this magic nights because you could see constellations, even with all the city lights." Jace kept rubbing her shoulders, wishing she'd never gotten entangled in this.

He wished she'd moved away to a small town where nothing bad happened and she could sell her estate items without a care in the world. Certainly without seeing two teenagers dead on a faded orange sofa, looks of shock and terror on their young faces.

Two teenagers who had their lives stretched out before them, who would never again play video games or ride their crotch rockets through rush-hour traffic, scaring motorists. He felt sick, remembering their bodies on the sofa.

Jace squeezed her shoulders as she straightened up and handed her a bandana he fished out of his pocket.

She blinked, dried her nose and eyes. "You always keep these on hand?"

"When I'm around a lady, yeah."

Kara flashed a brief smile and then her mouth wobbled again. "So much blood. There was so much blood... Why would anyone kill them? They were barely babies."

"Babies who carried weapons and committed felonies. You okay now?"

She nodded.

He glanced around. They had to leave. Now.

The sun was starting to climb in the sky as he pulled up to Kara's driveway. Jace cut the bike's engine. The others would be at the clubhouse or the garage, starting the day's work.

Discovering the dead bodies and missing jewels.

The Devil's Patrol clubhouse had always been known as the Devil's Den.

Today it fit, since they'd left behind hell and three dead young men who would never again see the light of dawn.

He studied her sedan as Kara hurried into her house. It was a new model. A sticker on the back windshield was the only decoration.

Watch for motorcycles.

Jace blinked. Son of a gun...she hated bikes. Why advise other drivers to be careful of them on the road? It made no sense.

Jace went inside. Kara had brought her love of antiques into her home. Even his untrained eye knew the few pieces in her living room were expensive. Jace went to a round table and a squat lamp sitting on it. A lead crystal vase stood next to the lamp, filled with dried lavender.

Something else adorned the table. Jace's breath hitched.

He picked up the clear crystal frog nearly hidden behind the lamp. Swore. His fingers traced the edges, noting that the frog had been carefully dusted, since each crack and crevice was clean.

Jace pocketed the frog.

"Pack only what you need," he called as he walked down the hallway. "No suitcase filled with makeup or false eye-lashes."

"I'm not high-maintenance, Jace."

He stood at her bedroom door. "I was teasing."

Open on the bed was a Louis Vuitton overnight case. Kara stood at her dresser, a fistful of lace panties in one hand. He swallowed hard at the sight. Despite the threats trailing them, the grim scene they'd left behind, Kara holding her silk-and-lace underwear made his imagination go wild.

Down, boy. Get her the hell out of here. Yet he had to find out. Jace removed the frog from his jeans pocket and held it in his palm. "I saw this. Why did you keep it?"

Kara glanced at the frog, and color suffused her face. "I don't know." A shrug. "I like frogs. Maybe I found it hard get rid of it."

He stared at the frog. "I remember the day I gave you this. We had only been dating a short time. Went to that antique fair and you were educating…well, trying to educate me on the finer points of valuable antiques. I bought this because—"

"I said you were like the frog prince, except instead of kissing a frog and turning him into a snobby handsome prince, I kissed a handsome prince and he turned into a real man, who liked hot dogs as much as he enjoyed a gourmet dinner and wasn't afraid of a woman knowing more than he did."

A slight smile touched his mouth. "Yeah. That was a special day."

They'd gone to his condominium that night and he'd cooked her a simple dinner of spaghetti and meatballs. They'd killed a decent bottle of red wine and made love for the first time, long into the night. The little frog had sat on his nightstand, a witness to their tangled passion, a secret smile on his crystal face.

They had it good back then, when he thought nothing would separate them. Felt as if he'd found the woman who knew his soul, a woman he wanted to make happy for the rest of his life. He'd felt it deep in his bones that Kara was the one.

Jace turned away and placed the little frog on her dresser. Those days were long gone. "Hurry up."

To his surprise, she picked up the frog, wrapped it in a shirt and tucked it carefully into her suitcase.

As she came into the living room, Kara gripped her suitcase.

"Do you think whoever killed those kids will come here looking for me? That biker, Mike, he saw me with you, Jace."

"He'll come looking for me before he targets you, babe. But you have a great security system and even better neighbors."

She bit her lip. "Where are we going?"

"Someplace safe."

"Not good enough, Jace. I need to know where, because if you don't tell me, I'm driving to the bank and a safe-deposit box."

"For your underwear?" Jace frowned, totally confused.

"You are such a guy."

Kara squatted down, unzipped her case and withdrew a velvet bag. After she opened it, he stared inside.

Jewels. Diamonds, emeralds, rubies, sapphire jewelry.

"It's the rest of my stock from the Vandermeer sale. I didn't want to leave all of it in the store. I can't risk anyone taking these as well, so they're going with me until I can get a safe-deposit box."

Kara tossed the case inside and zipped up her overnight bag. Jace looked around. "Don't worry. We're headed to someplace safe, where you and the jewelry will be protected. We'll take my bike."

"I'm driving."

"I want to get there today, not next week." Jace sighed.

Kara scowled. "I don't drive like an old lady."

"No, an old lady is a NASCAR driver compared to you, babe." He took the keys, jingled them. "Fine. I don't have time to argue. The sooner you're away from here, the better I'll feel. You follow me. Let's go."

As he wheeled her suitcase out to the car, she looked around as if for the last time. Kara hugged herself as he opened the trunk and deposited her suitcase.

"Will your friends object to me staying there, and you ringing their doorbell this early? It's barely six."

"They're early risers."

He itched to get her to safer ground, leave her where no bad guys could find her.

But Lance's reach had many tentacles. He only hoped she'd be safe, and out of danger.

Chapter 10

The drive to the house of Jace's good friend seemed to take forever. Kara kept mulling over the events of the last day. Her life had flipped upside down. She'd lost most of her inventory and there would be hell to pay.

But none of that mattered as much as the dead bodies in the clubhouse and a terrified Dylan being on the run.

If the person, or persons, who had killed them found Dylan before they did…

She shuddered as Jace turned down a street toward a driveway she recognized.

Kara glanced at him as he spoke briskly into the speaker next to the gate.

As the gates swung open, she followed him through.

Jace drove up the curved drive and parked in front of the stately mansion, with its soaring architecture. As she opened the car door, some of her tension fled.

She felt a sense of discovering yet another new thing about him, yet this discovery relieved her. "You know Jarrett and Lacey Adler? Lacey's a friend."

"I know him."

Nothing more from him, only the tense look that hadn't left him since he'd hustled her out of the clubhouse with its miasma of blood and death.

Jarrett opened the front door and came outside. He clapped Jace on the back and gave her a wide smile.

"Kara. Great to see you again."

Lacey's handsome husband, an ex-navy SEAL, could have been greeting her to a tea party instead of offering refuge from members of a murderous biker gang. Typical Jarrett, always putting people at ease, but behind his sunny expression she knew he was a man fiercely devoted to his wife and family, who wouldn't hesitate to break someone's arms if they posed a threat.

"Lacey's inside with the baby. Flor is already at school. Lacey's anxious to see you again."

He picked up the suitcase Jace had placed on the drive and wheeled it toward the house. After they went inside, Kara hung back, watching Jace talk in a low voice to Lacey's husband. Suddenly, it struck her how much these two men were alike, both with military erect posture, quiet determination and a strong protective streak.

This chivalrous persona, a reflection of the old Jace, clashed with the insouciant biker who valued freedom and outlaw living more than family and friends.

It was almost as if Jace was putting on an act.

She'd barely had time to wonder when Lacey hurried into the living room.

Kara rushed over to her friend and gave her a hug. Lacey laughed and stepped back, searching Kara's face.

"What happened? This isn't a social call."

Lacey didn't need to worry. Kara pasted on a bright smile. "Maybe it is. Maybe it's about time I met your son."

She glanced back at Jarrett and Jace, still talking quietly. "Come on. You look like you need a break. Or a cup of strong coffee."

"Try two," Kara muttered.

* * *

Relieved that Lacey steered Kara away to the nursery, Jace felt a little tension leave. At least here she would be safe. Jarrett's house was a fortress.

"Care to tell me what the hell is going on?" Jarrett folded his arms across his thick chest.

"No."

His friend nodded. "Fair enough. No questions. You texted you need Kara to stay here because she's in trouble."

"Big trouble. The less you know, the better. It has to do with a criminal gang who stole from her."

Jarrett flexed his fists. "She'll be safe here. I'll take good care of her. Lacey will enjoy the company, too. I'm guessing you're not staying."

"No. Need a favor." He took Kara's keys from her purse and removed the car key, pocketing it. "Now she can't follow me when I leave here. For now, can I borrow a laptop?"

Without hesitation, Jarrett headed down the hallway and entered a stately library. Books lined the walls and a large mahogany desk sat before a set of French doors that overlooked the pool beyond. Jarret switched on the computer, typed something.

"All yours. Take your time."

When Jarrett left, he texted Rafe that he needed any and all information on Dylan, telling him Dylan was a witness who could ID Marcus. Rafe's response was a string of stunned Spanish words. Jace had to grin.

I'm hitting the road to search for Dylan.

Be careful, his boss texted back.

Jace set down his cell phone. He deleted the messages,

then checked his email. In a few minutes, Darkling sent him everything she could find on Dylan Moore.

He worked steadily, without interruptions, making notes on everything in Dylan's past. Jace shook his head. Dylan had been messed up at an early age, in and out of school. Therapy from a trauma, no mention of the trauma, but the strain caused his father to divorce his mom, leaving Wanda a single parent.

Jace's mouth tightened as he scrolled through the records. Dylan never had much of a chance. He'd gone from living in a wealthy subdivision with a father who seemed to care, to a single-parent household where his mom struggled to pay the bills, and then had to adjust to a stepfather who was less than stellar. No wonder Kara worried about him.

After clearing the history and shutting down the laptop, he made a few calls. Satisfied, he tucked away his phone.

Now, all he needed to do was leave before Kara got wind he was gone. Jace ducked out of the study. Laughter and the sound of a baby gurgling came down the hallway. For a moment, he smiled. Lacey and Jarrett having a baby after their miscarriage and infertility was a reminder of the good things in this world.

A reason why he had to keep fighting the bad guys.

Palming his keys, he hesitated. Should say goodbye to Kara, but it was best if he simply left.

He started for the door when he heard her call her name. Jace turned to see Jarrett, a worried-looking Lacey and an angry Kara.

"Jace, are you sneaking off without me?"

Feeling a tinge of guilt, he shrugged. "Caught me."

"You bastard," she breathed. "You're dumping me on Lacey and Jarrett."

"You're no imposition," Lacey began.

Kara ignored her friend. "Jason, how dare you!"

"It's safe here. Where I'm going, it isn't."

Not waiting for an answer, he walked out the door.

Kara followed him as he slid a leg over the bike seat.

"Where are you going?" she demanded.

"To find your cousin and the jewelry he took before the Devil's Patrol does and turns him into roadkill."

Harsh words, but necessary. She paled and stood her ground.

"So am I. I'm leaving the jewels here, with Lacey. They'll be safe here. But I'm not staying." Her blue gaze turned stormy. "Dylan is my responsibility, Jace. He's family. I'm going to find him myself."

"The hell you are." Jace turned on the engine and revved it, drowning out her angry protests.

He backed out of the driveway as Jarrett opened the gates for him. Jace blew kisses to a worried-looking Lacey and a grim-looking Jarrett. For Kara, he couldn't bring himself to give her even that simple gesture.

He was too damn worried. Jarrett might lock down the compound, and his friend was adept at protecting his own, but Jace knew he'd put a heavy burden on the former SEAL. The Devil's Patrol could track Kara here and endanger Lacey and the children. All it took was a well-aimed bullet.

He wished there was an alternative, but he couldn't take Kara, and there was no safe space for her. Not without blowing his cover.

Less than an hour later, he arrived at his apartment complex.

Jace pulled into his assigned spot and scanned the area, as always. Tension rode his neck muscles as he pulled off the black helmet. This place had been a Florida motel in the heyday of pink flamingoes and signs advertising Color Television and Air Conditioning, but it was a dump even then. More of a dump now. Still, it was safe for this assignment. Most tenants never spoke to one another and minded their own business. He dismounted and headed up the stairs, avoiding the rusty iron railing that wobbled with each touch. Landlord didn't care about repairs, only the rent getting paid.

A tingle rushed down his spine as he neared his apartment. Jace stopped, scanned the area again. No one around. Not even the stray cat that chased away the rats snacking on the garbage overflowing the dumpster. He inched closer, muscles knotted with tension and awareness.

His door was slightly ajar. Perhaps a crack. Jace removed the Glock tucked into the back of his jeans.

With the tip of one steel-toed boot, he kicked the door open. Son of a... The postage-stamp studio looked like someone had dumped the contents into a blender and then everything had been spat out. Frayed sofa torn open, stuffing spilling out. Same with the old armchair he'd found at a thrift shop. Coffee table broken and lying in pieces.

Weapon cupped in his hands, he advanced. It took less than a minute for his head to assure him "all clear" and he tucked away the Glock. He studied the open refrigerator, the eggs spilled onto the floor and the bread smashed. Inching closer, he saw the clear indent of a biker boot on the store-bought loaf. Yeah, no surprise here. Lance sent his crew to upend Jace's place to search for the stolen jewels. He peered at the fridge's wire shelves and shook his head. Beer was gone as well. No surprise there, either. The gang never wasted a beer, not even when they wrecked someone's place.

Good thing his laptop was secure, back at the FBI headquarters. Jace did all his work on his phone, not leaving anything of value or importance in the apartment. Except for his weapon.

He heard a noise out front. With extreme stealth, he palmed his Glock and waited. Maybe the bastards who did this had returned.

Footsteps sounded on the cheap linoleum. Not the heavy tread of boots, but a lighter step. Female.

Jace stepped out of the bathroom, gun pointed ahead.

A startled yelp. "Please don't hurt me!"

Rolling his eyes, he lowered the weapon. "Dammit, Kara, I could have shot you. What the hell are you doing here?"

"I followed you."

"How…"

"Since you took my car key, I borrowed Lacey's Mercedes."

Jace scowled. He'd sorely underestimated his ex. "You need to go back."

She gingerly sidestepped parts of sofa stuffing. "I told Lacey and Jarrett I couldn't endanger them and their baby, if things were as bad as I thought. Jarrett tried to stop me, but you know me."

He did. No one could stop Kara when she made up her mind. Curiously, she'd been more stubborn in the past about others being endangered, but not herself. She seemed to care deeply about the welfare of others more, which had led to a few fights when she drove him wild with worry.

"What happened here, Jace?" Kara shuddered. "You should call the police."

"No cops. Someone got angry at me for something. It's no big deal." Jace crossed the room, tucking the gun into his waistband. "What the hell am I going to do with you?"

"Take me with you. Or I'll go myself. But I would rather have you with me." Her expression remained guileless. "To be honest, I don't exactly relish the idea of going alone and possibly running into your gang."

"They're not my gang," he said absently. He looked around the wrecked room.

His cell buzzed. Caller ID indicated Lance.

Jace pocketed the phone without answering. Not now.

"I know Dylan must have taken the jewelry. With or without you. I have to find him before it's too late. I can't lose him the way…" She bit her lip.

"The way what? What aren't you telling me, dammit!" Something wasn't right here. Kara had a secret she wasn't sharing and he didn't have time to be polite.

She shook her head. "Nothing. I need to talk to my aunt. She'll know where he is."

Jace gritted his teeth. He didn't need her as baggage around his neck, a possible target that would put him and, worse, her in jeopardy. "Kara, I'll talk to your aunt. These guys don't mess around. Is the jewelry worth the risk?"

"I saw the bodies." Her big blue gaze was clear and direct. "I know what the risks are, Jace. I have to find Dylan. I know he's terrified and all alone. It's not the jewelry. It's him."

Admiration for her rose a few notches. More than a stylish and wealthy businesswoman intent on recovering her property, Kara had a kind and gentle heart. He'd forgotten about that, dammit, and one of the reasons he'd fallen hard and fast for her.

"Try showing up at my aunt's house and she won't open the door for you." She lifted her chin. "But Wanda will talk to me."

Grudgingly, he admitted she had a point.

"Take me to your aunt's house and we'll talk to her together. Soon as we're finished, I'll take you to your parents' house."

Kara's mouth trembled. "I'm not a fool, Jace. I don't want to do this. I'd rather be back in my shop, filing an insurance claim. I have to do this. Maybe someday I'll explain it."

After grabbing a small backpack from the closet, he went to the bureau drawers and tossed in clean clothing, underwear and socks.

Kara had a small smile on her face. "I see you still prefer boxers."

Jace considered. "Naw, not always. Some days I go commando."

Grinning at the delicate tint of red on those high cheekbones, he added extra ammo for his Glock, then grabbed toiletries from the bathroom. Jace slung the pack over one shoulder, checked his weapon and then tucked it into the back of his jeans.

Jace texted Jarrett to inform him Kara was safe, and would be staying with him, then instructed him about the location of Lacey's car.

They left the apartment and descended the stairs.

Kara hovered around his bike, studying it as if it was a great, growling beast she feared. His heart skipped a beat. If anything happened to her, he couldn't bear it. The thought of how close they'd come to meeting with the killer who had no compunction in killing two teens made his blood run cold. Kara needed to be someplace safe.

Kara stared at him. "So how are we leaving here?"

Jace opened a leather saddlebag, stuffed his backpack inside and then closed the lid. His gaze flicked to her. The blue-and-white flowered sundress she'd changed into billowed in the wind. He caught a glimpse of long, tanned legs and shapely feet encased in white strappy sandals.

Hugging herself, the motion lifting her breasts, she stared

at the bike as if it was a writhing spider. "I can't ride on that thing."

Jace blew out a breath. "Yes, you can. Jarrett is sending someone to pick up the car."

"I'm in a dress."

All her arguments were feeble. Jace gestured to the flowing dress. "Doesn't matter. Get on."

If Jace had asked her to walk over live coals, she could have handled it far easier than riding on a bike.

Terrified, Kara stared at the motorcycle. Her heart beat like the drums she enjoyed listening to at the club where she and Jace used to go to listen to live music.

Kara had avoided motorcycles ever since Conner's death. She didn't like them, didn't like being around them and vowed to never ride one.

Now, she had no choice. Even as the thought shot through her head, the upstairs door next to Jace's apartment opened and a man came outside. He peered into the parking lot at them and pushed the glasses up on his thin nose.

"Hey, Jace! Everything all right? I got home a little while ago and thought I'd heard someone in your apartment. I'm keeping an eye on it for you, you know."

Jace waved a hand. "Thanks, Oscar. All's fine."

Kara peered up at the man, who looked as if he was more of a paper pusher than Jace had been before her ex had married the biker lifestyle.

Jace gave her a reassuring smile. "Get on first and brace your back against the bar. It's easier for you to throw your leg over the seat. Watch your balance. Wait until I'm on and then use these—" he tapped at pegs at the back of the bike "—to rest your feet. Make sure to avoid touching your legs to the hot exhaust. You'll do great, Kara."

She stared at the big bike. "Is it like riding a bicycle?"

"Yeah. Once you start, you never forget." He winked at her. "Just like sex."

Oscar hurried toward the stairs.

"I don't have time for this guy. Oscar's a black hole with convos and a biker wannabe, and I'll never get rid of him. Get on the bike. Please," Jace urged in a low voice.

Gingerly, as if mounting a horse, she hoisted a leg over the thick black saddle. She did exactly as Jace instructed, and as he climbed on in front, she took the helmet from him.

Jace's neighbor descended the stairs. His gaze was fixated on her bare leg, the skirt riding up almost to her panties. Biting her lip, Kara pulled down her skirt, feeling as if cockroaches crawled on her skin. The guy looked like a nerd, but something in his eyes hinted he was slimy.

Her stomach roiled. Kara looked away.

"Look, man, appreciate you keeping an eye on my place. Me and the old lady are taking a short run up to Sugarland. We're running late, so I'll catch up with you." Jace waved a hand at his neighbor.

"Sure you don't need help?" Oscar eyed her the way she'd seen hungry people eyeball steak at restaurants.

"We're fine," Kara called out.

"You're more than fine, mama," Oscar said. "In fact, you're…"

Jace started the engine, drowning out Oscar's words.

Now she had to go through with this or she'd look like a scared princess too high-maintenance to ride with Jace. Even through the helmet's tinted visor, she could see the pure lust on Oscar's face. Something about him made her more uncomfortable than riding on a motorcycle.

Isn't it always the quiet ones you have to be aware around?

Kara wrapped her arms around Jace tightly and leaned against him.

Jace backed up and then took off, at a slower pace than she suspected he normally drove. The seat beneath her felt comfortable and vibrated with the purring engine. Still, she shut her eyes. Opened them. If they were going to wipe out, she wanted to see what was going on. If they were going to crash, she wanted to try to grab some control.

Even though she felt none.

But Jace took it slow and easy to the address she'd given him.

Kara's aunt Wanda never visited family. Since Dylan had begun working for Kara, she'd only seen her aunt when she visited the house. Then, when Bruce, Wanda's husband, started leering at her, Kara stopped visiting.

Wanda's house was far more modest than the luxurious, waterfront home her first husband had owned. Her aunt hugged Kara after opening the door. Kara hugged back gently, mindful of the bruises probably on the woman's arms. Her anger surged at the thought of Bruce beating her aunt, but she managed to keep her emotions at bay.

Inside the living room, Kara perched on the edge of an armchair and studied the woman who had always welcomed the neighborhood kids with lemonade and cookies after school. In her late fifties, Wanda had a haggard look, with pain time-stamped on her face. Her long dark hair was gone, replaced by a serviceable cut. Despite the heat, she wore long sleeves.

Not only had Kara's family been torn apart by the accident, but Dylan's had also been damaged.

Too many people suffered because I had to take the car out without my parents.

Family photographs lined the walls, along with a photograph of Conner and Dylan at a Little League game. Bile rose in Kara's throat.

Wanda gripped her hands tightly in her lap, anxiety clear in her dark eyes. Her red-and-white polka-dot shirt was bright and lively, a contrast to the shoulders slumped within the clothing. Gone was the plump woman who looked healthy and happy. Wanda had lost weight and had an air of desperation.

Jace explained they were searching for Dylan because he was in danger. He studied Dylan's mother with an intensity she'd witnessed previously that reminded her of a cop scrutinizing a possible suspect. Jace wasn't law enforcement. He'd make a good cop. Too bad he'd chosen a different path in life.

His rugged charm and quiet determination reminded her of the old Jace, the man who hesitated at nothing to acquire what he wanted, especially if that something helped someone else.

As he finished, Wanda grew even paler. Her hands twisted in her lap, as if she didn't know what to do with them.

"We need your help to find Dylan before the gang members do," Jace added. "If he stole the jewels, and I am certain he did, he's in extreme danger."

But Wanda shook her head, her mouth compressed as if holding back secrets. Kara knew Jace would get nothing further out of her. Her motherly instinct to protect her son at all costs clashed with the desire to trust them. Wanda needed to be assured.

Kara joined her on the sofa, slid her hand over the woman's trembling palm.

"Aunt Wanda, I should have seen Dylan's desperation and given him a loan. I had promised him a large raise once I sold the Vandermeer jewels. I didn't realize he couldn't wait, because you are his entire world. I'm so sorry."

Jace cut in, his voice direct. "Does Dylan have any friends upstate who might help him sell the jewels? Or relatives with connections to jewelers who wouldn't question where the jewels came from?"

"No. I don't know." Wanda wrenched her hands out of Kara's. "My Dylan is a good boy. He wouldn't do anything wrong."

Jace came closer, his manner and tone gentle. "Mrs. Moore, we need to find him, fast, before the bad guys do."

Wanda's gaze darted between Kara and Jace, her eyes reflecting a mix of fear and desperation. "I don't understand. Dylan wouldn't do something like that. He's a good boy."

Jace's voice cut through the tension, firm but compassionate. "We know Dylan cared deeply about you, Mrs. Moore. We believe he might have taken the jewels to help you with moving out."

"I would never ask him to do anything like that!"

"You didn't have to. Sometimes children will do anything to help their parents," Jace said quietly. "Even resort to crime."

The woman's face paled at the realization. Kara wondered at the resigned tone of his voice, as if Jace had more than a nodding acquaintance with this fact.

"Please, Aunt Wanda, help us. We want to help Dylan. The people who orchestrated the theft won't give him a second chance."

The woman looked stricken. "He always talked about going to Georgia. Or North Carolina—he likes the woods…"

Jace shook his head. "Tell me about your brother, Phil Pierce. He lives in the mountains of western North Carolina. Moved there in eighty-nine, retired from working as a radiation tech at a hospital, now owns and rents cabins there to tourists."

Wanda paled. Kara felt utterly confused. "How do you know this, Jace?"

He made a brief dismissive gesture. "We want to help Dylan. You have to trust me on this. We've got to find him. The motorcycle gang wants these jewels back and they're hunting him."

"I don't know," she blurted. "How do you know about Phil? I haven't spoken to him in years…"

"What about Dylan?"

She seemed to shrink into her skin. "Maybe. I don't know."

Why was he badgering her? And how had he found out that information? Jace was always friendly, but this was a hard-edged side of him she'd never seen. He was quiet, determined and intense. It contrasted severely with the insouciant biker who enjoyed freedom more than responsibility.

Wanda's eyes filled with tears. "Please, if you find Dylan, don't hurt him."

Jace nodded. "I'm going to do everything I can to make sure he's safe. Is there someplace you can stay until all this is sorted out? Someone you can stay with?"

"My parents," Kara said quietly. "Please, Aunt Wanda."

Wanda shook her head. "No, I won't impose. I'll go to my friend Sissy's house in North Park, a couple of hours away. She's pressured me to visit, but I couldn't take time off work." Wanda wiped her eyes. "Not that it matters now, anyway. With all the work I've missed at the factory, they fired me."

The woman was hurting for money. As Kara thought over the contents of her bank account, and how she could help, Jace pulled out his wallet. He thumbed through several bills and placed them on the scratched coffee table.

"Here's one thousand dollars. This will tide you over for a while. I'm sorry it cannot be more."

Wanda shook her head. "I can't…"

"Dylan would want you to have it," Kara insisted, her voice filled with conviction, though she wondered where Jace had gotten the money. "He would want his mom to be okay. You're his entire world, as much as he is yours."

Wanda picked up the money, nodding in thanks. Her gaze darted over to Kara as she picked up her cell phone and texted.

They walked outside as Wanda told them goodbye. Kara studied the big Harley in the cracked driveway. "Jace, where did you get all that money? And why are you carrying that much in your wallet?"

"I like cash. Easier to deal in cash."

"How did you know all that about my uncle? Jace, what's going on here?"

"Nothing I want to talk about, Kara."

"Nothing you can talk about or want to talk about?"

"Drop it."

His voice was guarded and he avoided her gaze. Kara's pulse raced. Was Jace also dealing in something illegal? He'd joined a criminal biker gang, and though he'd always been squeaky clean, almost like a Boy Scout, he'd changed.

Or maybe not something illegal, but the opposite. Was the biker persona all an act? Was Jace working for the police? It would explain a lot. Kara knew she had to keep quiet on this, for his sake.

"Are you hungry? Want some lunch? We can eat at my parents' house." Stomach in knots, she couldn't eat if someone forced her, but politeness made her ask.

"Sounds good. That cup of coffee at Jarrett's barely did it." He cocked his head at her. "Your parents still employ Lucy, the cook? She always made a terrific Spanish omelet. I've a hankering. Much better than diner food."

"Yes. She's been with the family forever." Kara was impressed Jace still remembered Lucy. A brief smile touched her face. "Extra peppers, right?"

"You got it, babe." He winked.

Kara hesitated. Once he'd called her that as a term of endearment. They were no longer together, and it stung.

"Please don't call me that, Jace, especially in front of my parents. I...don't want them to think we're together again."

His gaze was long and steady. "Sorry. I slipped. My bad. Fell back into old habits."

Once she'd wished they both could fall back into what they had shared. But the pain of their breakup still radiated deep in her bones.

She gestured to the bike. "I wish I could just call an Uber. It's not too late for me to try, and you could meet me at my parents' house."

He gave her a scrutinizing look. "Was it really that bad, Kara?"

Instinctively, she knew he was talking about them, not the bike.

"No, it wasn't. But there was simply too much to overcome, Jace," she said so quietly she wasn't certain he heard her.

Her cell rang. Kara's heart raced as she saw caller ID. Dylan.

Thank heavens he's alive. "Jace, I have a call. I'll be right back."

Kara walked over to the side of the garage as Jace climbed onto the motorcycle and started it. For the first time, she was glad of the motorcycle's coughing roar. Jace couldn't hear her conversation.

"Where are you?" Kara tried to keep her voice calm. "Dylan, your mom and I are worried about you. I just spoke to her."

"I know. She texted me and told me to call you."

"Please, tell me where you are and I'll come get you."

"No! I'm okay, Kara. I took the jewelry from the gang. Had to. I'm so sorry I had to steal from you, Kara!"

He sounded scared and lost, like the little boy who came to Conner's funeral, wondering why his best friend had died. Kara swallowed hard.

"The jewelry doesn't matter. You do. Jewelry can be replaced. You can't. Please, Dylan, I'm so worried about you."

"I didn't want to steal, Kara. But Lance threatened me. I had no choice." He paused. "He promised me at least two thousand for the job, and when I asked Big Mike about the money, all I got was a line of crap. They had no intention of paying me. You're the nicest person I know and you didn't deserve this. So I took from them what they took from you."

Something inside her eased. Kara peered around the garage. Jace still sat on his bike.

"I want to return it to you, Kara. I can hide it and you can get it. I'll find a place and let you know where it is."

"Dylan, tell me where you are."

"I can't, Kara. I saw something." His voice broke. "I'm in big trouble. They'll kill me if they find me."

She drew in a breath. "Like the others?"

"I saw who killed them."

Her stomach roiled. "Oh, dear heavens."

"I saw them, Kara. I was in the garage, taking Royce's bike, and heard two big hogs pull up. Two guys… Big Mike, and he called the other guy Marcus. I went to the clubhouse and peeked through the windows. I saw who killed them. There was so much blood, I was so scared I wheeled my bike out to where they couldn't hear me and then I just took off and I've been hiding ever since."

Nausea rose in her throat.

"Did they see you, Dylan? Did they?"

Because if the bikers knew Dylan witnessed the murders, he was as good as dead.

"No. I'm sure they didn't. I was careful, got away from the clubhouse before they came out. Unless they checked the security cameras."

"Jace disabled the receiver before he left. Long story."

Kara gripped her cell so hard it was sure to leave imprints on her palm. "Stay where you are. Stay there and I'll come and get you. The police will go easy on you, Dylan, if I vouch for you."

"No. I can't risk it. I'm sorry, Kara, but I can't."

"Please, Dylan. If you truly are sorry, you'll let me help you."

Silence for a moment and then he finally said, "Okay. Not now. It's too risky, I'm in a place where I'm too visible. Tomorrow, I'll call you at five in the afternoon and give you details where you can find the jewelry. Not in Florida. Marcus has spies all over Florida."

"Where?"

"Georgia. Gotta go."

The line went dead.

Her palm was clammy and cold as she put away the phone. Kara behind Jace and put on the helmet he handed her.

"Client problems?" he asked, backing out of the driveway.

"Sort of."

"You got it worked out?"

"I will."

She had little time to get to Georgia and save Dylan.

Before Marcus and the other bikers found him first.

Jace drove slowly on the motorcycle to her parents' house as Kara clung to his waist. Snuggled against him, she couldn't help feeling a little of the old thrill when they'd been this close.

Always touching each other, holding hands in public, Jace never hesitating to show his feelings.

Now, he was distant. Cold. She should be glad for it, but instead, felt stabbing regret.

When they finally reached the pristine gated community of Coastal Woods, she relaxed a little. Her family had moved here after Conner's death to start over, and if it hadn't been for her father's real-estate business, they might have left Florida entirely.

Kara keyed in the code at the development's gate and the guard nodded as they roared through. Jace turned down tree-lined streets decorated with tasteful plantings, flowers and ornate streetlights until they reached Clover Lane, and the third house on the right.

As he pulled into the driveway of the sprawling, modern house on a deep-water canal, she breathed a sigh of relief. Relief turned into concern as she saw her mother scurry out of the double-glass front doors toward them. Claudia wore a light blue sleeveless dress and high heels. She'd never seen her mother wearing anything casual.

Except after Conner died, and the two weeks where her mother barely made it out of bed…

Kara pulled off the helmet and dismounted, then smoothed her skirt as Jace switched off the engine and put the kickstand down. Claudia had a tendency to clutch her pearls when presented with troubling circumstances.

"Kara. What are you doing on a motorcycle?" Her mother sounded puzzled, but not alarmed.

No pearl-clutching moments here. Kara swallowed hard, feeling all of seventeen years old again. She handed the helmet to Jace, who dismounted and then hung the helmet on the bar on the bike's back.

The sissy bar, they called it. Funny how she remembered things like that at moments when her mind was foggy. She'd barely gathered her composure to reintroduce Jace when he pulled off his helmet. Claudia's expression changed.

"Do I know you?" she asked slowly.

"Aye, matey, I've sailed the seven seas with you," he said in a pirate accent.

Kara bit her lip in a smile at the memory. Her mother brightened.

"Jason? Is that you under all that fur?"

He gave a little courtly bow. "One and the same."

"Oh! Jason. How lovely to see you again. We've missed you."

Jace embraced her mother, who hugged him like a long-lost son.

Gently disentangling himself from her mother's grip, Jace grinned at her. "Kara, your mouth is open."

After shutting it, she looked her ex up and down, squinting in the bright sunlight, trying to make sense of things. When they broke up, her parents had been upset, but now she wondered if they were more upset over losing Jace as a future son-in-law than her own pain.

Claudia gave the motorcycle a cursory glance and then studied him with calm assessment, as if Jace was driving a BMW instead of a motorcycle, his hair shaggy.

"Jason, are you on a special assignment?"

Jace was quick to speak up. "Yes, ma'am, my assignment is to deliver your daughter to you, safe and sound. Here she is."

Kara gave him a puzzled look. "It's a long story, Mom. I'll tell you. We just came from visiting Aunt Wanda."

Her mother's quick gaze darted between the two of them. "Well, no use standing in the sun. Come inside and have coffee."

"Yes, ma'am. Thank you. I was rather hoping to get a quick bite of breakfast, if you don't mind."

Claudia actually smiled. "Now, Jason, you know I cannot abide the *ma'am* title. I'm Claudia. I recall you like Spanish omelets with extra peppers. Coffee, black and strong."

Jace grinned and nodded. Her mother was the only one who seemed to get away with calling him the more formal Jason.

Still slack-jawed at her mother's reaction, she followed her into the house like an obedient puppy. Before she could fill in her mother on Dylan's disappearance, Jace told her a brief version, indicating they needed to find Dylan because he was in deep trouble.

Kara watched him. He didn't lie, but evaded details, probably out of concern for her mother. Jace always liked her mother and never wanted her to worry.

Claudia listened, nodding, her face tightening. "Dylan has had a hard time of it in recent years. I hope you can find him, and straighten out all this, Jace. He needs a mentor like you."

A mentor in a criminal biker gang? Kara shook her head and went into the kitchen to greet Lucy, who was cooking at the stove.

Lucy turned down the heat from the cast-iron skillet and beamed at Kara in greeting.

But with Jace, Lucy ran over to him, exclaiming in Spanish as she hugged him. Their cook stood nearly half a foot shorter than Jace, who laughed and hugged her back.

Claudia poured coffee into a large mug.

Jace nodded. "Thank you."

He eyed the lanai and the boat docked out back. Whistled. "You still have it. Sweet."

Kara followed his gaze. *Claudia's Dreamboat*. Sleek and polished, the yacht was her father's pride and joy. The boat was a constant reminder of her little brother, and how much Conner had enjoyed being on the water with them.

How Conner adored sailing! His little fingers learning to work the lines with her father. That time he'd never listened and leaned over too far and fell overboard.

Kara had fished him out as her mother fussed and scolded. They had shared a shaky laugh.

A few years later, he was gone.

"We sailed to Bimini last year, but Chuck is too busy this year with a large deal he's been working on for months. Perhaps some time you'd like to take her out yourself."

Kara felt as if she'd stepped into an odd time warp. Was her mother trying to set her up with Jace?

"Mom, remember? Jace and I are no longer together."

Claudia smiled. "I know, honey. I was inviting Jason, not you."

Ow. That stung.

"Thank you. Maybe sometime." With a nod, he opened the sliding glass doors and stepped out into the lanai, shutting the door behind him.

Kara turned to her mother. "What the hell, Mom. I mean, Mom! What are you doing? Can't you see? Even if we didn't break up, Jace is… He's in a criminal motorcycle club."

"I doubt it."

Couldn't her mother see reason? It was as if Claudia still glimpsed Jace as the same clean-cut and stoic man he'd been while they dated.

Claudia went to the sliding glass windows and studied Jace as he walked out to the dock. "Honey, did I ever tell you your father did a background check on Jason Beckett right after you announced your engagement?"

"No. Why would you do something like that?"

Claudia turned around. "You know your father, how protective he was."

Curiosity got the best of her. "What did you find out?"

"Perhaps I'll share that information with you some day." Claudia smiled gently. "There's nothing to fear with that young man."

Something bizarre was going on. "How would you know?"

Her mother sighed. "About a year after you and Jason broke it off, we received a phone call asking about Jason. He'd put our names down for a reference."

"Job reference? What kind of job? Stockbroker?"

Jace's firm had been a money-management company and many of the younger employees like him fast-tracked to becoming investment advisors.

"Did he tell you what he's done since you broke up with him?"

"Obviously, he's turned into a full-fledged biker." Confusion filled her. "Isn't he?"

"If he hasn't told you, he has good reason to right now. I'll leave it up to him to share such information. But know you can trust him. We do. Jason was good for you, Kara. I always thought that you two belonged together. We were so disappointed when you broke off your engagement and stopped seeing him."

It stung to think her mother still adored Jason and knew more about his present life than she did. Once more, she felt like a little girl whose parents lectured her about bad choices and wanted to control her life.

"Stop idolizing him. He's in my past and we're no longer

together, and except for finding Dylan, I have no intention of ever seeing him again. For anything."

"I think that will be the biggest mistake you will ever make, Kara."

Staring, she felt her emotions boil over into a lather. "I broke up with him. I'm not going back to the past."

"You're right. You cannot. But I always felt Jason and you shared a bond, Kara. I never saw you glow around other men as much as you did with Jason. He makes you happy. He wanted to make you happy." Claudia sniffed. "Jason was always much more mature, even at twenty-five, than those college boys you dated who thought the world revolved around their favorite sports team."

Keeping her voice level presented a struggle, when all she wanted to do was shout at her calm, refined mother, who rarely showed any negative emotions. "He made me happy. But there's too much baggage between us. Why are you trying to set us up again? You see what he's turned into!"

"Kara, Jason Beckett is no ordinary man. We've always trusted and liked him, and he has a high sense of morality and ethics." Claudia's smile was gentle as she tucked back Kara's hair. "Whatever Jason is involved with, it's for a good reason."

"Maybe you should have married him," she muttered.

"Kara Marie Wilmington, watch your mouth." Claudia touched her pearls. "Jason is a good man. I know this."

Kara wondered about Jace and the whole drastic shift to embracing a biker lifestyle. Was all this a masquerade for some greater purpose?

"What is he involved with, Mom? What aren't you telling me?"

Claudia shook her head. "I don't know, and it's not my

place to say if I did. I'm sure he's under tremendous pressure now to find Dylan."

"He's under pressure? Mom, Dylan is my cousin. Dylan stole from me. Jace belongs to a criminal biker gang and helped in the theft. I'm going to find Dylan."

Her mother's smile slipped. "You cannot. It's too dangerous. I'm sure this is why Jason brought you here, to keep you safe."

"Don't you see?" Kara grabbed her mother's hands. "It's my fault he got into this mess. He had a good life when he lived near us, when Conner was his best friend. He was happy and his parents were together. It wasn't until after…he got messed up and needed help his father refused to give him. He's a good kid at heart and if not for me…because of…"

"Because of the accident?" Moisture glistened in Claudia's blue eyes. Blue like her own. Like Conner's had been.

"Kara, it was an accident. You didn't know Conner was hiding in the back of the car. It's more my fault… I knew how mischievous he was and how you were itching to take out the car. We should have taken the keys, removed temptation. I should have…I should have known. Conner loved that car, too. He wanted to ride in it as well."

Claudia's voice dropped to a whisper. "We spoiled him too much. He was too used to getting his way."

Kara's mouth opened and closed. All these years, her mother hadn't mentioned the accident, hadn't ever shared how she felt.

"Mom, I drove the car. I was responsible."

"You were a headstrong teenager, honey. A teenager with a new car she was anxious to test out. It was an accident."

"I should never have taken the car out."

"We should have taken the keys with us when we left. It was too tempting. I've tried to shield you since then…how I wish the world were kinder and I could keep you from every harm. We've tried, we've tried so hard, but sometimes it isn't possible. I worry constantly about you."

Now, two huge tears slipped down her mother's cheeks. For the first time, Kara noticed she was showing her age. She'd always thought of Claudia as timeless, as strong as a towering rock. Cracks showed in that rock now, cracks Claudia hadn't displayed to her previously.

Suddenly, she understood the reason for her mother's helicopter parenting. It wasn't that her mother thought she was incapable of making wise choices.

Her mother didn't want her to make a wrong choice that might result in Kara getting hurt.

"I know you didn't blame me, Mom. So please, don't blame yourself. It was an accident. Please, don't worry about me anymore. I'll be fine. I can take care of myself now." Kara slid her arms around her mother.

For a few moments, they clung to each other until Kara sensed Jace approaching. She stepped free of Claudia's embrace and wiped her face as Claudia slipped away, presumably to gather her lost composure.

Her mother never cried in front of anyone. Not even when Conner died. The display of vulnerability troubled Kara, and yet she was glad for it, feeling it had brought them closer together.

I am not alone in my grief.

Jace opened and shut the slider. His quick gaze darted to the tear tracks on Claudia's face as her mother entered the living room.

He headed for the kitchen, ignoring her mother's obvious distress. "Lucy, that omelet is calling my name."

"It's ready, Mr. Jace," Lucy told him.

Like old times, Jace slid onto a stool at the kitchen island.

Never one for formality, unless the occasion called for it, he blended in well with so many situations. For the first time, she wondered about that and her mother's odd mention of a background check.

And that mysterious mention of an assignment. Kara sat on the stool next to Jace, as he dug into his meal with gusto, praising Lucy's cooking and making her flush with pleasure.

He glanced at her. "Want to get in on this? It's a huge omelet."

"I'm not hungry, thank you."

Jace shrugged. "Missing out here."

Missing out on more than food? She began chatting with Lucy in casual Spanish, asking about her teenaged daughter, who was preparing for her fifteenth birthday and the quinceañera celebration to honor the occasion.

Kara glanced at Jace. "Sorry to speak in Spanish in front of you. We were talking about her daughter's quinceañera."

Jace replied in Spanish, "I know what it is. My boss Rafe's niece is celebrating her quinceañera soon."

Her jaw nearly dropped. "Since when do you speak Spanish?"

Jace's mouth quirked in a quick, mysterious smile. "Since about ten years ago."

"You knew Spanish the whole time we were together? I never knew!"

A guarded look came over him. "Maybe there's a lot you don't know about me, Kara."

Pieces of the mosaic were beginning to fit together. "I see. Such as this boss of yours. I thought Lance was your boss, since he owns the garage where you work as a mechanic."

Busy polishing off his omelet, Jace didn't answer. He downed his coffee, wiped his face and thanked Lucy in English as he placed his plate and mug into the sink. Then he dropped a quick kiss on her cheek.

"You're the best," he said, and Lucy beamed.

As her mom entered the kitchen, all trace of tears gone from her cheeks, Jace nodded. "Thank you, Mrs. Wilmington. I'd better get going."

A sinking feeling swirled in the pit of her stomach as he jingled his bike keys. "Going where? To find Dylan?"

At his nod, she compressed her lips. "Then I'm going with you, Jace."

He gave her a long, steady look. "Kinda thought you'd say that, Kara, which is why I really brought you here."

She slid off the stool and smoothed down her wrinkled skirt. "I'm going with you. If there's any chance of saving Dylan before those bikers find him, he'll listen to me. I can convince him to do the right thing and turn himself over to the police."

Narrowing his eyes, he stared at her. "Not a chance."

"Kara, please listen to Jason. It's safer for you here." Her mother drew in a breath. "I know you wish to find Dylan, but…"

"He called me."

Now they both turned to stare at her. "What the hell," Jace finally said.

"He called me, Jace. He apologized for stealing from my store and told me how scared he was, but that he had no choice but to flee with the jewels." Kara drew in a deep breath. "And he was hiding outside when the others were killed. He saw who killed them. The biker named Marcus and Big Mike."

Jace released a string of curses in Spanish, glanced at Lucy and apologized. His gaze narrowed. "When the hell were you going to tell me this, Kara?"

She met his angry gaze head on. "I know you, Jace. I know your protective streak and knew you brought me here to leave me. I'm going to find him. All you need to know is he is in hiding and safe in Georgia."

"No, you're not going anywhere. Tell me where he is and I'll go. It's too dangerous."

"He doesn't trust you. He's terrified."

Jace gave a grudging laugh. "Of course, the kid is scared! He's a material witness to a double homicide and he's the only person who can identify the real leader of the Devil's Patrol, a guy as lethal as a Mafia boss. Damn." He rubbed the back of his neck. "Stay here. I have to make a call."

As he stepped out onto the lanai again, heading for the boat dock, she threw an apologetic look at her mother, who looked pale.

"Now, can you understand why I must find Dylan? He's terrified, Mom. I made a promise to myself to take care of him and I'll be damned if I break it. Jewel thief or not. I owe it to Conner to make sure his best friend lives."

Her mother steepled her fingers and buried her face into them, a clear sign of agitation. "Kara, please, I cannot lose you, too. Please, stay here with us and let Jason find him."

Guilt surged through her. "I'm sorry for putting you through all this worry, Mom. Dylan trusts no one but me right now and I have no choice."

Finally, she raised her head. "Very well. As long as you promise to go with Jason and follow his lead. Don't go anywhere without him. I trust him. Promise, Kara, or I will lock you into your bedroom."

Kara blinked. "I'm not ten, trying to sneak out to a late movie, Mom. I'm not a little girl."

"Promise, Kara."

Such faith and trust in her ex. "Mom, why do you trust him so much? We're no longer together."

"Promise me."

"I promise. I'll follow Jace's lead."

Kara swung around as the sliding glass door opened. Jace shut it behind him. "I'm hitting the road."

"So am I. With or without you. Dylan's promised to call me to tell me where he's hiding. He's going to return the jewelry to me." She took a deep breath, feeling perched on the edge of a dangerous cliff. "Me, Jace. Not you."

Jace heaved a deep sigh. "This isn't a road trip to look at sights, babe."

Ignoring the endearment that sent a tingle down her spine, she threw back her shoulders. "I know. But you need me, Jace. Dylan needs me. I have until tomorrow afternoon to get to Georgia before he calls again at five. He's going to give me instructions then. It feels like a ransom, but I have to play along with him. He's holding the cards."

Jace leaned against the wall. Glanced at her mother. "You approve of this?"

"No. But I trust you to keep her safe, Jace. She will do this and if you are with her, you'll protect her. I know you will." Claudia's gaze turned steely. "You had better, Jason."

"I will." Jace saluted and then kissed his fingertips and touched them to his heart. "I will put her safety above my own."

Emotion welled in Kara's throat, not from his solemn words, but the gesture he made. How many times had Jace used that special gesture to signify a promise to her? A promise she was the only one for him. A promise he would be faithful and look out for her needs. A promise to make her happy as her husband.

But never a promise to stop riding his motorcycle and put her first.

Maybe you didn't promise to try to understand because you were too scared to reach out to him.

It was too much for one day. Kara bit her lip to regain control of her lost composure. "I'm going to pack some essentials I have here, and call Lacey, ask her to send the suitcase I left at her house."

Jace consulted his cell phone. "Never mind calling Lacey. I'll call Jarrett, ask him to send someone with your suitcase to a place where we can meet on the road. We have to get going. You can't wear that dress, Kara. Long pants—jeans—are best for riding, and a long-sleeved shirt. Shoes or sneakers, no heels. Take a small pack if you have one. There isn't much room in the bike's saddlebags."

In the bedroom her parents had always set aside for her, Kara found jeans, a white blouse and tennis shoes. She dressed, then retrieved a backpack, clothing and her emergency stash of cash. Then she started down the hallway and paused.

Conner's room. The door was always closed. Kara took a deep breath and opened the door.

It felt like stepping back into a time warp. Unlike her bedroom, which had changed as she grew older, her little brother's room remained the same from the day he died.

Bed still unmade. Toys scattered around the room, several miniature cars as well. Posters of favorite sports stars and a photo on the dresser of Kara and Conner.

She crossed the room and picked it up. Someone had dusted in here—Lucy, probably.

In the photo, Conner stood behind her on a raised surface, his skinny arms around her neck as he rested his head on her shoulder, grinning at the camera. She looked impatient and yet amused.

How well she remembered that day. They were about to set sail and Conner climbed up on the deck box and threw his arms around her because she wanted to go sailing alone with her friends, and he pestered her until she capitulated and agreed.

We spoiled him too much.

I spoiled him as well, Mom.

Conner always got his way. Until that day. Kara wiped the tears trickling down her face.

She closed the door behind memories and mourning. Time to forge ahead and try to save someone else. It was too late for Conner. But she would save Dylan, even if Jace didn't want her along for the ride.

Chapter 11

The sky overhead was clear, cloudless and baby blue. Though the sun beat down with relentless heat, riding on the bike of Jace's Harley provided a sufficient breeze.

Gradually, she lost her fear and began to relax, her grip loosening around his lean waist. Kara began to notice things she'd never seen while driving, or riding shotgun with friends. Horses grazing in a pasture off the highway. The way the sunlight glinted off the smooth surface of a drainage lake. How the pine trees clustered together seemed to stand aloof and alone, devoid of wildlife, until she saw a lone osprey perched on a pine bough. The clean, fresh smell of newly mowed grass.

Jace stuck to the back roads instead of the interstate to "get her used to riding."

This was not the busy Florida she knew, with concrete streets, sandy beaches and traffic. This was a different Florida, with plenty of wide-open spaces, and palm-tree farms that bordered orange groves.

Kara grew more appreciative of her home state as she clung to Jace's back.

He stopped in Manatee Island. Jace pulled into the crowded parking lot of the marina and aquarium. She eased off the motorcycle, her bottom a little sore, her nerves still rattled by their narrow escape from the clubhouse.

Jace removed his helmet and dismounted. He turned, her reflection showing in his mirrored sunglasses.

"Jarrett sent an Uber here with your suitcase. Good ol' Louis Vuitton won't fit in the saddlebags, but you can take what you need from the suitcase and leave it here with Brandy, the director. She's going to bring us snacks and water for the road as well."

She removed her backpack from the leather saddlebag and hoisted it over one shoulder. "I've met Brandy at fundraisers for the sea-turtle hospital."

"Jarrett said she's a good person and can be trusted."

Could anyone truly be trusted?

Wincing, she walked bow-legged toward the building. Jace stood back, a wide grin on his face.

Kara scowled. "What are you looking at?"

"You look like a greenhorn after her first long horse ride."

"My bottom hurts."

"Want me to rub it?" He winked.

Kara started to frown and make a snappy reply, but decided against it. "Not unless you plan to get naked."

Behind the mirrored sunglasses, his expression was difficult to read, but his breath hitched.

"Don't tempt me," he muttered.

The sun felt warm on her bare arms as she stretched, working out the kinks in her legs and arms. Kara felt as if she had been running for days on adrenaline and caffeine. Jace, on the other hand, looked a little windblown, but handsome and deliciously rugged. It wasn't fair. Men could make a bad-hair day look like a good-hair day and lack of sleep only made Jace's blue gaze heavy-lidded and sexy.

The way he used to look at her right before they made love.

Not a good thought to entertain right now.

Jace headed for the building, then pulled on the door. Locked. He squinted in the sunlight at the handmade sign on the door.

Closed for Renovations. See You Next Month!

He walked over to some bushes, retrieved her suitcase and handed it to her. Kara kneeled and unzipped it, and removed necessary toiletries and clothing, stuffing them into the backpack.

"The rest can't fit, but I'll leave it here. Brandy is supposed to meet us here?"

Jace ran a hand through his long hair. "She's probably on her way to meet us. I have to make a call, Kara."

He indicated a picnic table set beneath the shade of sprawling trees.

"Go wait over there, and I'll be back."

Gripping his cell phone, he walked a short distance away. Close enough for her to still see him, but far enough for privacy. Kara wondered what kind of business calls he made. More and more she doubted Jace had embraced the criminal lifestyle of the other Devil's Patrol members.

But what was he doing, associating with them? Certainly there were other bike clubs he could join to indulge his love of motorcycles.

The parking lot had only a few trucks with empty boat trailers. Another truck pulled into the graveled lot, parked closer to the aquarium. A man wearing a tan ball cap, faded khaki shorts and a white T-shirt climbed out and fetched a fishing pole from the back. The pole looked expensive, even from a distance.

Jace rejoined her, studying the newcomer with intensity. He fiddled with his sunglasses.

"Something about that guy," he mused. "Did he just get here?"

Kara nodded.

As the fisherman walked down the dock, Kara's unease grew. Something seemed off. On the surface, it was a serene place to stop and rest, with the clear blue sky overhead, the brilliant sun, the water gently lapping at the pilings. Yet she felt anxious.

Making an impatient sound, Jace shook his head. "We can't wait much longer. This is odd. Brandy seemed reliable. Let me call her... Damn, signal's weak in this spot."

Kara watched him as he headed into the sun, pacing back and forth.

Returning to her, he pocketed his cell phone. "Brandy got delayed. She apologized for not meeting us."

Kara's stomach rumbled. "I guess I should have eaten back at Mom's but I was too upset."

He reached over, ran a thumb across her cheek, making her shiver. Once his touch had drawn them closer. Now, it only served as a reminder of what they had lost.

She pulled away and climbed down from the table. "Where is she?"

The frown denting his forehead made her uneasy. He removed his sunglasses, his gaze hard against the glare from the water. "She's at least twenty minutes out. I don't think we should wait."

"Me, either."

He scanned the marina and his gaze landed on the fisherman, who set his fishing pole into a holder at the dock. Jace's body tensed.

"See that guy over there?"

She nodded.

"Notice anything unusual?"

Her stomach did a flip-flop from anxiety instead of hunger. "He's fishing without any tackle. Or bait. Just the lure on his pole."

"Right. Let's get the hell out of here."

As they headed back to the bike, Jace kept looking at the fisherman, who had turned to watch them. The man seemed to sense their departure, for he abruptly abandoned his fishing pole.

Jace quickened their pace. "Hurry," he urged her.

Kara ran to the motorcycle, put her pack into a saddlebag and then climbed on. She put on the helmet as Jace reached for the handgun tucked into the side of his jeans. Not caring about his obvious interest, the fisherman hurried down the dock, but suddenly, as if by a stroke of good luck, his pole jerked in the holder.

"You got one," Jace called out. "Better run if you don't want your gear in the drink."

As Jace tucked his gun away, mounted the bike and then started the engine, she heard the man's curses as he did an about-face and ran to his fishing pole. It suddenly flew out of the holder and into the water.

Kara didn't look back to see if the man followed his pole into the bay to retrieve it as they roared off, heading on the causeway toward the interstate again.

It was probably nothing. Only her tired and quite overactive imagination seeing shadows behind shadows.

But she had a bad feeling about all this. Someone was following them.

Kara hugged him tight as Jace headed north on the interstate, making good time.

His quick call to his boss proved worrisome. Word on the street had spread about the clubhouse murder and Dylan was a suspect. The local law enforcement, local LEOs, as they called them, wanted him for questioning.

If the DP discovered Dylan had seen Marcus, that put him in even more peril, more than simply taking the jewelry they had stolen.

The incident at the aquarium rattled him. Perhaps it was all innocent and the fisherman was waiting for someone else or playing a part, maybe even a private detective spying on one of the yachts anchored close to the marina. However, paranoia proved healthy in the past. Had the guy come after him when Jace was alone, he could have easily taken him. Perhaps gotten some answers as to who was following him.

With Kara, he didn't dare take chances. Maybe it was better that way because, as his boss always warned, Jace could sometimes throw caution to the wind.

It was one reason Rafe had hesitated to assign him to this case. If not for Jace's family background and his old man being a member of an outlaw bike club, Rafe would have selected someone else.

Kara had no clue what this was truly all about. One thing about his ex—once she dug her heels in, she stayed. Even when it grew dicey. Especially when her family was concerned.

If he had pushed even a little to stay together and asked her to work things out instead of walking away six years ago, Jace knew she'd have caved. But he hadn't. Too many times in the past had he built those walls to keep from getting hurt, like his family had hurt him. His family, who were so different from Kara's.

He thought about the warm reception her mother gave him. Damn, he held strong affection for both her parents. Claudia and Chuck treated him like a son, and when he and Kara broke it off, he missed them as much as he missed Kara.

Claudia had been more of a mother to him than his own

mom, fussing about him, always worrying, ensuring his favorite meals were cooked when he came over. Inviting him on their family excursions.

He'd even traveled with them to the Bahamas to stay in their vacation house. Chuck invited him fishing and they'd had some mighty fine male bonding that day on the deep blue sea. Caught a few good snappers and had a great time grilling them later for the ladies.

They made a couple of stops for snacks and drinks, but Jace kept pushing on.

Finally, much later, knowing she needed to eat, Jace pulled into the parking lot of a small diner in a small town. It seemed safer here, more anonymous.

The DP had a long arm in Florida and he intended to avoid that arm.

As Kara walked inside to use the restroom, his cell rang. Lance again. Jace went outside. This time, he stabbed the answer button. This was a convo best had in private.

"Yeah, Lance. Thanks for trashing my place."

A volley of foul words followed.

"You think what the guys did to your sofa is bad, Gator? When they catch you they're going to cut you into so many pieces the gators will have trouble finding all of you."

The man's voice lowered. "There'll be nothing left of you to bury. Not even bones. Your own mother won't recognize you."

"Sure." He managed to sound bored. "She won't give a damn. You'll never find the jewels that way."

He expected more swearing but heard only silence. Finally, Lance said, "Go on."

"If I stole your stash, and killed those kids, think I'd bother talking to you? I think I know where the kid is and I'm going to find him and get the jewelry back."

"Where's Dylan, you bastard? I warned you to watch him!"

Jace released his own string of swear words. "I couldn't watch him every second. What the hell do you want from me?"

"Your life, you bastard, if you don't find Dylan. Find him, or you're dead meat."

Lance hung up.

Blowing out a breath, he pocketed the phone. *That went well.*

The diner wasn't busy this time of night and he was glad of it. Jace ordered a burger, medium rare, with a salad, then excused himself to the restroom. After, he called Rafe. No answer. Worry needled him. His boss never shut off his cell phone.

After he finished eating, Jace glanced at the round clock over the diner's counter. Nearly eight, and Kara's head was bobbing over the bacon, lettuce and tomato sandwich she was struggling to finish.

Jace consulted the internet and found a small motel. He tossed a few bills on the table, took a long swig of his iced tea and slid out from the booth. "Come on. We need to find a place to crash before you fall off the bike."

A few miles later, they pulled into the motel parking lot. Only two other vehicles were parked, and they were closer to the office of the U-shaped motel. Jace's practiced eye roved over the tiny office as he went inside, saw the bullet-proof glass shielding the sleepy desk clerk who came out to answer the bell Jace rang.

Seeing Kara, the clerk immediately perked up. He smoothed down his oily hair, flashed a grin in Kara's direction that raised Jace's suspicions.

"Hello. Need a room for the evening…or the hour?"

The man's sly grin widened as he stared at Kara.

"All night long." Jace locked gazes with the man and didn't drop his until the man did.

Jace turned to Kara. "Honey, why don't you wait outside in the fresh air?"

The clerk told him the amount. Jace opened his wallet and thumbed out the cash.

"Nice bike," the man suddenly said. "Been riding a while?"

Kara yawned and rubbed her bottom. Jace caught a glimpse of well-known ink on the man's arm. Devil horns in crimson with a snake threading through them.

Guy was a DP. Damn. Yet maybe not. He might be a wannabe or prospect.

"A while. You ride?" Jace asked.

"Had to sell my bike." The man's gaze sharpened on his face, then he looked him up and down.

Jace didn't like how the guy picked up his phone and studied it intently, as if getting word of the Rapture. All his instincts warned this dude was no good.

He needed to toss him a little misdirection in case the clerk was connected to the DP.

Jace picked up the motel key. "Going to Texas but first dropping this little lady off at a friend's. Got a little business to do—and I don't want the company. Not until tomorrow morning, after we both have a little fun."

Filled with distaste, Jace winked at the man.

The clerk nodded, counted the cash and put it away. Already his interest was elsewhere. "Have a good night."

Jace opened the office door but saw in the glass the clerk get on his cell phone. Not good.

Best to leave, now…

Aw, damn.

Sitting on the curb, Kara had propped up her chin on one fist, her eyes closed. She was dead tired.

Getting her to ride was impossible and risky. She'd fall off. No choice but to stay here for her to catch a few z's.

Arm around her waist as he supported Kara, remembering happier times when they'd snagged a room for the night to enhance their romance, he helped her into Number 9.

Soon as they got inside, he set Kara on her feet and yanked down the threadbare bedspread. His ex, whose expense budget probably covered five-star resorts with mints on the pillow and Egyptian cotton sheets, fell onto the lumpy bed and was instantly asleep. He removed her sneakers. Jace shrugged out of his leather jacket and tossed it over a chair at the scratched desk. He went outside, parked the bike in front of their room and grabbed their knapsacks from the bike's saddlebags.

Jace made sure to lock the door. He checked the exits— window by the bed. It overlooked a dark alleyway. Not good.

Sighing, he rubbed a hand through his hair. He grabbed shampoo from his bag and stripped, then stepped into the shower. Water spurted out. At least the pressure was good. He showered, using the postage-size soap the motel kindly provided, and washed the day's strain out of his hair.

Minutes later, he padded into the room, feeling a little more revived.

Sleep was impossible right now. He'd lived without it before. More important that Kara rested.

Maybe he could blend in with lowlifes, but Kara stood out, a diamond among costume jewelry.

Not for the first time, Jace wondered if he should have swapped his bike for a rental car. But the bike was faster and he had to stay in character. Gator would never drive a car, and as far as he knew, Lance trusted him to find Dylan and the missing jewels.

He didn't want to stay here. He wanted to push on. But

Kara needed rest. Jace accessed the internet using his phone and logged in to retrieve his messages.

Cold sweat trickled down his back.

Not only had the local law enforcement opened an investigation into the murders at the clubhouse, but he and Dylan were also wanted for questioning.

If he turned himself in, he'd blow his cover.

If he stayed in character, he risked arrest.

He couldn't turn himself in now. He was close to discovering Marcus's real identity. And there was Kara…who would simply continue onto Georgia without him, endangering herself.

Jace exhaled a sharp breath as he glanced at his ex. One hand was tucked beneath her smooth, flawless cheek. Her long hair spread out on the pillow. She was a breath of fresh air in a dirty, foul arena, the light floral scent of her perfume cutting through the smoky air and smell of old beer.

Stretching out next to her on the king-size bed, he tried to focus on resting. Fastidious Kara hadn't even blinked when he'd escorted her inside. No complaints.

He appreciated that side of her—hell, had appreciated it when they were together. Just never showed it. Maybe if he had, they'd still be together.

Suddenly he could no longer keep his eyes open. During his time with the Army Rangers, he'd trained himself to fall into REM sleep for short intervals. Jace lied down on the bed and in minutes, was fast asleep.

He woke to sounds of the shower running. Kara. Jace closed his eyes, wishing he didn't have such an active imagination.

When she emerged from the bathroom, he closed his eyes and pretended to sleep.

It seemed like minutes later he woke up. No reason.

Two o'clock. So much for a quick nap. He glanced at the luminous numbers on the ancient clock radio on the scratched bedside table. In her lacy bra and panties, Kara was lying on the lumpy king-size bed, fast asleep once more. Her delicate features had softened in sleep, losing the worry that had etched her expression since they'd left his apartment. Outside, light from the lone streetlamp illuminating the back alleyway spilled through the threadbare curtains. Kara breathed slowly and deeply, soothing his frayed nerves. At least she was safe now.

All his senses were on high alert. Spending the night here was not his preference, but Kara was exhausted.

Finally, he drifted off again.

A crunching noise outside awakened him like a gunshot. Jace bolted upright, glanced at the clock, every cell tingling a threat.

Nearly five. Glock in hand, he padded over to the window, lifted the dirty lace curtains with the back of his left hand. He could see clearly outside. In the darkness, he knew no one could see inside their room.

The narrow back alleyway, flanked by straggly trees and scrub brush, was little more than a dirt road mixed with old coral rock. In a thin wash of pale moonlight, he saw them. Two figures in black, striding down the alley. At the window of each room, they paused and peered inside. He didn't need to see their clothing to know they were wearing leather, and biker boots. Judging from how tall they were, one was Big Mike. The other, maybe Snake.

Looking for them.

A chill raced down his spine. Jace had insisted on the room at the end. Good thing, for the pair had started at the opposite end.

Pressing against the window, he held his breath as he watched the shadows creep closer. Pale moonlight dappled the ground as their boots crunched the gravel. Moonlight glinted off the metal barrels of the handguns they held.

Damn. He considered his next move. Stay here? Obviously not, for they'd be as good as dead. Flee, but where? They'd hear the bike, guess what happened and pursue them once more.

Unless… Jace smiled.

Dropping the curtain, he raced over to the bed, jiggled Kara awake with a gentle shake to her slim shoulders.

"Let's go."

Only two words, but she was awake, rubbing her eyes and drawing on her jeans and T-shirt. He made a brief, protesting sigh as all that lovely, pale skin was covered in cloth, but at the same time he was sheathing his sidearm in his back holster and grabbing their packs, heading toward the warped door.

"Do I have time for the bathroom?" she whispered.

"No."

No protests from her as she raced outside with him. Jace opened the saddlebags and tossed their gear inside. He held a finger to his mouth. She walked with him as he wheeled his bike away.

At the edge of the lot, he stopped.

"Get on," he whispered. "I'll be right back."

Fishing a big knife out of his duffel, he ran over to the two bikes parked by the motel office. One, two and the deed was done. Air hissed out of the tires he'd punctured.

Jason ran back to his bike and started the engine. Sweet deal, it turned over easily. He grinned as he accelerated out of the parking lot, craned his neck to turn and see the two men run around the side of the motel and head for their bikes.

Seemed like Big Mike shook a meaty fist at him in the rearview mirror.

"Won't they follow us?" Kara pushed back her hair.

"It'll be a few hours until they can get those fixed. We'll be long gone," he assured Kara.

"How did they find us?"

"I don't know. But I sure as hell am going to find out."

He stopped at a 24-hour convenience store and escorted Kara inside toward the restroom. Keeping an eye on the women's room door, Jace bought a couple of colas and paid cash. The clerk, a kid in his teens, looked more interested in his phone than Jace.

Waiting for Kara, he paced the aisle and called his boss. Rafe answered on the first ring. Finally.

"Where the hell have you been?" he demanded.

A huge yawn. "Sorry, man. Phone died... It's been...a day."

"They found us. How, I have no clue. I took precautions. Lots of them," Jason warned.

"Damn. You know the local LEOs are looking for you. And Dylan."

"I know. Got my messages."

"You still headed to Georgia?"

"On our way."

"You need to come in," Rafe said suddenly.

Jace's heart sank. "No way, man. I've put too much into this case and so have you. I'm close, Rafe. Dylan contacted Kara and if I can get to him, I can get him to turn state's evidence. He witnessed the murders and he can ID Marcus. I'm the best chance you have at exposing this son of a bitch."

Silence for a moment, and then Rafe sighed. "Knew you'd say that. I'm no longer in south Florida. This is my op and

I intend to see it through. Took the team to a small Georgia field office. Where you at?"

Jace told him. "I think they've got eyes on me, somehow. I hate getting rid of my bike, but I need new wheels."

"No problem. I'll handle it. Remember the abandoned warehouses where we did that raid two years ago and busted up the drug ring?" Rafe named a town in north Florida.

A small smile touched his face. "How could I forget it? It was my first op. Our first op together. A real meet cute, where we began our bromance."

But Rafe failed to laugh at the joke. "Good. Meet me there around, say, eight o'clock. We'll swap vehicles. Can you make it there by then?"

"I can, if I push it. Rafe, what's wrong?"

Rafe heaved a deep breath. "This op is going south, fast. Now, my best guy undercover is a wanted man and Darkling says the chatter has increased that Marcus has his target sighted and his plan is in motion."

Jace swore in a low voice as the women's restroom door opened. "What's the target?"

"Something public and wealthy. The rich will pay. That's all we got. Keep your head down and stay alert, Jace. I don't want to lose you."

Rafe hung up.

Jace palmed his cell as Kara joined him and took one of the cold colas from him.

The game had suddenly gotten a whole lot deadlier. He needed to get to Dylan and get Kara away where she wouldn't be endangered.

Before both of them ended up dead.

Chapter 12

By 8:00 a.m., Jace and Kara arrived at the location Rafe had given him.

He guided the bike down the pothole-strewn street and pulled into a parking lot, accelerating until reaching the back of the warehouses.

Jace's gaze assessed the ruins of the decaying, abandoned warehouses with boarded-up windows and peeling paint. Once they'd housed businesses and storage, but Hurricane Igor a few years ago had ripped off roofs and smashed glass. The owner never restored the buildings, as he was waiting for an insurance dispute to resolve legally. After the hurricane, they served as hangouts where drug dealers met at night to exchange cash for cocaine. The FBI had conducted more than one raid here, cleaning up the area with the help of local law enforcement. Few people ventured there now, scared off by the Feds. Place was as silent as a ghost town, flanked by abandoned railroad tracks.

It made for a perfect location to swap vehicles.

The big bike roared down the cracked pavement, sound bouncing off the buildings. Jace halted by the railroad tracks, engine still running. If someone had followed him here, he needed to make a quick exit.

"Can I get off now? My butt is sore," Kara told him.

"No." He spat out the word with more worried urgency than he cared to show. "Wait."

"Wait for what?"

"Our ride."

Gritting his teeth, he hoped the hell Rafe had come through, and not with an SUV that looked like a typical Fed vehicle. He needed to look innocuous, but on short notice, he worried Rafe wouldn't be able to pull this off.

He turned his attention to the train tracks. Early morning sunlight glinted off a still unrusty section of railroad track. A dense canopy of tall, spindly Australian pines flanked the tracks, swaying in the breeze. Trash littered the tracks—soda cans, orange peels, candy bar wrappers. Brush and sun daisies grew between the tracks. The colorful yellow flowers softened the sense of decay and neglect. Grackles crowed in the nearby trees. A few dropped down to forage for scraps in the litter lining the railroad tracks.

Nature takes over everything eventually, if given enough time.

A few minutes later, a sleek black sedan drove up behind them and stopped. Engine still running, the driver's side door opened.

Jace breathed relief as Rafe stepped out of the vehicle, leaving the door open. Never one to drop his guard, his team leader scanned the surroundings, not once, but twice, before putting distance between himself and the car. The car was an older model, nondescript, but gleaming in the harsh sunlight.

"Now we get off," he told Kara, turning off the engine and dismounting.

As Jace grabbed their backpacks from the saddlebags, Kara removed the helmet and placed it on the seat next to the one he'd placed there. They walked over to the car. Jace bent down and peered inside. He rolled his eyes at the rearview mirror.

"Fuzzy dice?"

"My cousin's car. He likes to gamble. Borrowed the wheels from him."

Kara looked over Rafe as one might scrutinize a new ally. Or an enemy. Her gaze whipped back to Jace. "You look somewhat like Jace."

Rafe offered a dazzling smile. Jace couldn't see the resemblance. Yeah, they were about the same height, bearded, similar slender but muscle-toned build and had dark hair, but the resemblance ended there. Rafe's skin was sun-darkened, hinting of his Hispanic origins.

His hair brushed the collar of his white dress shirt, where Jace's was down to his shoulders.

"Hello. You're Kara. Heard much about you, but Jace never mentioned how beautiful you are," Rafe said in his deep voice.

"Funny. Jace never mentioned you," she said.

Rafe gave a sharp bow. "Rafael Jones Rodriguez, at your service, Miss Wilmington."

"Jones?" Kara's brow wrinkled.

He shot her a toothsome, aw-shucks grin that usually made women melt. "I'm Cuban, on my mother's side. My dad is Joshua Jones. Old family joke is keeping up with the Cuban Joneses."

Kara's pretty, glossy lips quirked up in a faint smile. Rafe's dark eyes gleamed with intensity as he studied Kara. Rafe might be his friend and a top-notch, dedicated Federal agent, but he was a guy as well. Real ladies' man, and the ladies loved him back. Kara, however, only sniffed and turned back to Jace.

He felt an utterly juvenile thrill that Rafe's charm hadn't had any effect on her.

"We're leaving the bike with him?" she asked.

"Yeah. The car is less conspicuous. Just hope she's fast."

"Fast?" Rafe shook his head in apparent amusement. "We're talking my cousin Luis, who's a mechanic and swapped the original engine for real power. New tires, the works. Got a full tank of gas as well." Rafe spoke to him but kept looking at Kara.

"Good enough. If they start shooting, I can always toss the fuzzy dice at them," Jace drawled.

A joke to ease the uncomfortable tension, but Rafe's smile dropped.

"That's not funny, Jace."

"I promise I won't get any blood on the seats."

"They start shooting, you get the hell away, Jace. That's a direct order. I'll be damned if I lose anyone else."

Gone was the ladies' man. Rafe turned into the stoic FBI agent who'd witnessed two of his men gunned down in a hail of bullets.

He didn't like the dawning questions on Kara's face, as if she was starting to put pieces together.

Raising his hand to his ear, he signaled Rafe he'd call him later. Rafe gave a brusque nod and walked around the car to open the passenger door for Kara.

Ever polite, Kara nodded. "Nice to meet you, Mr. Jones Rodriguez."

Rafe didn't answer but shut the door when she was settled inside. He helped Jace toss the two packs into the trunk. Then he fetched the extra helmet from the bike and tossed that inside as well.

"Here. I can't use two helmets."

Jace reached inside the car, removed the dice from the rearview mirror and handed them to Rafe. "Return these to your cousin. I can't guarantee the car will be in terrific condition when he gets it back, but at least the dice will be intact."

"We need to talk." Rafe's gaze flicked to Kara as he peered inside the car. "Alone. Excuse me, Kara, if I seem rude."

He began speaking in rapid Spanish to Jace. Kara held up a hand. "Sorry. I'm fluent in Spanish. You're saying something about critical information at this juncture?"

Rafe stared while Jace grinned. He didn't know why, but he liked Rafe underestimating Kara.

"Let's talk over here a minute. But only a minute. I have to get on the road."

"*We* have to get on the road," Kara pointed out.

"I'll be a minute. Stay there."

Jace steered Rafe over to the side of a warehouse, out of hearing range for Kara. Stomach tight, he jammed his hands into his pockets.

"What's up?"

Rafe kept scanning the area. "They want those jewels Dylan took. Or more likely, Dylan himself. The heat is on, Jace. You're sure to have a tail on you because Lance's crew knows you're out to find him."

Jace nodded. "I promised Lance I'd find Dylan. Soon as they get hold of him, adios, I'm sure. Lance wants that jewelry back."

"Which is why you can't take her—" Rafe jammed a thumb toward Kara "—with you. Too dangerous. What the hell are you thinking?"

Something didn't make sense. "You're holding back on me. What is it?"

Rafe's face tightened. "I'm almost ready to call you in, Jace. You're in deep, but too deep. It's getting dangerous."

"I'm in deep, which is why I'm the best man for the job. Dammit, Rafe!" He blew out a breath. "Talk to me. What happened? And why the hell couldn't I reach you yesterday?"

The other man's shoulders slumped and his gaze turned empty. "We lost John Myers yesterday."

Holy crap. "Johnny? He was working on Devil's Patrol angle from the outside."

"He got intel from Parker, a DP who promised to hook him up with a member who reported to the top man, Marcus. He offered to take him to a meeting. Johnny went, against my express orders. It was an ambush. They set him up." Rafe swore a string of curses in Spanish. "Local LEOs found his body in ditch off US Twenty-seven this morning."

Damn. Jace's chest felt hollow. Lost another one, a good agent, a nice kid who only tried to make life safer for civilians. Johnny was young, eager to prove himself. Now, he understood Rafe's concern.

"I'm sorry, Rafe. Johnny was a damn fine agent."

Rafe's dark gaze glittered. "We got a break with Parker. Tracked him down and arrested him for peddling drugs at a local club. He told me a few things."

Jace blew out a breath. "Good."

If anyone could make a suspect blather, it was his boss.

"I want you to come in, Jace. This assignment's gone south. I won't lose another member of my team." Rafe sounded broken. "Not you. They knew, somehow, that John was an agent. It won't take much for them to realize you're one as well."

"I'm not John. My cover's good. Lance knows I'm after Dylan to get those jewels back."

"I doubt that numbnut even knows he's being outmaneuvered and Marcus is using him. The jewelry is a drop in the bucket, Jace. Why do smash-and-grabs for jewels when Marcus is bringing in more than ten million dollars a year using the Devil's Patrol for drug dealing, extortion and gunrunning? I think the jewel thefts are a cover for something else. Something Marcus wants more than money."

His knees felt weak. "What? Any idea?"

"We don't know. But it's personal. More than power, Marcus wants something and is planning to blow up a target because of it. He killed those kids, not because they stole the jewelry, but because they knew too much. Maybe they overheard something they shouldn't have. Dylan as well. Marcus didn't want to leave witnesses behind."

Jace's stomach roiled.

Rafe caught his shoulder. "Jace, we can't be sure that Johnny didn't talk before they killed him. If he did…"

His stomach tightened as he looked at Kara, pacing back and forth by the railroad tracks. "Marcus would know I'm a federal agent. And come after me."

"Right now you're the best means of finding Dylan. They're certain to follow you, not to get the jewelry back, but to finish what Marcus started."

"Unfortunately, Kara's the only one who has a clue where the kid went. She has to go with me. Dylan trusts her."

Rafe's mouth compressed. "Maybe it's better she does. Then you'll take extra precautions with her around. I'm damn sick and tired of losing my team. Too many damn funerals."

Jace felt grief at the loss, and more than a little concerned for Rafe. He'd grown a lock of gray hair since getting shot more than a year ago and each loss he took personally, as if losing a member of his family. He squeezed the other man's shoulder.

"You need to go to a wedding. Remember the good things about life."

A short laugh. "Right. I have a wedding the same day as John's funeral, can you believe it? My cousin Christina on my mom's side. Had to cancel and my family is furious. Weddings are mandatory on my mom's Cuban side of the family. The only good excuse is you're either in the hospital or below ground. Good thing my *abuela* considers me her favorite, or I'd be toast."

"Your grandmother has good judgment. Nice lady."

Rafe laughed. "Oh, she'd smack me down if she thought I was getting out of line. And then probably make me a huge meal and force me to eat because she thought I was too skinny."

Such family devotion was foreign to Jace. His family didn't care if he went to funerals, weddings or any gathering. He was almost invisible. Hell, he couldn't even remember the last time he saw his maternal grandmother. As for his father's side of the family...those grandparents were long dead and his uncles and aunt were lowlifes somewhere out west. He had met them only once, and once was enough.

Jace felt a tinge of envy for such close connections, which also came with their own set of problems, from what Rafe had told him.

"Some days I think I should give up. Turn in my shield. Retire early."

Now, real concern shot through him. "No way, man. Not you. Your career."

Rafe snorted. "What good is a career when you keep losing members of your team?"

"You can't quit, Rafe. You're too good. We need you." Jace glanced backward at Kara. "People like her count on you. The world's a dangerous place that keeps shattering and you're one of the good guys who glues the broken pieces together."

Rafe gave a brusque nod. He looked as if he wanted to say something else, then cocked his head. Alert, tense.

Recognizing the sound, Jace's heart raced, adrenaline flooding his veins. Motorcycles. At least two big hogs. He ran to the railroad tracks. Two big bikes roared on the street on the opposite side of the tracks, the sound growing dimmer as they headed south. But that street was a dead end. Soon, they'd turn around.

He wanted to believe they were out for a leisurely drive. Knew better. Jace cursed, whipping his gaze around. "How the hell did they find me this fast?"

Something flickered in Rafe's gaze. "If you were followed, then they tracked you a different way. Who has access to this bike?"

"Anyone. Everyone, when I park it in the open."

"I'd bet my sweet *abuela's* secret family recipe for *comida criolla* they put a GPS tracker on your bike."

Jace swore. He didn't like the idea of Rafe being a new target. "Yeah, I figured as much, which is why I want you to take Kara and leave. I'll find the tracker."

"Change clothing with me. It'll buy you time. Kara said we resemble each other a little. We're about the same size."

He didn't like it, but Rafe had a point. Jace sat on the ground to tug off his biker boots while Rafe toed off his shoes. They stripped and exchanged clothing. Rafe's white cotton button-down shirt and linen trousers felt odd after months of going casual.

The clothing was a little loose on him, but it worked. He eyed Rafe in his T-shirt, black leather jacket, worn jeans and biker boots.

"Now I know where your salary goes, bruh. Nice threads," Jace said.

Rafe tucked his weapon into the back of the jeans. He climbed onto the bike, saluted Kara.

"Stay safe," he told Jace, and then he was off, the big bike roaring and the sound finally fading away.

Jace watched him leave. Getting to Georgia and finding Dylan was imperative now. They had to get to the kid.

Before Marcus launched his op to blow his target sky high.

Chapter 13

The car Rafe loaned him was immaculate, and rode like a dream, with a V-8 engine that purred at the speed limit and accelerated like a bullet when he needed speed. The seats were soft leather that provided plenty of comfort for long driving. The air-conditioning worked, and he could Bluetooth his iPhone to the speaker system and play soothing classical music.

Why then, did he feel so uneasy as they drove north through the sleepy back roads of Georgia?

Wasn't that he merely missed his bike and hoped the hell Rafe had been able to evade his pursuers. It was Kara, riding shotgun next to him, the delicate scent of her perfumed skin tasing him like an electrical shock. Kara, who had snuggled against him on the motorcycle and wrapped her slim arms around his waist, hanging on for dear life. Kara, who now hugged the door as if ready to open it and jump out of this car.

They'd driven all day, stopping briefly for rest stops. Jace glanced at the clock on the dashboard. Two hours until her cousin was due to call. He could understand her tension, but not the anger radiating from her like a heat signature.

"What's eating you?" he asked.

Kara turned her head. "Nothing. I'm fine."

"The hell you are. You've barely spoken since we left Rafe." Jace blew out a breath. "You insisted on being on this ride, Kara. Now, you're acting like I forced you to come along."

"What's going on with you, Jace?" she blurted. "Stop lying to me and tell me what is really going on. I know there's more to all this than my jewelry getting stolen. That guy you know—Rafe—you spoke to him like he was law enforcement and you work for him."

His shoulders sagged. He avoided a pothole, slowed down as they came into a tiny town where the speed limit was more conducive to a brisk stroll. A post office, mini market and gas station and two churches flanked them as he drove down the main street.

At a red light, he turned and regarded her. "Let's stop and get a bite. You have a couple of hours until he calls and you look famished."

Kara shook her head. "I'm not hungry and I can't eat until you promise to level with me. I can't do this anymore, Jace. I'm too upset over Dylan and I need you to stop acting like everything is a secret."

Her mouth compressed. "Because if Dylan is in real trouble, not just wanted by the local cops and these gangbangers you call friends, I want to know every single detail. I won't risk losing him, just as your friend Rafe told you to run if anyone starts shooting because he won't risk losing you as well."

She turned to look out her window. "And I…don't want to lose you, either, Jace."

Whoa. This went in a different direction than he'd anticipated. Jace's hand tightened on the steering wheel. "Nothing bad's gonna happen to me, Kara. I can handle myself. As for your cousin, I'll do everything I can to save him."

Without waiting for an answer, he used his phone's GPS to look for a quick meal and found a diner up the road. He'd prefer a more anonymous chain restaurant, but this rural area offered few options.

Jace pulled into the parking lot of the Good Times Diner.

Lots of pickup trucks, some older sedans. Definitely a locals' hangout. He rolled up his shirtsleeves. Maybe no one would recognize him. He held the door open for Kara, taking a deep breath as all convo stopped and they stared at her.

Kara was stare-worthy, oh, yeah. Put her in rags and she'd still stand out like pure snow on blacktop. But he wished he'd gone further, maybe found a fast-food stand. Too late now. At least no sheriff's deputies sitting at the counter, jawing about the weather and such, and criminal bikers on the run from law enforcement.

When they were seated at a booth near the kitchen, him facing the door to survey who came inside, Jace tried to concentrate on the grease-splattered menu. Too many questions, and he had answers he couldn't give her.

Kara was already involved and he needed to cut her out of this equation.

"Jace?" Her voice was quiet, troubled. "Please talk to me and stop staring at the menu as if it holds all the answers in the world."

"I wish it did. Maybe life would be less complicated." He set aside the menu as a waiter scurried to their side.

He ordered a thick juicy hamburger with cheese, fries on the side. Kara settled for a salad. She was too thin and she needed protein.

When their drinks arrived, he was ready to tell her a partial truth without blowing his cover. With the noise from the kitchen, and most of the locals gathered near the counter, they had a modicum of privacy.

"Kara, I work in the garage the Devil's Patrol own. Yeah, I'm a member. But I'm not like the others." He sipped the sweet tea. One thing about this section of the South. Sweet tea was guaranteed and it was mighty fine.

He sipped more tea and then continued, "Neither is your

cousin. I did a little digging and found out Dylan is in deep debt to Lance, the club president. Lance bought him the Ducati, the bike he owns, and as payback, Lance has forced him to steal. Smash-and-grab burglaries. Dylan didn't want to participate, but Lance threatened to break his fingers."

Blood drained from her face. She took a long drink from her water, and then patted her mouth. No lipstick on the napkin. No makeup. Only Kara, natural face and way too pale right now.

"He never told me. I wish he had. We're close but I guess not close enough. I could help him, my parents could help him... We have to get him out of this, Jace! How much is that bike?"

When he named the price, she didn't blink. "My dad would transfer the money to your president..."

Not my president. "No dice, babe. Lance doesn't want money. He wanted Dylan under his thumb to steal for him. His puppet. Until Dylan himself stole the jewelry from under the gang's noses."

"He might have taken it from the gang because they're my jewels. He's family, and we look out for each other."

"If he is, why is he so desperate to help his mother? Your family has money..."

Kara looked away, biting her lower lush lip. "We tried. We did give her money, but her husband, Dylan's stepdad, took it, and instead of using it to pay hospital and doctor bills, the rat bastard used it to gamble. Until Wanda can get out of there, he'll take everything she has. He doesn't care if she lives or dies. I'm going to find a way to get her free. I will."

Her voice held a note of fierce resolve. "As for Dylan, I can convince him to turn himself in, once I see him face-to-face."

She was awfully involved with Dylan. Understandable. Family came first with Kara, which was one reason he didn't protest when she broke off their relationship. He could never measure up to her expectations regarding closeness with family members. Not with his history.

The waiter brought their food. Jace took a huge bite of his burger, too famished to be polite. As he chewed, he considered everything she'd told him. Something was off about all this because she had a zealous attitude about Dylan, almost as if he was a brother and not a cousin.

Jace wondered.

The records he found regarding Dylan had been mostly sealed, due to him being a juvenile at the time of the offense. Darkling had gone over Dylan's social media and found a brief, but poignant posting about a boy named Conner, Dylan's best friend when they were both kids. Conner had been killed in a tragic car accident and his death had "messed me up for a long time," Dylan had posted.

Jace needed to ferret out more about the mysterious Conner. He found no obituary, or even mention of a funeral home. Kara must know who Conner was since Dylan was close to the boy.

He reached for the salt, shook a generous amount onto his fries. Nibbling on her salad, Kara shook her head.

"Keep that up, Jace, and you're going to have a coronary by the time you're in your forties."

"Better than becoming a rabbit," he joked, eyeballing her greens. "I don't always eat like this. It's a special occasion."

At her puzzled look, he added, "I'm hungry."

The sound of her light laugh cut through the tension and made him smile. "I've missed that," he admitted. "Hearing you laugh."

Kara stopped, her gaze locking to his. "I miss you making me laugh, Jace."

So much he missed about her, yet, busy with his career,

he hadn't filled in the gaping hole in his life until he'd run into her again. Talk about avoidance. He'd thrown everything into his career with the FBI, taking classes in undercover work to be the best. Always striving to be the best, making up for the screwups in his younger days.

Making up for the screwup with Kara.

Words he wanted to say remained stuck on his tongue. Jace bit into his burger again, chewed, uncomfortable with the silence between them. Good time to bring up their past, where they went wrong, maybe what they could do to fix it.

Because suddenly he realized he did miss her fiercely. Not just the hot sex and passion Kara brought out, more than any other woman. He missed everything about her, from her cute habit of nibbling on her lower lip while deep in thought, to her incredible determination in achieving her goals. The FBI had run a check on Kara after the theft, to make sure she wasn't orchestrating it for insurance. Every bit of information Darkling had sent about Kara indicated she was honest and had a sterling reputation. Kara had taken a mediocre estate-sale business and made it into a thriving company, sharpening her skills while treating her clients fairly.

He was proud of her, Jace realized suddenly.

Say it. The words were on his tongue. Damn, he wanted to say them, but he couldn't. Because in the back of his mind he hated starting up something he'd have to end.

This assignment came first. Not his personal relationships.

Kara glanced at her cell phone. "We need to be some place with a strong signal when Dylan calls. We'd better get out of here soon, Jace. Hurry, please."

Polishing off his burger in a few bites, leaving the fries, he signaled for the check. Paid it, leaving a generous tip. Kara didn't even fight him for it. How well he remembered her stubbornly insisting on splitting the check during their time together. She hadn't changed.

Worry was overriding everything else.

Outside in the parking lot, Kara grabbed the keys from him. "You've been driving forever. My turn."

He obliged but raised his eyebrows. "I was hoping to get further north by today, not next year."

"Ha ha. I can drive fast."

"Wonders never cease," he muttered, climbing into the passenger seat.

When they were on the road again, he glanced at the dashboard clock. Growing closer to five.

"How's your signal?" he asked.

Holding her cell phone, Kara nodded. "Good. I'm pulling over into that shopping plaza to wait for his call."

The plaza looked deserted, with a few businesses that were closed. Kara parked at the end under a shady tree and left the engine running. Overgrown bushes provided privacy from the main road.

Anyone searching for them would have to enter the plaza from a side street. Still, he kept glancing around, a well-developed sense of preservation honed over the years.

It had started with his old man, who liked to beat him up at times. Jace had learned to read the signals.

Kara had such a different upbringing. Still, he wondered what ate at her. Something clearly had and he'd always had the feeling deep down that she hid a family secret.

Good time to ask more about Dylan, before the kid called and forced them into a corner.

"Tell me, who was Conner? Dylan mentioned he misses him and the kid's death when they were both nine messed him up."

True enough. He neglected to add he discovered this through Dylan's social-media posting.

Blood drained from her face. Kara glanced at him, her eyes wide.

"How…when did Dylan say that?"

Ignoring the question, Jace persisted. "Was he a neighborhood kid?"

Pulse beating wildly in her neck, sweat forming on her temples and not just from the anticipated call. Jace turned up the air-conditioning to cool the car more, but he sensed her nerves, more than the heat, had caused the reaction.

"Who was he, Kara?"

She pushed back at the long fall of her hair. "He was a good kid. Dylan's cousin. Maybe a little too impulsive and inclined to get into trouble."

"Did you know him?"

That question evoked an uncomfortable silence. Jace persisted. "You must have known him since you're so close to Dylan."

Finally, she looked up. Stunned, he saw her clear blue eyes filled with tears.

"I knew him. I knew him well, Jace. Oh, God, I did. And every day, I miss him, too. My parents…they will never stop missing him."

Insight suddenly hit him. "Conner wasn't just Dylan's cousin and friend. He was your brother."

At her jerky nod, he blew out a breath and sank back into the seat. Felt like someone had punched him in the stomach.

"Damn, Kara. You never told me. You never talked about him. Your brother? Holy crap…"

"The accident was my fault, Jace. My fault! I was driving…" Her voice rose and then fell.

Her eyes closed as tears dripped down her cheeks. Jace

dug into the pocket of Rafe's trousers and found a clean linen handkerchief. Guy always carried them. He once said it was to comfort women who cried on him.

Made him wonder exactly how many times women cried on the guy.

Kara took the cloth, wiped her nose and eyes. Jace waited. Couldn't push her, not now. Not after all these years, she'd kept the secret. He wished he'd coaxed her into sharing her tragic past with him when they were together years ago, but he understood, maybe more than she knew.

Some family secrets were too painful to share, even when you thought you were close to someone.

"Conner was my brother. He was several years younger than me…"

Sensing the dam was about to spill, he waited. All he could do was listen and be there for her now, instead of regretting he hadn't been supportive when they were together.

He listened as the words spilled out, tumbling over each other. How she'd taken out her new car for a test drive, not realizing Conner was hiding in the back seat. The motorcycle that seemed to come out of nowhere.

The screech of sirens, flashing red lights and her brother lying oh-so still on the roadway as paramedics worked to save his life.

The dead biker who rammed into her car. The motorcyclist who ran a red light, seeming to come out of nowhere. She'd seen his face before a cop tactfully draped a yellow cloth over the body, his eyes staring sightlessly at the sky.

Everything made sense now. Her devotion to charitable causes, especially the organization dedicated to teaching young drivers. Kara's hatred of motorcycles and why she always drove slow and took no risks.

Her determination to save Dylan at a personal risk to herself, because she couldn't save her brother.

Kara gripped her hands so hard her knuckles whitened.

"Conner didn't die right away. They kept him alive…life support. He was on life support for two days and then my parents made that awful decision no parent should make."

Jace sucked in a breath. "Damn. I'm so sorry."

"Do you know what an honor walk is in a hospital?"

He nodded.

"They did that for him—the nurses, doctors, hospital staff, even the maintenance guys lined the hallway as a nurse wheeled my little brother down to surgery to remove his organs after they would take him off life support. It was the only way my mother would agree…so he would give life for someone else. They wheeled him down the hallway and I walked behind him. Someone threw a few flowers on the hospital bed… I was numb. I couldn't speak. Cry. Anything. I walked down the hallway on crutches because I'd broken my leg in the accident."

She drew in a breath. "I broke my leg but my brother's death almost broke my mom."

Jace felt emotion clog his throat, thinking of a young Kara, watching her little brother be wheeled into surgery so his life could end, and another could live. He couldn't imagine the heartache her family had suffered.

Every instinct urged him to offer solace. But how could you comfort someone who had suffered crushing loss and still believed it was her fault, after all these years?

No words existed. Jace reached out and held her hand, letting her feel his presence.

Letting her know he listened. And he cared, because damn, he did.

Tears glistened in Kara's eyes. "I miss him, Jace. He was

only eight and could be a brat, but he was *my* brat, my little brother. I miss him so much at times. I—I went into his room when we were in Mom and Dad's house and kept looking around, expecting him to come bursting out of the closet to yell 'gotcha' or tease me or ask me how high school was... He always followed me around like an eager puppy. I miss him so much I can hear the ghost of his voice in my mind and I turn around, expecting to see him, but I see only silence. So much quiet."

Jace let her grip his hand and nodded. "I understand."

Because even if he hadn't lost a brother like she had, he knew what it was like to lose a family member. He'd lost his dad years ago, long before he was imprisoned. Lost his mom the day his dad got arrested.

Her gaze turned stricken.

"Do you know when someone you love dies and their room remains the same as it did the way they left this earth, it becomes more of a memorial than a tombstone? It's a place-holder covered in memories that are so sharp and painful they make you bleed inside, and yet you don't want to get rid of the grief because it's the last, lingering connection you have to him. When the grief is gone, he'll be gone for good."

Lifting her hand to his mouth, he gently kissed her knuckles, wishing he could kiss away all her pain. Jace reached up and gently wiped away her tears.

"I'm sorry, babe. I am truly sorry. I'm sorry you had to go through that alone and you never told me. I'm glad you finally did. Thank you for trusting me enough to tell me about Conner. He sounds like a special kid."

"I found out who the biker was, Jace. His name was Archie Turner. He was divorced but had a son. I wanted to contact the son, but my parents wouldn't allow it. I think...they helped to pay for his funeral, anonymously. I still felt guilty. It was my fault, Jace. The accident was my fault."

"How? You were a kid, sure, the ink barely dry on your learner's permit. Yeah, you disobeyed your folks in taking the car when they weren't there. But you had the green light. The biker didn't."

"I killed two people, Jace."

"No, babe. Two people, including your brother, died in a tragic accident. Did the cops charge you with anything?"

Biting her lip, she shook her head.

Jace cupped her cheek and caressed it in a lingering stroke to wipe away her tears. "All law enforcement have homicide investigations when someone dies in a crash. They do it for a lot of reasons, but the main one is to discover what happened and who was at fault."

"My parents told me the biker was at fault because he was speeding and ran a red light. I went on the green light, maybe too soon…"

Jace nodded. "It wasn't your fault, babe. Believe me. You were punished enough. Stop punishing yourself for a mistake you made when you were a kid."

As he drew his hand away, Kara wiped her eyes. "Thanks, Jace. Thank you for saying that."

He glanced at the dashboard clock. Another time he'd ask her about the good memories because he'd learned the good memories needed to balance out the bad ones.

"You okay? Because Conner's best friend is gonna call any minute now and you need to get yourself together. For the sake of your little brother, not just Dylan. Your brother would want you doing this."

As if she reached down deep inside and found an inner core of strength, Kara sat straight and wiped her eyes and composed herself. She found lip gloss in her purse and used the visor mirror to apply it. Pasting on a wide smile, she nodded.

"That's my girl."

Her lower lip wobbled. "Thank you, Jace. Thanks for listening and doing this."

He wanted to pull her into his arms, reassure her as he'd done in the past when they were together. For a moment, the temptation tugged at him, then the pragmatic agent nudged it aside.

A black SUV pulled into the shopping plaza lot and parked near them. Jace assessed the newcomer. Blacked-out windows, engine still running. What the hell were they doing here? Driver wasn't getting out, either.

Not taking chances, he gestured to the vehicle. "I'm driving so you can focus on Dylan's call. We're out of here. I don't like the looks of that SUV."

They changed seats. Kara bit her lip as they drove past. The driver of the SUV made no attempt to follow.

"It's almost five, Jace. He's going to call."

At precisely five, her phone rang. Kara glanced at him, and mouthed, *Dylan*.

Jace nodded.

She answered, the phone held away from her ear so he could listen, her gaze never leaving Jace's. "Dylan. Thank heavens. I've been so worried about you. Hold on a minute, the car's in motion and I can't really talk."

Not much on this lone stretch of country road, but he spotted a white steeple with a cross. He pulled into the parking lot, parked and shut off the engine. Irony struck him—sitting in a church parking lot, hoping Kara's cousin would have a come-to-Jesus moment and turn himself in, or at least give them a hint where he was hiding.

Before the DP caught up with him and sent him firsthand to meet the good Lord in person…

"Okay, I'm back. Are you all right?" Kara asked.

"Is Jace there with you?"

Her brow wrinkled. "Why would he be?"

"He wouldn't go anywhere without you. I know it! Don't play games with me, Kara!"

From the sound of it, kid was falling apart. Jace gently took the phone from Kara and pressed the speaker button. "I'm here, Dylan, and you're on speaker."

"Good." His voice was shaky, but strong. "Make sure you're someplace where no one can hear you. I have something to tell you."

"Where are you?" Kara asked.

"Someplace you can't find me, but I'm okay. I'll be okay." Dylan's voice dropped. "I'm sorry, coz. I didn't want to help them steal from you. You're the last person I wanted to hurt."

"Dylan, that's not important," she began.

"Yes, it is! It is to me! You and your family have been so good to me. I want to make it up to you, at least a little. I hid the diamond necklace from the robbery, the one you said was almost worth two hundred grand, and I'm going to tell you where to find it."

Jace's questioning gaze flicked to her. Kara bit her lip. "All right. But, Dylan, please, we need you to come in. The police are looking for you."

"Everyone is looking for me. It's why I can't meet you guys. I've got a target on my back. I've got to go it alone."

"I can help you, Dylan," Jace said, cutting in. "I have resources."

"You're not going to turn me over to Lance? I checked his email and that's what he says."

"How did you…?"

"Hacked into his account when he wasn't looking. The guy is more oblivious than a bag of rocks. Except with guns. How can I know you won't turn me over, Gator?"

You can't. Except I'm not turning you over to a cold-blooded murderer. Just my supervisor.

"I have no intention of letting Lance know where you are, Dylan." That much was a truth he could dole out.

"Dylan, please, let us help you," Kara pleaded.

"No can do, coz. But I can help you."

He gave them the GPS coordinates. Jace memorized them.

"The necklace is inside the cabin in a velvet bag in the fireplace."

"You put my diamond necklace in ashes inside an unlocked cabin?" Kara sounded incredulous.

"No one goes there. Everyone in this town says it's haunted. A guy was murdered there ten years ago."

"Terrific," Kara muttered.

"You afraid of a ghost story?"

"No, Dylan. I'm afraid for you. Please, let us help you."

"Sorry."

The phone went dead.

Jace took the phone from her trembling hands and looked at the number, memorizing it. Even if it was a burner phone, at least he now could contact Dylan.

He knew Kara. She would face a horde of zombies to help her family. Admiration filled him. She held no concern for her own welfare, only her young cousin.

Such bravado and selflessness made his job more difficult, because Kara had a tendency to make reckless decisions as long as she thought someone threatened one of her family members.

"Let's go get your necklace and then revert to Plan B."

"Plan B. Where you leave me someplace and go off to trace

Dylan. I don't give a damn about the diamonds." She swallowed hard. "Don't dump me someplace and go off without me, Jace. The diamonds mean nothing compared to Dylan."

Jace gently tipped up her chin with a thumb, caressed her soft skin. She bit her lip, her woebegone gaze regarding him.

"Listen to me, babe. You're coming with me right now. We're going to find the diamonds and then put them someplace safe. Dylan will be okay. I won't stop until he's found and protected. I know how much you care."

Moisture glistened in her big blue eyes. "I do. Care."

For a moment he dared hope she meant him, not merely her cousin. Jace dropped his hand and returned her cell phone.

Suddenly, hair rose on the nape of his neck. Sirens sounded in the distance. He cursed a blue streak. "I knew it was too good to be true. I bet that's for me."

Kara turned around. "Oh, no. Is that a cop?"

"Yeah. Local LEO, probably responding to the BOLO for me. Cops put one out after the murder. I'm wanted for questioning."

At her stricken gaze, he added, "One reason I didn't want you along for the ride, babe. I don't want you mixed in with this mess."

Her chin took on that stubborn tilt he remembered well. "I bet someone in that diner reported you to the cops."

He thought hard. If he dodged the cop, he'd bring every single LEO in town after him.

Blowing his cover remained the only option. But he wasn't ready for that. Not yet, not when he'd put so much into this case and Dylan remained at large. They were close.

"I've got a plan." He popped the trunk.

They got out. Jace climbed into the trunk. "You've got to sound convincing. Sorry, babe, but you have to play the, excuse me, naive girl to the cop. You picked up a hitchhiker, treated him to lunch because he needed a meal and dropped him off someplace."

Kara nodded, bit her lip and shut the trunk. Jace centered his breathing. The trunk smelled like oil, grease and suntan lotion.

He heard the car pull up, a door open. Kara calling out through her open window.

"May I help you, Officer?"

Her voice so sweet and guileless. Jason grinned. *You could charm ants out of honey with that voice.*

He heard the cop say in a gruff tone something about a citizen spotting her with a dangerous biker wanted by authorities. Was she all right? Did she know the guy?

To his credit, the sheriff's deputy didn't act accusing, but was more concerned.

"Oh, my heavens, Officer! I didn't know! My word. I felt sorry for the poor man. He was hitchhiking and looked harmless. A criminal, you say?"

More mumbled words.

"Sorry, Officer. I dropped him off after we left the diner." Kara named a location twenty miles south. "I had no idea he was dangerous!"

More mumbling, but this time closer to the trunk. *Aw, damn.*

"Open the trunk, miss."

Jace bit his lip. Okay, think fast…

The trunk lid opened and he found himself staring at the face of an amused sheriff's deputy and Kara's worried expression. The deputy consulted his phone, and then spoke into his shoulder mike.

"Got him. He's here, hiding in the trunk."

Okay, Jason Beckett, how the hell are you getting out of this one?

Chapter 14

Kara's heart sank to her stomach. Caught, and rotten timing. Maybe she could call her father, ask him to beg a favor from one of his friends in law enforcement, the local DA, but this was Georgia, not Florida.

Her father's reach didn't go that far.

As she ran through the list of possibilities, the deputy's grin widened. The man was slightly portly, with gray hair and a suntanned face. He took off his mirrored sunglasses, squinted into the trunk.

"Jace Beckett. The one and only. What the hell you doing in there, son? Get out."

Jace blinked, took the hand the deputy offered and climbed out of the trunk. He dusted off his jeans, gave them a rueful look.

"Can I help you, Officer?"

So polite, and grace under pressure. Kara doubted she'd have the same dignity and confidence after climbing out of a trunk, knowing she'd been caught by the law.

"No, but you sure need some help," the deputy drawled. "From the looks of it, you sure do. Where's your bike?"

Jace blinked, losing a little of the confidence. He studied the deputy, who made no move to cuff him or read him his Miranda rights. "I know you?"

"Not exactly. Name's Bill Blakeson." The man stuck out a hand and Jace shook it. "You rode with our club last year to raise money for the benefit fund for the widows and orphans of our local deputies."

Jace squinted, grinned. "You don't look like you did on that ride. What's with the car?"

Deputy Blakeson snorted. "That ratty thing. I'm motorcycle patrol, but my bike's in the shop."

"Your uniform threw me off," Jace told him.

"Your duds threw me off and my boys as well. One of them was off duty at the diner, spotted you and saw the BOLO. An off-duty deputy followed you. Was going to bring you in, but we got an alert from the FBI to notify Raphael Rodriguez if you were spotted. Most of the guys here don't trust the Feds, but I rode with you, and I do. So I called Rodriguez and he told me you're clean. Sure appreciate what you and your team are doing to clean up the bad guys, even if it isn't in this area. Damn DP are everywhere, ruining things for legit bikers."

Kara stared at Jace, totally confused. Jace threw her a guilty look. Then it dawned on her and fury bubbled up.

"Officer, what exactly is Jace's team?"

Too late, the man shut his mouth, clammed up tight. Jace folded his arms across his chest, his mouth compressed.

The deputy touched his hat. "I'll be going now. Unless you need me for anything. Just call. We're on your side."

Kara couldn't believe it. Her mind felt like it was spinning in circles. Jace, working undercover. She should have known he hadn't turned criminal. But she was so stunned by the biker gang, so filled with fear for Dylan and contempt for the bikers, that she'd let her emotions cloud her.

As Deputy Blakeson nearly ran for his car, Kara turned

to Jace. "What the hell is going on, Jason Leroy Beckett? Whose side are you on?"

Swearing wasn't in her vocab. Not Kara, the good girl who always tried to do the right thing. But there was no other word to express the sheer anger, hurt and betrayal she felt right now.

Jace straightened and dropped his hands. "Kara, I'm undercover. I infiltrated the gang a few months ago, working deep undercover."

"Undercover for the local sheriff's office?"

"No, the FBI." He heaved a deep sigh. "Now that my cover's officially blown…"

Jace stuck out a hand. "Special Agent Jason Beckett of the South Florida Federal Bureau of Investigation."

Kara stared at his hand, then her gaze traveled up to his face. That face, sincere and hard in the sunlight, a flicker of uncertainty in his blue eyes as he dropped his hand. The well-trimmed beard, ragged hair threaded with gold streaks from the sun—now, she saw the contrast with his always military erect posture. He'd succeeded in blending in, a chameleon in wolf's clothing among dangerous, criminal wolves.

Anger faded. "Jace, why didn't you tell me?" Kara rolled her eyes. "Never mind, that's a rhetorical question. You couldn't. I suppose there's a lot you can't tell me."

Clues had been there, even last year when she saw him in formal dress at the fundraiser for the sea-turtle hospital. Or how Jarrett treated him like an equal, not like a dangerous criminal. Jarrett was as straight as they came.

Her own mother suspected and gave her a gentle warning.

"Please, answer one question. Did you go undercover to catch my cousin stealing?"

His shoulders lost a little of their tension. "No. We've been watching the DP for nearly a year, when we got wind they were connected with a terrorism incident that we subverted. Two months ago, they started their smash-and-grabs at local jewelry stores. I had no idea Dylan joined them until I became a member."

"You actually became a member? Incredible."

A rueful smile touched his mouth. "Yeah. Initiation was not fun. They beat you up, with chains. Still have one mark on me."

Horrified, she stared. "Jace, you let them do that to you?"

A shrug, as if he'd admitted to them patting his head. "Had no choice, Kara. I got that far, further than anyone else. A beating seemed a small price to pay for inside information."

His expression softened. "That day at the Tiki Bar, Lance forced me to flirt with you. Part of my initiation as a prospect. I didn't want to insult you, Kara. I'm sorry for making you so uncomfortable."

But still, she sensed he was hiding something, not to do with the assignment, or his FBI work. Something else that ran deeper.

"Why you, Jace? Why not someone else in the FBI?"

Now he turned away, jammed a hand through his messed hair. "Long story, babe. Let's just say that the beating I got from the DP wasn't my first. I know all about biker-gang culture."

So many questions. She searched his face, the barely hidden anguish below the surface. Kara cupped his face in her hands, gently stroked the bristles on his taut jawline.

"Perhaps someday, you'll trust me enough with the full story, as I trusted you."

Kara dropped her hands and walked to the passenger side. This time he did not open the door for her, but slid behind the wheel, saying nothing.

She wasn't certain what troubled her more—Jace's reticence about his past, or the fact he couldn't trust her with it.

* * *

Damn and double damn. He could do many things, but keeping the truth from Kara presented him with a challenge he'd rarely experienced.

He'd expected his cover to be blown. But he'd hoped it wouldn't happen until he had the chance to level with her. So much for that.

In the car, he plugged in the GPS coordinates into his phone and sent them via Bluetooth to the sedan's system.

They drove in silence for an hour, neither talking as he headed down a twist of backcountry roads in northern Georgia. Nothing much he could say to her right now, no answering the questions she asked.

The sun had started to descend by the time they reached the small town Dylan had mentioned. A freshly painted sign boasted Welcome to North Crystal Lake, the Friendliest Town Around!

Pristine, tree-lined streets greeted them as they drove on a narrow main street, where shops with colorful flower baskets advertised everything from a barber shop to clothing. Pedestrians strolling the swept sidewalk seemed less interested in the sedan than the street vendor playing a wicked fiddle on the corner. Someone else joined in with a banjo.

"Hard to believe this place is haunted," she murmured. "Or had a murder."

Relieved she'd finally spoken, he grinned. "Local gossip. I looked it up. Guy wasn't murdered, he hung himself and the townspeople said his ghost haunts the place."

He parked at the edge of a county park with a hiking trail. Jace looked around. Their car blended in with the others in the lot. Most of the owners seemed to be sitting on metal bleachers, watching a softball game being played on the field.

Navigating the steep, mud-strewn path, they arrived at

a small clearing surrounded by trees and flanked by thick brush. Soft green moss carpeted the clearing and he heard a stream nearby.

In the center stood an ancient, dilapidated shack with a single door hanging precariously from its hinges. Jace recognized it from Dylan's description. This was the place where he had hidden the necklace, but wow, he'd picked a hell of a hiding spot. Open to anyone.

Anyone who dared to come here, anyway.

Not that he believed in ghosts.

Place looked like it had once been home to a campground, perhaps. Jace's imagination flicked to the old *Friday the 13th* movie.

Kara shivered as they made it to level ground. "This place is spooky. Like Camp Crystal Lake from *Friday the 13th*."

He blinked. Oh, it wasn't the first time they held the same thought, but it had been a long time since they were in sync. Jace grinned.

"Sure is. And I'm Jason."

At his suggestive wink, a shaky laugh ripped from her throat. "Just tell your mother to stay away from me."

His grin slipped. *My mother is busy enough staying away from me. Prolly for the best.*

They stepped over trash scattered on the ground. Dead leaves crunched beneath Jace's shoes as he advanced to the front door. Motioning for Kara to hang back, he withdrew his gun and then opened the door.

It creaked on rusty hinges, sounding like a cliché from a horror movie. The cabin was one room, with a fireplace cluttered with ashes, moldy furniture and a table beneath a broken window. Looked like vagrants had called it home for a while. He went to the fireplace and combed through the ashes.

A blue velvet bag peeked through the grayness. Jace lifted it and opened the bag. Whistled.

Gleaming diamonds nestled inside the velvet. Clutching it in his left hand, still gripping his gun in his right, he ran outside.

Kara stared at the bag as he handed it to her. She started to pull out the necklace. He stayed her hand.

"Wait. Anyone might be spying on us."

They trekked back to the car and drove away. Only when they were on a main road did Kara pull out the necklace. Diamonds glittered in the sunlight as she held it up.

"It's the Vandermeer necklace. Not a replica."

"How can you tell?"

"I'm not a trained gemologist, but I've learned a few things along the way. With diamonds you look for cut, clarity and color and carat, what's referred to as the four C's. I look for clarity—the fewer imperfections, the greater the clarity grade. But with this necklace, there was a small imperfection…not in the diamonds themselves, but the clasp."

Kara pointed out the lobster-claw clasp. "It's crooked. I meant to get it fixed. Besides, Dylan wouldn't have had time to replicate the necklace. Or the resources."

"Unless he worked with a third party."

The necklace dropped into her lap. "Jace, he's not like that. He's a scared kid. Stop acting like he's a suspect."

"Which he is."

"And so were you. Or is your real mission to find and arrest my cousin instead of that criminal gang?"

With considerable effort, he curbed his temper. "Your cousin is in extreme danger. If Lance and his gang find him before we do, or the police do, Dylan is a dead man. He's the only one, that we know of, who can identify Marcus, the real power behind the Devil's Patrol."

He hated scaring her like this, but Kara needed to know the threat Dylan faced. She ducked her head, staring at the velvet bag. "I'm sorry, Jace. I didn't mean to snap. I'm worried about him. And I trust you'll cut him a fair deal when he's found. Promise me."

At least she'd cut him that break. He gestured to the necklace. "I promise I will do what I can. What about that bling?"

"Bling?" She laughed and consulted her phone. "I wouldn't call six figures in diamonds *bling*, Jace. I need to store this in a safe place. A bank deposit box… There's a branch of my bank in Atlanta."

"I'm afraid I can't do that." He drew in a breath. "That necklace is evidence."

"Evidence! It's mine and Dylan returned it to me… What, are you going to hand it over to that murdering biker who wants the property he stole back…? Wait…"

Jace waited. Yeah, he knew she'd make the connection sooner or later. Surprising it took this long because Kara was sharp. Worry about Dylan had consumed her.

"Evidence," she repeated slowly, tucking the necklace back into the dusty velvet bag. "Cop talk. I forgot. How absurd of me."

Tucking the bag into her jeans pocket, she shook her head.

"What about Dylan? Are you sending your squad after him?"

Jace sighed. "I don't have a squad, Kara. I told you, my concern is the same as yours—find the kid and get him into protective custody. You have to convince him to turn himself over to us. It's for his own good."

Trusting him now was important. They were close to getting Dylan to come in. If not, the kid would keep running, and Lance and his crew had spies everywhere.

"All right. I'll try."

Kara called Dylan and put the phone on Bluetooth speaker. Dylan answered.

"You got the necklace? You see, Kara? I'm not a thief. I always meant to return it to you."

"Thank you for returning it to me, Dylan. I know you are not a thief. Now please, Dylan, you have to come in. You can't keep running forever," she said in a gentle tone.

Silence.

"Will you trust me on this? Please?" Her gaze flicked to Jace. "If I share something in confidence, will it convince you to turn yourself over to Jace?"

"Jace?" A bitter laugh. "He's okay, but he's still one of them. What's to prevent him from tossing me to Lance to end up with a bullet hole to my head?"

Kara looked at him. Jace cleared his throat. Now or never. He'd already blown his cover. But maybe it could work in his favor this time.

"I'm not a real member of the gang, Dylan," he said slowly. "I'm working undercover, investigating Lance and his crew."

"Huh." Dylan's voice filled with suspicion. "Like one of those television journalists?"

"No. I'm FBI."

A long whistle. "No kidding? You're a Fed? A Fed! Damn."

For a few minutes, her cousin laughed. "All this time I thought you were a little easygoing mechanic who liked to ride and hang out with criminals. And you're a Fed."

"And you're in trouble. Big trouble, not so much with the law but Lance's crew. Name a place and I'll meet you, Dylan. I promise to speak to the US attorney on your behalf."

It was all he could do.

For a few moments, Dylan said nothing and Jace feared the kid wasn't going to agree. Then a tiny sigh.

"Okay. But a place on my terms."

Dylan named an abandoned campground in southern Tennessee. "Meet me by the railroad tracks at five tomorrow afternoon. Bring Kara. If you're who you say you are, Jace, I'll surrender to you. But if not, I'm outta there. Kara, I'm sorry I dragged you into this mess."

So was he, and everyone else. But at least now Dylan was close to being safe. "You got it."

"Dylan, thank you. Remember, we're family…"

"And family does for family. Got it. Thanks, coz."

He hung up.

Kara turned the cell phone over in her hands. "I'm so worried about him, Jace. What if the bikers find him before we do?"

He reached over, squeezed her hand. "You have to trust that won't happen, babe. Dylan's evaded them so far. Even evaded us. He's smart. It runs in the family."

She glanced at him. "Smart, huh?"

"Who else could take a business and turn it into a success?" He consulted his phone. "We need to find a place to stop for the night and rest."

They stopped at a fast-food restaurant near Tennessee for a quick dinner. By the time Jace drove them to a nondescript motel near the main road, he was exhausted and Kara looked ready to drop from stress.

He let her use the bathroom first to shower, his imagination going haywire at the sounds of the water running. By the time it was his turn, he was no longer exhausted, only tense and wired at spending yet another night with her.

Kara slid beneath the covers and seemed to be asleep. He finally emerged from the bathroom and saw she'd placed her suitcase on the other bed.

Well, he could handle this. Jace climbed into bed with her.

Jace sighed as Kara snuggled up against him, closing her eyes with a smile. Damn, this was tough, feeling her soft, sweet body lying next to him. Old habits died hard. He wanted to wrap his arms around her, pull her close, start those long kisses she loved. Finish with both of them naked, panting and worn out from the good loving.

He couldn't afford distractions. Jace slipped out of her grasp and curled up on the other bed with her suitcase for company instead of Kara herself.

But it was a long time before he slept.

Chapter 15

They met Dylan at the campsite as planned the next afternoon, and never had she seen her cousin more scared.

Or relieved.

Dylan had cut his shoulder-length hair and dyed it blond. He looked much younger than his years, and vulnerable.

Jace treated him with courtesy but remained firm. Her ex in action seemed a totally different man from the casual biker who had given the impression of insouciant living and partying. He took Dylan formally into custody, read him his rights and called to have his motorcycle picked up and stored in a local impound lot, giving Kara the information to retrieve it later. Dylan handed Kara the rest of the jewelry, which she combined with the diamond necklace. Kara dropped the bag into her purse.

Nothing carefree about him now, Jace was all seriousness as they drove, Dylan riding quietly in the back. She had trouble reconciling the tough FBI agent with the biker who called her "babe." Maybe that was part of his persona, and what made him blend so well.

"Jace, you're headed the wrong way. Atlanta is southeast, not southwest."

"We're not going to Atlanta." He turned off the road and

headed for the interstate. "I'm headed to the FBI field office where my boss is working this case."

"Rafael. Rafe. *He's* your boss. Your real boss."

"Boss and friend. Team leader."

She wondered about that. "You've known him a long time?"

He nodded.

"How hard was it to go this deep undercover with the gang?" she asked.

Jace's jaw tightened. "Can't really talk about it."

"I understand. It's got to be like living two lives—your real life with the FBI and the life with the motorcycle gang, and then the lives start to blend and intertwine until you aren't certain which one is real and which is not."

He threw her a quick, startled glance, telling her more than words.

"It is, but I'm not into the lifestyle of OMGs, Kara."

"I beg your pardon?"

"OMG is an acronym for Outlaw Motorcycle Gang, such as the Devil's Patrol." Jace switched lanes and accelerated. "I love riding a bike, and enjoy the company of other bikers, but partying and girls, and the drinking and drugs and certainly the outlaw lifestyle aren't me. Never were."

"You seem quite certain."

"Hell, yeah, I'm certain. I saw what it did to others."

Judging from the tautness of his jaw and the cheek tic, Jace didn't like the conversation. Now or ever. If she had a hope of pulling him from his dark place, she had to try.

"Level with me, Jace. I told you the truth about my family and what happened. Is your father the reason you never wanted me to know about your parents or any of your family?"

For a few moments they rode in silence. Kara held her breath. Maybe she'd pushed him too hard. Then he released a heavy sigh.

"Yeah. Basically it." He glanced into the rearview mirror. "I'll tell you more later. Promise. But business first."

Something inside her cried out to provide comfort at such a painful memory. Kara slid her hand over his right hand. He glanced at her again but did not pull away. Instead, he squeezed her hand slightly and then released it, his expression serious once more.

Two hours later, he pulled into the parking lot of a one-story office building with offices for rent.

Hand on Dylan's arm, Jace escorted him into an office with an FBI sign stenciled on the glass. Inside, a blast of cold air greeted them. A man sat at a reception area earnestly typing on a laptop. He glanced up.

"Special Agent Beckett?"

Jace nodded.

The man dialed a number and Rafael appeared out of the back, this time dressed in black slacks, a white shirt and a tie loosened at the throat. Rafael inclined his head and Jace led Dylan away. Before he did, she gave her cousin a reassuring smile and squeezed his hand.

Dylan looked terrified. She supposed they would formally charge him.

Kara regarded Rafe as if the man was an enemy. "I see you made a safe escape on Jace's bike after we left the warehouses."

Rafe didn't blink. "I was faster than the guys chasing me."

"I suppose I should be polite and say I'm glad to see you again, Agent Rodriguez, but I don't like lying. I will let you know I am here against my wishes."

He cocked his head at her. "It's Supervisory Special Agent, but please, call me Rafe. Miss Wilmington, you're under no duress. You are free to leave, if you wish. I'm not placing you under arrest. But the jewelry in your possession is evidence, I'm afraid. May I?"

With a gaze as hard as the diamonds themselves, Kara handed over all the jewels. Rafe opened the bag and removed the necklace. The agent sitting at the desk whistled.

"Sweet. What are they worth, at least six figures?" the agent asked.

Kara didn't bother replying, only kept eyeing Rafe. The temperature in this office probably dropped at least twenty degrees with her attitude, but she didn't care. She was too concerned about Dylan.

Rafe closed the bag and handed it to the agent, who walked away with it. "Thank you for turning over the evidence."

A casual shrug. "It's not as if I had a choice."

She stepped outside, into the humid Georgia air, to call her parents. Kara made her call brief, sticking to the facts, suggesting her father call his sister to give her the news.

Maybe, finally, her aunt would agree to receive the help her father had always offered. No matter. Her father, always concerned about his sister, would hire one of the best attorneys in Florida.

When she returned inside, she asked about Jace and was told he was meeting in the back with the suspect.

The suspect. Her cousin. Kara's chest felt hollow with grief. How had Dylan gone from a kid who only wanted to race his bike to being involved with a gang who stole and murdered?

She sat on the sofa in reception to wait for Jace. Kara scrolled through her phone, too anxious to focus. Jace had promised the prosecutors would take it easy on Dylan. Surely, he would deliver on that promise.

She banked on it. Finally, after about an hour, Jace came out of the back office, his mouth tight.

"Kara, I'm going to have someone drive you to a local hotel. I'm going to be here quite a while."

Her fingers gripped the purse straps. "What's going to happen to Dylan, Jace? Please. I can't leave here until I know."

To her relief, he sat, putting them on an equal level. "I promised I'd do everything I can and I will, Kara. But it's up to the US attorney. He's facing serious charges. However, he is also material witness to a double homicide, and our best bet for catching Marcus."

"And what about my cousin, Jace? He's all alone now. He needs me. I need—"

"You can't see him."

Clipped, curt words.

She stared. "You promised to help him…"

"I promised to try and I am trying."

Images haunted her—Dylan sitting alone in a jail cell, looking betrayed and hurt.

"Jace, I know you have to do what you must, but please, don't lock him up. I don't want him rotting in a moldy jail cell with a filthy mattress and bugs…"

For the first time, he looked impatient. "Kara, he's not going to rot in a jail cell. Stop being dramatic."

"He's not your cousin."

"He's not your responsibility," he shot back.

"But he is. He's family."

He glanced at his buzzing cell phone. "That's all I can relay for now. If I have solid news I can share, I'll let you know."

Jace signaled to the agent working on a laptop. "Wayne will drive you to a hotel. My expense account."

Hotel. Expense account. Jace dismissed her as if she was of no more use. *I suppose I am not. He has what he was after—my cousin.*

Kara stood and smoothed out her wrinkled trousers. "Not necessary. I'll procure my own lodging, and transportation. Surely they have an Uber in this section of backwoods?"

He stood, rammed a hand through his hair. "Kara, we can get you a room…"

"No. I don't want your hospitality. I've had quite enough." She consulted her cell, messaged for an Uber. "Good-bye, Jace."

"I need to know where you're going…"

Kara summoned the iciest look she could manage for all the hurt swirling inside her. "I'm going to find a motel and sleep, Jace, and return in the morning when my father gets here with an attorney. Dylan needs good representation since you cannot deliver on your promise."

She couldn't reach the door fast enough. He made no attempt to follow or stop her. In fact, by the time the young agent named Wayne opened the door for her, Jace had vanished into the back once more.

Her cell pinged a message. Kara glanced down.

Babe, I'm sorry. Let me send an agent with you, please.

Kara ignored the text and put away her phone.

When the driver appeared, she asked him to bring her to the nearest motel.

The seedy roadside motel suited her mood. Kara paid with her credit card and took the key. Inside the room, she sat on the bed, staring dully at the walls.

Jace had betrayed her. He'd made a promise and his duty to the FBI came first.

She wasn't certain if she could ever forgive him again.

Chapter 16

The FBI field office in Georgia was functional but beginning to resemble a typical government working environment. Blue carpeting helped absorb the noise caused by agents talking on the phone and typing furiously into their computers.

A glass-walled conference room with a large screen and a whiteboard sat off to the side, with blinds for privacy. Banks of computers and keyboards lined a long table near a maze of cubicles.

Gray cubicles filled the main room, with laptops, calendars and desk lamps at each working space. Jace spent time in the small, private interrogation room interviewing Dylan.

He'd hit a brick wall.

The kid wasn't talking. He made his one phone call—to Kara's father. Then he shut down, saying he wasn't speaking another word until his attorney arrived tomorrow. He wouldn't even give them a hint about Marcus.

Rafe had let him handle the interrogation, until deputies arrived to escort Dylan to the local jail just before midnight. Two agents accompanied them.

He needed to find Kara, but first, he had business to deal with. Weary, the lack of sleep getting to him, Jace headed to Rafe's assigned office.

Three walls of glass formed the office. An American

flag sat in the corner near a small conference table and two black sofas. The wall behind the credenza was dark paneling, with built-in shelves holding law journals and manuals. Neatly stacked file folders lay upon the credenza, along with stacks of paper.

The wood desk was equally functional, with a desk lamp, blotter, pencil box and laptop. The only concession to decor was a silk plant in the corner.

In a crisp white shirt, sleeves rolled up his forearms, and a blue silk tie loosely knotted, Rafe sat at the desk, working on his laptop. He glanced up as the door opened. Jace didn't bother knocking. He was too angry.

"I knew this would happen. Kid's lips are sealed. He won't talk until his attorney is here. I told you to let Kara in the room. She could have reassured him."

"Against protocol and you know it. Where's Kara?" Rafe turned his attention back to his computer.

"She took an Uber to a hotel. A hotel of her choosing. Soon as I'm done here, I'm going to track her down. She's pissed at me, Rafe, and I don't blame her. I told her the prosecutor would cut Dylan a deal. And now I find out Dylan may be charged with a felony?"

"Never make promises like that." Rafe shook his head. "We're not the US attorney's office. We only find and arrest the bad guys."

He paced the floor, feeling as if they had missed out on something.

"Any more word on this big incident Marcus plans?"

"Nothing recent. It's gone quiet." His boss leaned back. "Your part here is finished, Jace. You're off the case."

He whirled and stared at Rafe, feeling betrayed. "Are you serious? You're not letting me in on the takedown?"

"Afraid not."

"Rafe, I've been trying to prove myself to you for more than five years. I worked my ass off on this case. I'm totally committed to this assignment and this job. You need me."

"I need you on my team." Rafe leaned forward, elbows on the desk blotter. "Yeah, I do. But you took risks, Jace. Risks that could have cost lives. You took Kara with you, an unarmed civilian."

Exasperated, yet knowing Rafe was right, he jammed a hand into his hair. "I know. My bad."

"Without Kara, we never would have found Dylan. He's our star witness. With Dylan we can take down Lance and the others."

Jace felt the rug yanked from beneath him. "What? Then why am I off the case?"

"Because you're too close. Because your cover is blown and your life is at risk. You need to lie low for a while."

Releasing a string of Spanish swear words, he paced the office. "I can't believe you're doing this to me."

"It's to keep you safe, Jace. You did well, despite everything." Rafe twirled a gold pen in his fingers. "Kara was right. Dylan never would have talked to you, or anyone else. He needed someone he could trust. Don't worry about Kara and the prosecutor. She'll get over it when the attorney her father hired arrives tomorrow. He's good. Seen him in action before, and the US attorney's office isn't interested in hanging Dylan out to dry on this. They need him and I'm sure they'll work out a good deal."

"Then why…?"

"Because in this business you can't make promises you aren't sure you can keep." Rafe stared at the wall, his jaw tight. "I promised my guys last year it would be a simple takedown. And now they're dead."

Jace blew out a breath. "It wasn't your fault."

"It was. But that's another matter. For this, I did have a backup plan."

He picked up his office phone. "Is she out there? Bring her in."

Stunned, he watched the woman walk into Rafe's office. Jace stared. "You?"

"Pleased to see you again, Special Agent Beckett." Allison Lexington removed her motorcycle helmet. A waterfall of shoulder-length dark hair spilled out. Still attractive as ever.

"How the hell did you get here?" he demanded.

"Rode my bike here for hours after he—" she jerked her thumb at Rafe "—told me to come in."

Jace frowned. "You a cop?"

"Confidential informant, not by choice." She scowled at Rafe, who gave a slight smile. "After I saved Lance, Rafe threatened to arrest me for interfering with an official investigation."

"She was at the bike rally where Lance was running guns and got shot by a rival gang member. She treated him," Rafe added, his dark gaze centered on Allison. "Aiding and abetting someone who committed a felony is a second-degree offense."

Allison narrowed her eyes. "I told you, I didn't aid and abet. I treated a gunshot wound. I did my job. I'm a nurse. What, was I supposed to let him bleed out?"

"No, you were supposed to inform law enforcement of what happened so he could be arrested, not let him slip through your fingers."

"Pardon me for living, Agent Rodriguez. The guy had a gun to my head."

"Supervisory Special Agent Rodriguez," Rafe corrected. "I paid you to be a CI. I don't recall any complaints about the money."

"Considering I had to give up several lucrative nursing jobs, I deserved compensation. I'm a traveling nurse and I make more than you do, Supervisory Special Agent."

"I'm sure you do." Rafe seemed amused.

Jace watched, sensing chemistry between them.

Allison tossed back her long, brown hair. "May I leave now, since this assignment has ended? I trust you no longer need me. Unless you have another BS charge you want to slap on me to force me into spying for you. Only this time, I'm not getting close to a criminal gang."

A shadow crossed Rafe's face. "I told you if you ever sensed you were endangered, to pull out. I'm serious, Allison."

She gave a mock salute. "Right. As if I couldn't handle Lance and his crew. They were all trying to get me into bed, especially Snake. I have better taste than that."

"I'm sure you do," Rafe said softly.

Allison glared at him. "If you'll excuse me."

When she walked out the door, Rafe followed her with his dark gaze. Then he leaned back, the leather chair creaking.

"We have a new lead on Marcus."

This was news. Jace sat down. "Spill it."

"It didn't come from Allison, or Dylan, obviously, and there's no way you could have gotten the intel, Jace. It had to come from someone deep inside, who knew the club's inner workings. Someone who had been there before."

I've got a bad feeling about this. "A former club member?"

"Your father."

I knew it. I knew the old man couldn't stay away.

Feeling even more betrayed, Jace released a string of cuss words. Rafe held up his hand. "Whoa. Slow down. He doesn't know about you, or your cover. He's working with me totally separately on this case."

"You went after my old man because you didn't think I could deliver? Dammit, Rafe!"

Rafe shook his head, his voice calm. "I didn't. He approached me, Jace. He got out on parole and wanted to help. He's changed."

"Changed, my ass! He's still the same selfish prick—"

"He wanted to make up for the past, and leave a legacy of doing something good, Jace. For you. He said he didn't want his only son remembering him as a son of a bitch."

Rafe drummed his fingers on the armrest. "He doesn't know about you being under. He mentioned seeing a prospect or a new member at the garage, and was asking about getting a job at the garage. Said the guy was cold."

Cold? Not cold enough, apparently.

"When the hell were you going to tell me my old man works for you? Want to recruit my mother as well? She loves money."

"Stop it, Jace." Rafe's dark gaze narrowed. "I didn't want you to know because I knew you'd react like this. You've done a damn fine job inside, and I wasn't going to compromise your safety."

"Right." Jace started for the door. "I've got a ton of paperwork. Rafe, next time you want to play mother hen on me, remember I'm a qualified, trained agent. If you coddle all of us, the criminals you want to put behind bars will never get caught."

He slammed the door on the way out.

Though she was bone-tired, sleep proved impossible for Kara. The thought of Dylan locked up in a dingy jail cell, terrified and alone, made her stomach roil.

No use in hanging around the field office, but she couldn't abandon Dylan. She promised to be there for him.

Jace had not.

She had showered and dressed in fresh clothing, too wound up to sleep. Kara looked at the television remote, shuddered and sat on the bed.

A knock stirred her from examining her conscience. Kara went to the door, peered out the peephole.

"Sorry, ma'am, there's a matter of your credit card being denied."

She started to reach for the dead bolt and stopped. Common sense overruled emotions. The man's voice was too rough, too deep, to be the same desk clerk who'd checked her into the room.

"I'll call the front office," she told the man, not unlocking the door.

"We need to take care of this now." The man jiggled the doorknob.

Kara's heart raced, her breath coming in shallow gasps. Ironic how she and Jace had remained barely one step ahead of the danger constantly chasing them and suddenly now, as she was alone, someone had caught up to her. The sickly fluorescent light outside provided little illumination for her to properly see who wanted to get inside.

"Go away," she said in a loud voice. "I'll call the front desk and leave another credit-card number."

No footsteps indicating the man walked off. Instead, he pounded on the door.

"Open the damn door!" He pounded on the door. "Bitch, open it now!"

She backed up. The flimsy door vibrated with a loud thud. It splintered and buckled as the man forcefully kicked it open.

Terror filled her as a hulking figure loomed in the doorway. The intruder was short, wearing a denim jacket with the sleeves cut off. Ink covered his bare arms. Most prominent was a Devil's Patrol tat on his left forearm.

His beer belly hung over a leather belt like a waterfall. And then she recognized him. Even though the lighting cast his face mostly in shadow, she knew.

"Lance," she said, stumbling back. "What do you want?"

Heart pounding in her chest, she backed away from him, frantically thinking of exits. He must be searching for Jace.

The man's face was a grotesque mask of anger and determination, his rough features twisted into a menacing sneer, accented by the scar on his cheek.

"You can't run forever. Got you. Finally."

Fear jolted through her. Her eyes darted around the room, searching for an escape, but the window was too small. Her phone was inside her purse, just out of reach. She was trapped. Her gaze dropped to his waist. The Devil's Patrol carried guns. But he made no move to withdraw a weapon.

Maybe he thinks I'm helpless. Let him think that way.

"What do you want with me?" she asked, trying to control her terror.

He grinned. "You. Someone special wants you."

The man licked his lips. "He didn't mind if I had a little fun first. Jace kept bragging about how you were a great lay."

Adrenaline fueled her body. She ran for the bathroom, closed the door and locked it. It wouldn't hold. It wasn't designed to keep out huge, hulking monsters who wanted to assault her.

Outside, Lance hammered at it, yelling at her. Kara whipped her gaze around for a weapon. Anything. Shampoo? Thoughts raced through her head.

Oh, God, what did he want other than to attack her? Why did the gang leader want her? Why couldn't she have done

as Jace wanted and let an agent take her to safer, more refined hotel?

She spotted the toilet tank. *This.*

Lifting the ceramic lid, she cringed at the thick layer of
ugly black mold ringing the cover. Kara waited, praying
Lance would stop. But, no, he was kicking the door…he
was inside, advancing toward her with a leer. No gun. No,
he planned to overpower her with brute force.

Kara swung at the man with all her might. The toilet
tank lid connected with his chin, and he released a surprised
grunt, and staggered backward, moaning as blood gushed
from his jaw. Lance released a string of violent obscenities.

Not waiting to see if he would faint, or lunge or shoot
her, she grabbed her purse and bolted, running for the office as she reached for her cell phone. Cool night air hit her
face felt like a welcome embrace. Her feet pounded on the
pavement as she sprinted into the darkness, praying that she
could outrun her attacker.

Favor was with her, as the night clerk was emerging from
the back as she stormed inside the office.

"Help, please, call the police! I've been attacked!"

Chapter 17

Jace couldn't speed to the motel fast enough after Kara called him. He showed up at the office quicker than the local police. Seeing Kara in the office sitting on a chair, her blue eyes huge, her lovely face pale and sheened with perspiration, he felt a surge of pure relief.

Heart hammering, he searched her up and down, looking for injuries. "You okay? Did he hurt you? Kara?"

She gulped down a sob as she stood. "I'm all right. Jace, it was terrifying."

As she relayed what happened, he folded her into his arms, glaring at the curious night clerk who was staring at him. Shaking, Kara took fistfuls of his shirt, clinging to him like a life raft.

Shouldn't have let her go alone. Damn, I promised her mom I'd watch out for her.

Sirens wailed outside. Jace glanced as two local sheriff's deputy units pulled up to the office door and four men climbed out. He gently disentangled himself from Kara.

"Babe, you have to give them your statement, let them know everything that happened. This guy is still out there," he murmured.

Kara nodded.

As they entered the office, Jace told them about the at-

tack. One of the deputies had a sergeant's patch on his uniform. The sergeant sent the three deputies to investigate the
ground-floor motel room, while he remained in the office.

"Can you tell us exactly what happened, miss…?"

"Kara, please, call me Kara." She turned around, her composure regained, though she still looked far too pale.

Relaying every detail, including the man's physical char-
acteristics and how he sported ink that sounded suspiciously
like a Devil's Patrol tat, Kara stayed calm.

The deputies returned from the room.

"We checked the room and others. There's a blood trail
leading out the door to the parking lot. Whoever broke in is
long gone. Probably a thief." The deputy shook his head. "A
beautiful woman alone in this area, kinda rough."

"He wasn't after my purse. He wanted to kidnap me. It
was Lance, the leader of the Devil's Patrol."

The sergeant gave her a dubious look. "Kidnap you? For
what?"

Jace's heart nearly stopped.

With remarkable control, she wiped her eyes and spoke
in a steady voice. "I don't know. He said someone special
wanted me."

Jace's blood ran cold. He clasped Kara's arms. "Did he
say anything else, babe?"

"Other than swear at me after I clobbered him with the
toilet tank lid, no."

"Good job," he said softly, rubbing a thumb along her
damp cheek, his mind racing. "You sure it was Lance?"

Kara nodded. "There wasn't much lighting in the room,
and I've seen him only once, but I'll never forget his ugly
face from the Tiki Bar."

His heart skipped a beat and dread shimmied down his
spine. Why did Lance want Kara? Was the gang leader hop-

ing to use Kara to reel in Jace? Use her as a hostage? Or get Dylan to remain silent by using her as a hostage?

He gently squeezed her hand. "I have to make a call. Sit tight."

Outside the office, he called Rafe and relayed the news. His boss swore in Spanish.

"Talk to the man in charge, tell him what you've learned and to get a BOLO out on the bastard. He can't get far. He's wanted for two federal charges now, attempted kidnapping and interstate transportation of stolen property." Rafe hung up.

Kara was his main concern now. With Lance on the loose and after her, he wasn't taking any chances.

Leaving the sheriff's office to the investigation and advising them of what Rafe told him, he told her he was taking her to his hotel room. She did not argue.

In his car, Kara sat quietly after he'd loaded her suitcase into the trunk. Jace couldn't leave the parking lot fast enough.

He glanced at her. "Toilet tank lid, huh? Good thinking."

She took another unsteady breath. "I was hoping I'd either knock him out or he'd suffer a terrible allergy attack from the black mold on the toilet tank lid."

Jace laughed. She was going to be okay.

His laughter died. Yeah, okay for now, but Lance tried to kidnap her. Possibly assault her. Squeezing his fingers tight on the steering wheel, he felt his blood pressure rise. Someone had tried to hurt Kara.

It didn't make sense. *I'm the one they want to harm.*

"You'll be safe at the hotel and surrounded by agents. We have rooms on the same floor. If anyone tries anything—" he hissed out a breath "—they'll have to go through me. I won't let that happen."

An hour later, Kara was asleep in his room, one arm

tucked beneath her, her face smoothed out. Jace sat on the bed, stroked her hair. He'd dropped the ball with her. Wasn't going to happen again.

Right now, he needed to find out why the hell Lance wanted Kara. His cell buzzed and he walked into the hallway to talk to Rafe.

"We found him. Son of a bitch broke into a drugstore to steal first-aid supplies. Local LEOs arrested Lance and he'll be arraigned tomorrow."

Should have felt relief, but Jace didn't.

"Did he say anything?" Jace asked.

"Wanted a lawyer. Said he would talk if he got a deal, but only after the lawyer gets here. His lawyer can't be here until tomorrow, during arraignment, so he's spending the night courtesy of the local jail. We've got him on federal charges, and he's scared."

They had Lance in custody. Dylan as a witness. But Kara's attack didn't fit the puzzle pieces. He knew something else was up.

"So he said nothing about why he wanted Kara. Or who wanted her," Jace mused.

"Lance may have targeted Kara in order to keep Dylan quiet. Insurance, so he doesn't talk in case Dylan turned himself in." Rafe released a deep sigh. "Or you, Jace. Maybe the bastard figured out you're a Fed."

"Seems too elaborate for him. If Marcus is pulling the strings, he'd simply order a hit on Dylan. Or have taken him out before Dylan landed in our custody."

"How did he find you so fast?" Rafe wondered.

"He didn't find me. He found Kara." Suddenly, it clicked. "Dammit, I should have seen it. He put a tracking device on Dylan's bike. He's been following Dylan the entire time. Check out the bike and text me."

Less than an hour later, Rafe confirmed Jace's suspicions through a text and said he'd meet him at the hotel's lounge.

Leaving an agent on guard outside his room, he headed downstairs.

Low lighting and elegant wood paneled walls loaned the bar a feel of intimacy. Jace sat at a back table facing the entrance and ordered a bourbon and soda from the server. Dylan was safe, in custody. Lance had been arrested. A key part of this puzzle remained missing.

Darkling had to have intel. He texted her. Any more chatter on what Marcus and the DP plan to do for a public target and making a statement?

She responded, None. It's like they abandoned that plan.

Abandoned because the target was no longer viable? Or was it a diversion?

He texted Darkling again. What's your thoughts on this? Are they attempting something else? Or was it a ruse to draw our attention away from the real target?

Her response sent a chill down his spine, making gooseflesh break out along his bare arms, despite the morning warmth.

Ruse. All I've picked up are references 'She's with him. Get her.' No details. That bit of intel was a slip because they've all gone dark since.

He signed off with thanks and set down his phone.

Get her. Then tonight Lance had attacked Kara.

Rafe joined him a few minutes later. Tie loosened, hair mussed, the normally urbane agent looked exhausted. He ordered a beer and waited until the server walked off.

"Simple tracking device hidden on the Ducati," Rafe said, his voice tight. "Should have seen it from the beginning.

Lance knew where Dylan was at all times and even after we seized his bike and impounded it, it was only a matter of simple deduction for him to figure out we had him in custody."

"It doesn't add up. He knew he witnessed the murder of the other two kids. He knows who Marcus is. Why leave him alive?"

"Unless he didn't want Dylan. He wanted you." Rafe nodded thanks to the server and drank the beer the woman delivered. "You said you were going after Dylan and he could have been following you. You broke the bonds of brotherhood and he wanted revenge."

"Lance doesn't wipe his own butt without orders from Marcus."

"I know. Your old man told me. He knew Marcus."

Jace nearly choked on his drink. He set down the glass. "What the hell?"

"Remember that name that you spotted on Lance's phone?"

"PrisonerXYZ? Darkling tracked it down?"

"She found it on a few message boards and traced it. Guy thought he was being careful. Anonymous. But his ego is too big. He posted a fake photo, and she did a Google search and found it was fake, belonged to some photographer who shot photos at a bike rally."

Rafe's smile widened. "The same rally where Lance was shot. Photographer got a photo of Lance talking with another biker just before the fight broke out. Your old man told me he remembers PrisonerXYZ from prison. His name is Gerald, Gerry. Al said he's sure Gerry and Marcus are the same person."

"How can he be sure?" Jace snorted. "No one knows Marcus's true identity. The guy went deep into the shadows when supposedly he was released from prison. And my old man would say anything to beat the rap."

"Not this time. We checked out his story and did facial recognition, and found Gerald did time for armed robbery and got out of prison a year ago. Gerald got paroled same time Marcus emerged as the shadow leader of the DP."

"It has to be him. Damn."

"Your cover is definitely blown and you were followed."

Jace sucked down a breath and then drained his drink. "Not surprised. Someone saw Kara with me, figured things out."

"The bikers who followed you both from the Florida motel and the guy they had tailing you at the aquarium at Manatee Island. Lance admitted that much before clamming up."

"What Lance knows, Marcus knows."

"You're not safe, Jace. These guys play rough." Rafe traced the bottle's label. "What if Marcus wanted Kara because she's your girl and he planned to smoke you out into the open? Kidnap Kara in exchange for your life?"

"Maybe. But they had plenty of chances to take me out before this. Seems too elaborate."

He considered. "And the moment I leave Kara's side, she gets attacked. I don't believe in coincidences."

Rafe drank more beer, wiped his mouth with a paper napkin. "Doesn't matter. I want you to vanish, Jace. Too much at risk, especially your life. Kara's in danger, and maybe she knows something she doesn't even know she knows. Kara could be an essential witness as much as Dylan is and she needs protection. Take her someplace safe until we nail Marcus."

"And until then? You'll work with my old man to bring Marcus down?" He laughed without humor. "My old man, an ex-convict, to save the day."

"Jace, I won't lose you. You're good and in deep, and you did great. But it's too risky now. You can't keep the cover."

Lost in thought, he didn't respond. Two bikers knew Kara was with him at the Florida motel, maybe even saw him with Kara and Dylan when they all met, since they'd put a tracker on Dylan's bike.

They could have easily taken him at several intervals. Yet they did not.

Now, Kara was in danger. Rafe made sense. If he was the target, then he couldn't remain on the case.

"Fine." He shook his head at the waitress as she asked about a refill. "I'm taking Kara out of here tomorrow, first thing."

"I need to know where you're headed."

He gave him a level look. "You said not to trust anyone, Rafe. I'll check in when I get there."

Chapter 18

Kara agreed to accompany Jace the following morning. She didn't even care where they went. Still numb from the attack, she struggled to find direction.

Maybe Jace couldn't keep all his promises, but he wouldn't let anything happen to her. Surely, she was safer with him.

Jace insisted on her calling her father, who would worry if she wasn't there at the jail to meet him when he brought Dylan's attorney.

She tried to sound cheerful and reassuring as she talked with her father. Then she simply couldn't put on the act anymore. Jace took the phone from her and said he wouldn't let anything happen to her.

"An FBI agent will want to sit and talk with you, go over a few things about Kara to see if we can determine why Lance targeted her. Don't worry, I won't let anything happen to her. She will check in from the motel when we arrive for the night."

When he hung up, he helped her pack and loaded their backpacks into an agency-issued SUV.

As he drove northward, she thought about how she'd awakened in a panic during the night. Her pulse racing, feeling groggy and disoriented, all she could remember was Lance's leering grin as he advanced.

Kara had wanted to bolt from the room, run away, and then she'd snapped on a bedside light and seen him.

Jace. Curled up near the door as if guarding it in case one of Lance's buddies managed to slip inside. Seeing him there, his big body acting like a doorstop, gave her the peace of mind she needed to slip back into sleep.

Kara closed her eyes, not caring where he took her. Someplace safe, he'd promised, where they could spend the night and figure out a plan.

Stopping only for a couple of rest stops and to get lunch through a drive-through, Jace made good time on the road as she dozed off. He stuck to the interstate and finally they arrived at a motel right off of it.

He checked them into a ground-floor room at the end, far from the office. She texted her father to let him know where they were.

Kara didn't say much during dinner at a local chain restaurant, but he filled the conversational gaps by talking about music and movies he'd enjoyed. They had a quick dinner and returned to the room. Small, with two queen beds, and faded carpeting and drapes, but clean at least.

Bone-weary, she longed for a shower and glanced at her toiletries, still in the suitcase. Unpacking seemed fruitless and she didn't want to get comfortable.

Jace, sitting on one of the beds and checking his gun, glanced at her. "Go ahead and shower. I'll be right here."

"Thanks. I…keep hoping the anxiety will vanish."

His deep blue gaze filled with understanding. "It will fade in time, babe. I've got things under control."

After showering and dressing in bright pink sleep shorts and a tank top, hoping the colors would cheer her up, she sat on the other bed. "Where are we headed to next?"

"I can rent a place through Jarrett. He has safe houses for women and children they help through SOS."

Kara shook her head. "I don't want to take up residence in a place he might need for those he helps. I have a better idea. My uncle Phil, you know the one you found out about?"

He didn't blink. Jace had a poker face. "Go on."

"Phil has a cabin in a remote area of western North Carolina. Not easy to find and he's family."

"Family." Jace's expression clouded a minute. "Yeah, I can see how you'd trust your family."

The bitterness in his remark startled her out of her mood. "You can't? You never did talk about yours."

"My family isn't trustworthy or someone you'd turn to in an emergency. Call him. I'm hitting the shower."

He grabbed clothing and toiletries and headed into the bathroom. Kara called her uncle, who was happy to loan her the cabin. When she hung up, she kept wondering what Jace meant by that remark.

Jace was up at dawn, but in the other bed, Kara still peacefully slumbered. He made coffee in the little pot the motel provided. Tasted like old dishwater, but coffee was coffee.

Less than an hour later, they went to the motel lobby for breakfast. Basic, but decent, and the coffee here was stronger and more flavorful. Jace ate quickly, glad she did the same, and they filled their cups to bring more coffee back to the room.

While Kara showered again, he sat outside. He knew what she was going through—saw it in other victims. Showering to wash away the stench of their attackers, scrubbing their bodies to rid themselves of scent and memory. His stomach roiled as he thought about what might have happened if Kara hadn't struck Lance and gotten away.

Clouds thick with rain hung in the sky, promising an afternoon downpour. Humidity hovered in the air, thick as a wet blanket. Jace sipped coffee, watching sleepy people making their way to the lobby for the free breakfast. His mind whirled with thoughts, trying to make sense of what happened.

Slowly, it seemed the puzzle pieces were falling into place. Problem was, he couldn't see the big picture—what it all meant.

Big Mike had seemed very interested in Kara when he caught Jace in bed with her. Lance seemed interested in her. Why?

All his instincts went on overdrive. What if they'd targeted her store for a different reason?

What if Kara herself was the target? But why? Her store, yeah, she had inventory worth stealing. Lance attacking her made no sense.

Did Marcus want Kara, and if so, for what purpose?

He texted Rafe his thoughts, then asked Darkling to dig into his ex's history, her parents, anything that might be seen as a red flag and raise Lance's interest.

Rafe called him. "Jace, where are you?"

"Hotel in Georgia. All you need to know. We're headed soon to the mountains and cell service is dicey."

"I need a location."

"I'll let you know when we get there." He glanced at the parking lot and the travelers packing their minivans and cars to get on the road, hustling children and dogs into the vehicles. "Let me know soon as Darkling has anything on Kara. I'll question her from this end. There has be to a nexus in all this and Kara is it, but why is she the center of it?"

A thunderous roar of motorcycles punctured the air. Jace glanced at the road and froze.

"Gotta go."

Not taking chances. Too many bikes sent his instincts on full alert. He hung up and sprinted inside. Kara was combing out her hair, but thankfully, had dressed.

"Let's go."

Kara blinked. "What's wrong? I was going to grab us another cup of coffee from the lobby."

"We'll get coffee on the road."

He didn't want to alarm her, cause another panic. Jace grabbed their cases and tossed them into the back of the SUV. He herded her into the vehicle as the bikes rolled into the parking lot. Heart pounding, he watched them park near the motel entrance and dismount, then swagger into the lobby.

Another five minutes and Kara would have been inside, getting that second java for them.

They were DP. He recognized Big Mike's Harley with the ape handlebars, as well as the leather jackets the men wore. Ten of them at least.

They might be headed north to bail out Lance, or visit.

Could be a coincidence they were here.

Jace didn't believe in coincidences. He started the vehicle and went left instead of right out of the motel parking lot. Back road by the motel should suffice.

Kara's eyes were huge. She'd seen them. Her breath came in little gasps.

"Easy," he soothed. "We're leaving them far behind."

He hoped.

An hour later, they had left the motel far enough behind for him to feel confident the bikers couldn't follow them. He asked Kara to plug in the instructions to her uncle's cabin in North Carolina.

Glad she was finally relaxing and losing the tension gripping her, Jace smirked as she argued the GPS was wrong.

Jace switched on the radio. Kara gave him a pointed look. "Bluegrass?"

"We're in the country. I'm blending in."

"We're in an SUV, Jace. No need to blend in."

"You don't like banjo music?"

"You know I adore banjo music. But not in the woods."

"We're on the interstate. Hardly the woods."

"Those trees on the side of the road don't count?"

Jace chuckled and shook his head. "Okay, let's use your playlist."

She used the Bluetooth on her phone and the sounds of "Closer to Fine" blasted out of the speakers.

Side-eye time. Jace groaned. "Indigo Girls? Chick music?"

"It's a great song about the meaning of life. And we're driving." She flashed him a winsome smile.

"See if I invite you into my mojo dojo casa house."

Kara laughed. "You saw the movie *Barbie*?"

"Yeah. The girl I was dating at the time insisted. Was a pretty good flick."

"What happened to her? Your girlfriend."

Jace's stomach tightened. "The job got in the way. She got tired of waiting for me to clear my schedule. Or make a commitment."

"Sounds as if she wasn't right for you. She should have understood you are committed, but to the job."

He considered. Kara was right again. But it was a heavy subject for the road and he wanted to steer them to light stuff, considering what happened back at the motel.

"Mind if I switch my playlist? No banjo music. Spanish."

At her nod, he thumbed on his playlist and "Despacito" played. Kara nodded to the beat. He grinned.

"Like it?"

"Catchy. I didn't know you enjoyed Latin music. It's great dance music."

"I grew up listening to salsa, merengue. Used to hang out with Rafe and his friends a lot in Miami." Jace tapped his fingers on the wheel to the energetic beat. "Saved my life in a way."

Another heavy topic. But Kara didn't pursue it. Instead, she began seat dancing.

"Remember the times we went clubbing? That was fun. You're a good dancer. Great rhythm."

He grinned. "Yeah, you can't grow up listening to this kind of music and not be a good dancer, though Rafe, man, he's got amazing moves."

"So do you. On the floor and off…" Her voice drifted off and color suffused her cheeks.

Oh, yeah, he did have great moves in bed. With Kara, anyway. Always wanted to go the extra mile to please her and it seemed to come naturally, as if they fit together.

Like salsa and chips.

He swallowed hard, not wanting to go there, either. So many memories between them.

When the song ended, he gestured to her phone. "Let's try your playlist."

"How about good ol' rock and roll?"

Jace finally allowed himself to relax. How he remembered this—good times with Kara, going on road trips and singing to the radio as they headed for a quiet beach for a swim, or a hike on a swampy trail. Or put their bikes on his SUV and did a long bicycle ride on previously unexplored pathways.

Or those amazing times on the dance floor, followed by even more amazing times in bed…

Lost in thought, he went quiet, only noticing after a few

minutes she had turned the volume way down. Jace passed a slow-moving truck, glanced at her. "What's wrong?"

"Do you ever have regrets? Real ones, about life…about us?"

Time for the truth. He hated lying. Ironic. His undercover assignment depended on a lie. But with her, with this, he needed honesty.

"Yes. I have regrets about us. I thought we would get married, have a good life together."

"What happened, Jace? It wasn't my career. In fact, you always supported me in the business, told me to reach for my dreams." She drew in a breath. "It's one of the things I loved about you."

She said it so easily, without reservation, that it startled him. "And one of the things I loved about you. You were determined to make your business successful and not let anything get in your way."

"I wish my business helped people. Like you do."

He glanced at her. "Seriously? You help people, babe. People who have family who die, who feel helpless when faced with all the stuff left behind. Where do you start cleaning up? How much is everything worth? How can I sell it without worrying about someone ripping me off?"

Jace felt he needed to drive this point home. "People know they can trust you and you'll give them a fair deal. Remember that one family whose grandmother was killed in a car crash and they couldn't even function?"

"The family you referred to me."

"I worked with the dad. Funny thing, he was the type who could handle everything at the job, but when faced with his mom's death, he was helpless. You went through the whole house, had everything appraised, opened every single cabinet, organized, sorted between stuff they wanted to keep that was sentimental and stuff they didn't want. You spent days working with them, babe."

He smiled, thinking about that memory. "In the end, you didn't even take a commission because they needed the money to pay for her funeral."

Kara shook her head. "Not exactly true, Jace. They paid me later, when the house was sold."

"And you donated every dime to Mothers Against Drunk Driving."

She shrugged. "It wasn't anything special. I make a lot of money in my business, Jace. I'm no saint."

Her voice dropped. "Sometimes I wish I had chosen a more noble profession. Like you did. I should have known you'd never be a real criminal biker. I always believed in you, Jace. I wish you had believed in me."

Coffee. She'd wanted coffee. Seeing a fast-food restaurant off the highway, he drove there.

He parked and turned to regard her, knowing this was important. Not that he truly believed they had a chance to recapture what they'd both lost. This wasn't about him. It was solely about Kara.

"I did believe in you, Kara. Still do. I was too proud to tell you. You give people closure, sad closure with some clients, but necessary. Closure to move forward, say goodbye without clinging to stuff that clutters their lives. The volunteer work you did with hoarders proves it. I saw that one show where you had everything cleaned up, sorted, organized. You were so sweet with that woman who'd been hoarding for years. Got in there, got your hands dirty with a situation that would make strong people nauseated. You marched in there without judgment and got to work."

Kara blinked. "You knew about that?"

"I kept track." Tough to admit it—hell, he didn't want to

sound like he'd stalked his ex-fiancée. "I was damn proud of you."

Licking her lips, she stared at him. "Thank you, Jace. Thanks for telling me. It means a lot, coming from you. I always valued your opinion, more than anyone else's, even my family's. It meant a lot to me to have your respect, because I admired you so much for your strength of character."

The revelation startled him. He considered. "Guess we have our own mutual admiration society."

She rested her hand on his arm, sending his pulse racing. "You could say that. But it was always more. Much more, much deeper. With you I felt I could truly be myself. You made me come alive again, Jace."

He'd always been a guy guided by instinct. Instinct kept him alive in the Army. He'd honed instinct on the whetstone of adrenaline and danger until it became a razor-sharp weapon that saved his sorry ass more than once.

Ironic how he used instinct to survive on the job, but in relationships, he never did. Maybe if he'd learned to listen to his gut, they'd have survived as well. Maybe if he'd told her back then how he'd felt, his pride in her, instead of yammering about all the charity work as a way of lashing out because she'd lectured him about motorcycles, they could have worked things out instead of parting in anger and grief.

Instinct urged him to act now. Jace unbuckled his seat belt and leaned forward, cupping her face in his hands.

Kara tilted her head up and closed her eyes. Oh, yeah.

The kiss was slow, a test, a sampling of feelings and wants. Her mouth, heaven. Her lips soft, warm and promising. Memories flooded back, the long kisses they'd shared, taking their time, never worrying about hurrying into bed to get to the final act. Never had he enjoyed kissing a woman as much as Kara because they connected on a deeper level.

Taking their time…

Jace broke off the kiss. "Much as I enjoy this, Kara, we have to get going if we're going to make it to your uncle's house by dark."

She touched his face and his blood surged, his heart skipping a happy beat. Damn, she still did it to him.

"Long as we're here, can I use the restroom and maybe you can grab us that coffee you promised?"

He grinned. "Cream, two artificial sweeteners."

Kara dropped a kiss on his cheek. "Thanks. For this, for everything."

Jace escorted her inside and went to the counter, ordering two coffees. When she emerged, he handed her one cup.

"Want anything else? Maybe some more breakfast?" He winked at her.

"Are you trying to fatten me up with junk food?"

"Maybe I'm thinking of those Sunday mornings when we'd lie in bed, and I'd serve you breakfast. Although not as greasy."

She laughed.

They drank their coffee while Jace drove northward, fast enough to make good time, but not get pulled over.

For the next few hours, they talked. Caught up. Kara stuck to work discussions and movies and lighter topics.

Jace told her about a few cases with the FBI he had helped solve, cases that filled him with pride. Felt like he was getting to know her all over again, telling her about his current life.

"Why the FBI, Jace? It's a noble move, considering you were on the fast track to making money." Kara sighed and set her cup in the holder. "Not that making money is all that great. There's more to life."

"You have a successful business."

"Yet it feels stifling at times. Superficial. But I didn't know what else I could do, and couldn't disappoint my parents, so I took over the business."

"What do you want? Only you can discover your heart's desire."

"Do you know, no guy has ever asked me that?"

Kara stared out the window. "The social work I've done, the charities, it isn't the committee work and being recognized, Jace. I like helping people and I enjoy working with kids who are adrift in life and need guidance. Direction. Giving Dylan a job, I saw him blossom. His stepfather stripped away from him every iota of self, and with the job Dylan felt more confident and empowered. I felt like I accomplished more with him than I ever did in selling estate items."

He nodded. "So what do you want to do with your life, babe?"

"I'm good at what I do. I'm good at selling and buying and analyzing the value of items. I'd like to channel that into opportunities for others, especially teenagers with low self-esteem who need to be reminded of their own value. At-risk kids like Dylan."

Admiration filled him. Then he pointed to a fast-food sign. "Need a break?"

Making a face, she nodded. "Not that I'm fond of grease, but it's faster."

The restaurant was crowded when they went inside. Jace used his mobile app and grabbed their order. Kara stared longingly at an empty booth.

"Do we have time? For just a few minutes? I'd love a change of scenery from the car."

"Sure."

They ate lunch, Jace checking the window once in a while, while discussing the merits of mobile apps and ordering ahead versus chancing it in person.

"One time when I was in the Army on leave at a restaurant, the service was so slow by the time the waitress arrived to take my order, my leave was up."

"Oh, that's terrible. See? Always order ahead."

They laughed as Jace helped her clean up the table and pitch their trash into a bin. But the laughter died as she stared out the window. Her hand trembled as she pointed.

"Jace…"

He turned, swore and grabbed her hand. "Let's go."

Chapter 19

They were screwed. How the hell had the Devil's Patrol found them?

Only one bike, but one was enough. As he drove away, he caught a glimpse of the biker, face hidden by a helmet. But the DP on his leather jacket stood out like a neon sign.

Must be the car. Have to ditch it.

About an hour later, he pulled into the parking lot of a rental-car company. They went into the office, but no luck. All the cars had been taken.

All he could do was keep pushing ahead, hoping to lose them.

Or confront them head on. Dangerous with Kara in the car.

Confront the bikers in public, hope for the best. But not endanger Kara. No way he wanted her beneath a yellow tarp, her body left for police to identify.

He returned to the car, checked his weapon. Glanced at Kara. "We're about three hours from your uncle's cabin, if we stick to the interstate. I don't know how they're tracking us, but I say we keep pushing on."

Jace consulted the GPS. "If I pull off at this rest stop, I plan to confront this guy. Far as I can see, it's one guy tailing us. Need to stop him before he finds us at the cabin. I'll need you to do exactly as I say."

Kara took a deep breath. "Whatever you want me to do, I'll do."

In another hour, he found the rest stop, pulled off and parked beneath the shade of a sprawling oak tree. The area included green space, with a terrific view of the mountains, and picnic tables. A breeze ruffled the leaves and cooled the sweat trickling down his back. Jace scanned the tables and pointed to one occupied by a large family. She could easily blend in there and go unnoticed by whoever was stalking them.

After instructing Kara to hang near the picnic table and pace as if waiting for someone, he leaned against the vehicle and waited. Didn't have to wait long, for a motorcycle roared into the rest stop and parked nearby. The rider turned to him, ambled toward him.

Gun at the ready, Jace tensed.

As the biker drew closer, he squinted in the bright sunlight. The gait, rather a limp, seemed familiar. Not a DP he knew, though the guy wore the colors…

"Jace. At last, I finally get to see you."

Shock pummeled him as the biker removed his helmet. The gray hair, weathered face…eyes as blue as his own.

Swearing, he stared, but did not holster his sidearm. "Dad?"

"Son." Al smiled and sighed. "Been a long time."

Oh, hell no. Not long enough. Jace raised his gun. "You're following me. Why?"

Al held up his hands. "Whoa, stop. It's not what you think. I'm not here to hurt you…"

Not like all those times in the past. "Yeah? My boss told me you were helping him, but I don't trust you. You're just passing through? Why, so you can tag my location so the rest of them can nail me?"

"I'm here to protect you."

Jace narrowed his gaze. "Right."

Al opened his jacket. "Look, I'm not carrying. I can't, I'm a convicted felon. I'm not here to hurt you. Wanted to give you a heads-up. They're on to you, and Marcus gave orders through Mike to follow you and your lady friend."

Slowly he lowered the gun, still not trusting him. "And you know this?"

"They don't know you're a Fed. I do. Did some digging after I got out of prison so I could find you. Apologize for all the crap I did to you." Al sighed. "I didn't tell them your real identity, son. But that day in the garage, I realized you were undercover. I went to Mike, started hanging out with the gang again after you fled, trying to get information. And I went to the Feds to tell them I wanted to work for them as a confidential informant."

Jace still couldn't trust his old man. "Why should I believe you?"

Al eyed the gun. "Can you put that away if you don't plan to shoot me?"

Jace holstered the gun but left it in easy reach.

"I guess if I were in your shoes I wouldn't trust me, either. But I'm asking you to now. For her sake." Al pointed to Kara. "They don't know yet who you are, just that Marcus wants you and her. They've been following you all this time, asked me to ride ahead because Mike's bike needed repairs. Wanted me to keep tailing you. I'd say you have an hour at the most before they come after you."

Not that he truly trusted his father, but Al was right about Kara. "Why did Lance attack Kara?"

"Not sure. Like I said, there's a lot they're not telling me. I know Lance returned early from his trip up north to deal with Kara. That's about it. Marcus has his inner circle and

I'm not part of it. Been gone too long. I also know they're not worried about me losing you. I think they wanted me to ride ahead to lose me, not to find you. They know where you are, Jace."

He thought fast. "They must have a tracker on the vehicle somehow. Maybe they put it on the SUV while we were at the motel."

He eyed Al's big touring bike with the plush leather seat, saddlebags and sissy bar. Same bike his old man had when he'd been arrested more than twenty years ago. Looked to be in good shape, too.

"You really want to make up for all the crap you did to me? Give me your bike and take the SUV."

Al blinked. "You want me to ride in that cage?"

"It must have a tracker on it. That's how they're following me. I don't know when or how they did it, but it has to be it. You can drop it off at…" Jace consulted his phone and named a gas station off the interstate. "Then I'd vanish, if I were you."

Al hesitated a minute. Nodded. "You can have my bike but leave the SUV here. I'll get a ride. I didn't manage prison for all those years without knowing how to make my way around a tight spot."

Waving to Kara, he then went to the car, retrieved their backpacks as Al removed his pack from the bike. After Jace secured their belongings, he felt an unexpected surge of emotion.

How many years had he longed for his father's respect while growing up? If not for Rafe and his family, he'd never have known love or compassion. Al had changed in prison. Rafe tried to warn him.

As Kara made her way toward them, he shook his head. "Still can't believe you're working for Rafe."

Al smiled. "Let's just say the moment I figured out my son was undercover with the DP as a federal officer, I wanted to help all I could and do anything to protect him, keep him safe."

His father's smile dropped as Kara joined them. "I did a pretty crappy job with him growing up. I know I can't make up for that, but I had to try."

Al shuffled his feet as Jace explained to Kara the change in plans. Probably his father wondered if Jace would introduce him. Jace licked his lips.

"Kara, this is…my dad. Al Beckett."

Al stuck out a hand, which she shook. Kara didn't look shocked or confused, but graciously said hello. Relief surged through him.

Al glanced backward. "You'd best get going, before those fools catch up to you."

He went to turn, and Jace acted on impulse. Catching him by the leader-clad shoulder, he drew in a breath.

"Thanks…Dad. I mean it. Thank you."

Al shook his hand. "Wish I could have done more."

Jace handed Kara the helmet. "Here. Get on. Use the helmet and when we get into town, I'll get another for myself. But right now, we need to get the hell out of here."

They roared out of the rest stop. In the rearview mirror, he kept glancing at his old man standing on the sidewalk, until Al became a tiny dot and vanished altogether.

Chapter 20

Kara had promised the cabin was remote. Uncle Phil certainly believed in being alone.

Deep in the woods, the cabin was nine miles from town, but could be accessed by a long, narrow road with twists and turns through the mountains. He followed the instructions he'd memorized because the phone GPS didn't work in the mountains, and came to a dirt road leading to a wide, open field with three sturdy cabins. He rode to the middle cabin, a wood structure nestled against a flowing creek and a thicket of tall trees. He parked in the gravel space by the cabin and stopped her from getting off. An older model green pickup truck sat in the parking space by the cabin.

"That's Phil's truck. He leaves it here for hunting trips. Keys are inside."

"Wait here until I check things out," he instructed.

After using the combination Phil texted, he opened the door and inspected the cabin. Clean, perhaps a little musty. Basic furniture, one bedroom with a queen bed and a dresser, washer and dryer hidden in a closet. Tidy, cozy and well-kept. Sofa, coffee table, full kitchen and even a television set with a satellite dish. The back porch overlooked the creek, and trees marched upward in a slope from the creek.

He went out the back door and walked around the cabin.

Pretty here, with the crystal-clear creek set against the mountain slope, the pine and maple and oak trees, and a bed of moss. Two chairs were set before a firepit. Jace inspected the back of the cabin's exterior. The porch ran the length of the cabin, and concrete blocks supported the back half of the cabin, which was built on an incline. Great place for animals to hide. Squatting down, he saw a paper wasps' nest in the corner. Had to be careful, but wasps were the least of his concerns.

He returned to Kara, sitting patiently on the bike.

"Wasps' nest under the porch," he told her.

Jace assessed their situation. Phil owned all three cabins and had put a hold on renting them out.

Much as he appreciated the gesture, knowing it cost Phil plenty of money during tourist season, this place didn't sit right. It was too open, too accessible from the road. Anyone could come up the main road, park and take potshots at them through the trees.

He consulted his phone. No cell service, either.

Kara watched him. "Phil has a dish service and an emergency landline."

Terrific. If they got into trouble, he had a rotary phone. "Ever try to text from a rotary phone?"

Her tremulous smile wobbled. "Not recently."

"One way in, one way out. Where does that road lead to?"

"There's two, maybe three other cabins up there and the road dead ends. Uncle Phil said there's a hiking trail there leading to caves, where it's rumored the Cherokee hid from taking the trail of tears, when they were forced out of their homes and into a death march to reservations."

Hiking trail, and the other main road with the double yellow lines also dead ended. He felt like they were sitting ducks.

"We should leave, go to a hotel if we can find a room."

Even as he said the words, he knew it was pointless. Hotels made Kara vulnerable. Too many sets of eyes on her, and mouths that would gossip about the pretty blonde and the grim man with her. Until Rafe discovered who Marcus was and nabbed him, Kara remained in extreme danger.

"Who's going to know we're here except for Uncle Phil? Maybe we might run into a local who turns curious, or a hungry bear, but that's about it. Not in this section of woods."

Sweet, sensible Kara. But here in the deep woods, without any backup or reinforcements, he didn't like it. He turned to her. "I'll take my chances on the bear more than the locals. Does Uncle Phil have any guns?"

"Hunting rifles, and a shotgun in the bedroom closet. He owns the woods around the cabins and hunts during deer season."

"Good." At least the extra weapons and ammo might come in handy.

Breathing in the pine-scented air, he felt a little tension ease. Certainly, it was cooler here, and during normal circumstances, he'd enjoy hiking in these woods. Jace helped her dismount.

"Have I told you lately how great you're doing and how much I appreciate you riding on a bike and trusting me?" he asked as they took their backpacks and went up the steps.

Kara opened the door for him. "I don't feel like I'm doing great. Sometimes I feel like I'm screaming inside. But I have to hold it together. Not that I haven't done this before."

Inside the cabin, he dumped their packs and found the guns Kara mentioned as she inspected the refrigerator.

"There's some carbonated water and that's about it. We'll have to go food shopping. Phil said there's a grocery store in town. I really don't want to be on that road after dark. It's kind of spooky out here."

"I don't, either. Let's take the truck." He picked up the phone, heard a reassuring dial tone, and replaced it in the cradle. "Unless you want to relax a little first. We have time. I know riding the bike has to frazzle your nerves."

Kara's soft carnation-pink mouth curved into a smile. "It does, but in a way, it's good. I'm overcoming my fears."

"That's good." He went to the sofa, patted it.

As she sat next to him, Kara's expression filled with curiosity. "Jace, you introduced me to your father. You never told me he was a biker. Is that why you didn't want me to meet him when we dated? Why you told me he was dead...?"

He sighed, raked a hand through his hair.

"Yes, and no. It's complicated. He was dead to me for a long time."

She leaned back. "I'm listening. I won't judge you, Jace. Please believe that."

Too ashamed to delve into his family life, he hedged on telling her. Instead, he launched into an explanation about his profession of choice.

"My old man is a reason why I chose the FBI for a career path. I've been trying to find myself for years, babe. It took me a long time to discover what I wanted out of life. Not to get rich and have lots of stuff. People acquire stuff and eventually they want more, always more."

He stretched out his legs and studied the tips of his shoes. "All the guys I worked with were on the fast track. They were headed to Wall Street, becoming investment brokers. Not me. I didn't want that. I needed something more, something deeper than the almighty dollar."

He paused a minute, humbled by her quiet trust in him to tell his story. Because no one ever asked, not even Rafe, and he felt closer than a brother to his boss. She'd changed. Hell, he'd changed as well, hopefully for the better.

"I felt like a robot, a walking, talking artificial intelligence programmed to make money for others and myself. Couldn't resist the urge to follow a higher calling because I started getting afraid I was losing myself, before I ever really began. That might sound pompous."

"No, it doesn't." She put a hand on his arm, her gaze soft with understanding. "I get it, Jace. I do. After a while it feels like life in the shadows. You feel like a shadow of yourself."

Maybe they had spent so much time hiding their real selves from each other, being scared of the possible heartbreak and rejection if they shared their deepest desires, that they'd gotten lost in their own shadows.

"After my time in the Army Rangers, I realized I could still have that higher calling. Not work security like a lot of vets did, but actually help nab the bad guys. I wanted to be someplace where I could make a difference, where my life could make a difference before I leave this earth."

She smiled. "You already have, Jace. You have, more than you realize."

They found the grocery store and bought enough groceries to last a few days. After loading them into the pickup's back seat, he called Rafe.

"We made it to the cabin. Parking it here for a few days. No cell service, though, even here in town it's spotty. Get me up to speed."

"Nothing yet. Lance was supposed to be arraigned today, but they need to get him a court-appointed attorney and that won't happen until tomorrow. Think he's going to cave. Seems like it."

"Maybe my father can help you with Lance as well. I ran into him at a rest stop in North Carolina. He gave me his bike, but I'm still not entirely sure about him. Why you trust him is beyond me, Rafe."

Silence for a minute. "Need your location, Jace. Where are you?"

"Someplace safe." He blew out a breath. "I think someone on your team is in league with the bikers, Rafe. How the hell else could they find us so quickly? Someone had to have planted a tracker on the SUV, which is why I told my old man I needed his bike."

Rafe swore in Spanish. "Jace, these agents are loyal and they know you. They're your friends, for God's sake. No one's betraying you."

"I'm not taking chances."

"Then check in with me every six hours. I have to keep in touch with you."

Jace shook his head. "Once a day, Rafe. Texting won't go through. I'll call you on the landline. You hear news, you contact me. I need to know what's going on. Gotta go."

When they were on the road back to the cabin, he couldn't stop feeling a little betrayed. Yeah, he understood Rafe not telling him about Al's involvement, but still...

Kara seemed more relaxed than Jace felt. He still felt uneasy about this location. On the way back to the cabin, he had to take it slow, shifting the truck's gears and making them grind, much to Kara's amusement.

The long, winding road seemed to go on forever, twists and turns that he loved taking on a motorcycle on his time off. Not in a pickup truck with Kara riding shotgun, where local vehicles appeared out of nowhere going fast, crossing over the double yellow line.

Dusk draped over the valley by the time they were on the country road to the cabin. Sunlight dappling the trees grew thinner. He hated this road, and how tight it seemed, because he didn't like being in spaces that had no real exit plan. Anyone could come down this road and ambush them, and they'd be screwed. At least on the motorcycle he could make a quick exit with Kara.

He had navigated another twist in the road when Kara cried out, "Oh, stop!"

Jace stepped on the brakes, avoiding the truck fishtailing by twisting the wheel the opposite way. A low curse tumbled out.

Her door opened and Kara bolted out of the truck. Jace pulled off the road and followed her.

A dog. Trotting alongside the road, the mutt stopped as he spotted Kara. As if sensing a friend, or food, the dog ran up to her. Jace groaned. They didn't have the luxury of pet-the-dog time and this one looked like a stray. He called out a warning.

"Hey, be careful. He could bite."

"He won't bite me. Will you, buddy?" she crooned, holding out her hand. The dog, a beagle mix by the look, came up to her as if she was a tasty bone. He sniffed her hand and wagged his tail, looking up at her.

"Oh, Jace, he's half-starved. No collar, either. Do you suppose he escaped from home?"

"He's probably a stray."

"Uncle Phil did say sometimes people come here to dump dogs." She sniffed. "He's always trying to find homes for them. I bet this is one of the dumped dogs."

He came closer, held out his hand. The beagle sniffed his hand and stared at him with large, brown eyes that seemed almost soulful. Aw, damn. Damn dog looked almost like Rocky, the beagle mix he'd been forced to give away when he was thirteen. Rocky, who went to a rich kid who had always wanted a beagle and offered five hundred dollars for Jace's dog.

His mom decided they needed the money more than the dog, who was "eating us out of house and home."

Some moments you never forgot. Rocky was one—the dog howling as his mom drove him away, Jace hanging out the window, Rocky running alongside the car until he became a tiny blip on the horizon, the tears making him into a fuzzy dot...

He did not need this now. Baggage.

Kara was already headed back to the car, digging into the plastic grocery bags for the roast beef and tomato sub he'd bought. She pulled the roast beef free. Instead of giving it to the dog, she handed it to Jace.

"Here. It's your food. I only got a salad."

Great. Now he was feeding strays. Jace held out the meat and the dog swallowed in one gulp. Yeah, dog was starving. He looked hopeful, as if Jace had more.

"We can't leave him here, Jace. Please."

He jammed a hand through his hair, realized it was the same hand covered with roast-beef residue and released a laugh.

"I don't know..."

"Jace, please." Kara turned her big baby blues to him, at the same time the beagle looked at him with big brown eyes. Two sets of soulful eyes, pleading for help.

He was a sucker for helping people, bringing justice to the world because he'd been an abandoned stray.

Jace looked around. The sun had almost vanished now behind the treetops. "All right. Just for tonight and tomorrow we'll look for his owner."

He opened the truck's back door. "In."

The dog jumped inside, and then wriggled into the front driver's seat. He sat there, grinning at Jace.

Jace glanced at Kara, who laughed and finally the tension between them broke.

"Guess he's driving," he drawled.

Kara opened the driver's door. "Back seat, buddy. Your paws can't reach the pedals."

The dog jumped into the back, tail wagging, and thrust his head between them as they both climbed back into the truck. Jace scratched the dog's ears.

"You need a bath, dog," he muttered.

"You need a name," Kara decided.

"How about Dog?"

She rolled her eyes.

"Duke?"

The dog whined.

"He's not a Duke. But definitely a *D* name. How about Darby?" Kara asked.

The dog barked as if agreeing. Then he nudged Jace's hand with his cold, wet nose as if asking for pets.

A lump clogged his throat as he obliged. Rocky had done the same. Oh, Rocky had a good home after that pitiful yelping and running after the car. The rich kid whose daddy shelled out the five hundred for him had bragged in school to Jace about all the tricks Rocky was learning. How Rocky slept in his bed every night and how they took Rocky everywhere, including a vacation to the mountains, where Rocky went hiking and fishing with them almost every day.

Each time the rich kid told Jace these stories, he hated himself.

Hated his mother more.

Even at thirteen, he knew he should have let go and walked away from the rich kid waxing poetic about Rocky, but like a guy who never got over losing the woman he loved with all his heart, he'd listened to every tidbit, every single story about Rocky.

Just to know his beloved dog was doing okay.

He'd done the same with Kara, when her father had met him for lunch a time or two after their breakup, asking Jace what went wrong. Listening to how she was doing, making sure she was okay because he still cared.

Even though he didn't want to care.

Thankfully, those tortuous visits stopped when he applied to become an agent and training started at Quantico. He learned to deal with life's curve balls and managed to forge ahead.

Yet he never forgot Kara.

At the cabin, Jace climbed out of the vehicle, opened the door for Kara. Darby bounded out of the car. Halfway expecting him to bolt for the woods, Jace was surprised to see the dog bound up the cabin stairs and stand by the screen door.

Kara laughed. "Look, he thinks he's home."

Such a delightful, sweet sound, her laugh, and it echoed in the valley ringed by mountains. It soothed him, made him smile and nearly forget the reason they were here.

Inside the cabin, they set about putting away groceries and the dog danced around them.

"Uncle Phil keeps dog food in the pantry for the abandoned dogs..." Kara opened a door. "Here."

She poured kibble into a stainless-steel bowl and set it on the ground, and put water out for Darby. He drank the water, sniffed the kibble and then looked at her, tail wagging.

Kara laughed and opened a package of cooked chicken, sprinkling it on the kibble. The dog began eating with a voracious appetite.

Out of habit, he checked his phone again. Nothing. Jace picked up the phone on the table, heard the dial tone and replaced it in the cradle.

"No selfies here," he mused and she laughed again.

He hadn't seen Kara this relaxed in a long time. Maybe this could be a good thing, hanging here for a few days, the place to themselves... He plopped down on the sofa and crooked a finger.

"C'mere."

She made her way to the plush sofa, but the dog beat her to it. Wagging his tail, Darcy jumped into his lap. Jace sighed as she laughed again.

"I guess he thinks he's first in your affections. Poor baby is starved for food and love. We have plenty of both."

Eyes shining, her soft mouth curving into a smile, she looked like heaven itself in the cabin. Jace took a deep breath. Yeah, a few days here might be exactly what they both needed.

Rafael Jones Rodriguez seldom underestimated an enemy. He'd remained alive in many situations because of this trait. When facing gunfire, he assumed the bad guys had more firepower, better ammo and a quicker exit. He always had a backup plan.

Even that hellish day when he'd lost Fiefer and Sanchez, two of his best agents, it hadn't been because he'd underestimated the danger they faced. They'd failed due to promised backup that never arrived from local law enforcement. Outnumbered. Outgunned.

By the time the local LEOs finally got their act together and decided to save the day, Dave and Carlos were dead and Rafe had been lying on the ground, struggling for his life.

Ever since leaving rehab, he'd vowed to never get caught like that again. Two good men dead, their families left grieving. He'd go through hell and back again before it happened again.

Certainly wasn't going to happen with Jace. Not Jace, his friend and a dedicated agent who hadn't wanted this assignment, but needed to go through with the grueling undercover work, forfeit his personal life to get the job done. Jace, who always trusted him in the past, and didn't trust him enough now with the cabin's location.

That hurt.

Rafe paced in front of the bullpen as his team worked. They were close to discovering the real identity of Marcus. Dylan had given him a description, which they circulated to law enforcement.

Lance was in custody, but not saying a word. Maybe the president of the Southeastern division of the Devil's Patrol was loyal.

Rafe doubted it. Guy seemed more terrified than loyal. Marcus had a long arm.

His cell rang. Tom, the agent he'd sent over to the local jail where Lance was imprisoned, to check on the prisoner. Rafe answered in a clipped voice.

The news made his stomach roil and his bad day worse. He told Tom to stay, find out what the hell happened.

The men and women in the bullpen looked up as he released a string of curses in Spanish that would make his beloved *abulita* slap him into next week. He heaved a breath.

"Lance is dead. Someone shanked him in the cell. He bled out before the guards could get to him."

Over at the intel desk, Sally, a crack cybersecurity agent, beckoned to him. "I've got chatter, Rafe. The DP social media is saying Lance got what he deserved." She glanced down at her laptop. "Not for getting caught by the Feds, but letting Jace slip away with the target."

His mind whirled. The target… Kara. Not Jace. "You've got something there. Get Darkling on Teams."

Someone dialed the connection and Darkling went online to participate in the brainstorming meeting.

Rafe went to the board and began writing on the whiteboard as he quizzed his team. "Right. So we've got Marcus, who wants Jace and Kara. Why not send an army of gang members after him from the start when Jace was easier to find? What's his game plan?"

"No social-media chatter or anything on blowing up a target," Sally called out. "No viable threats of domestic terrorism."

"And yet he has enough makings for a bomb. Who is the target?"

"Killing Lance before he spilled anything else, like the real reason Marcus wants Jace," another agent called out.

"Maybe Marcus isn't after Jace for personal reasons," Sally added. "What about the woman, Kara?"

Marker in hand, Rafe paused, his instincts surging, brain cells clicking like machine parts. He turned from the board. "Give me everything you have on Kara Wilmington. Everything. I want to know where she went to elementary school. Her best friend when she was five. Dammit, even her favorite breakfast cereal. There's a connection here we're missing between Marcus and Kara."

It had to be Kara, because nothing about this made sense. Kara was the missing equation tying everything together.

From her laptop, Darkling called out. "I got it, Rafe. I know why Marcus wants Kara. It is personal."

As she relayed what she'd found out, Rafe's stomach roiled. This changed everything. This was personal and made Kara a target they'd never anticipated.

It wasn't money.

It was revenge.

Biting back another string of curses, Rafe reached for his phone to warn his best agent. Jace's cell went straight to voice mail.

They had to find Marcus before Marcus found Jace and Kara.

Chapter 21

They had dinner and after walking Darby, settled onto the sofa as it grew later. Darby settled on an old pillow by the sofa and promptly curled up to sleep.

Jace watched her channel-surf. Kara landed on *ET*. "Oh, look! Didn't you love this movie?"

He considered. "Yeah. And no."

She playfully touched his nose. "Lots of good advice in it. Be good."

He jerked a thumb at the back porch. "No, bee careful or bee sting."

"Wasps are not bees, Jace." She laughed and tucked her feet beneath her legs.

Confession time. He had to tell her the truth.

She had become such a part of him, wriggling past the hard barricade he thought was his heart, and wrapping herself around it. Kara was in him, around him. He smelled her perfume when he took coffee onto the lanai to enjoy the sunrise and the sweet scent of jasmine. He heard her gurgling laughter in the childish giggles of his neighbors' children splashing in the pool. He felt her loving concern when everything in this life seemed so crappy and he thought he'd never overcome his equally crappy origins. She forced him to see the good in people and the joy instead of the grimness and despair. Kara made him feel like he was at last worthy of loving someone and being loved in return.

Jace wondered how she'd react. For years, he'd been ashamed of his parents, his dysfunctional childhood. And yet, now more than in the past, he wanted to come clean with her. Let her know the answers to all the questions she'd asked.

Gently, he took the remote from her hand and turned off the television, setting the device on the coffee table.

"Kara, there's something I need to tell you. Something I should've told you a long time ago. It's about my family, and why I never wanted you to meet them."

Kara took a deep breath. "Jace, I'm listening."

Jace turned his head, meeting her gaze.

The weight of his secrets pressed heavily on his shoulders, and he knew he needed to share them. She deserved to know the truth about the man she'd met back at the rest stop.

He leaned forward, elbows resting on his knees. "I wasn't always on this side of the law, Kara. You know I've been undercover in this motorcycle gang, but what you don't know is that my family has deep ties to this world. My father, the guy you met? He was a DP—in fact, a founding member."

Jace hesitated for a moment, struggling to find the right words. "My father lived for the thrill of the open road and the chaos of the club. My mother, she tried her best to keep us together, but it was tough. She worked two jobs just to make ends meet."

No judgment on her face, only concern. Kara listened intently. "Go on."

Hell, this was tough. He felt like his insides were grated raw. "When I was a kid, I looked up to my dad. I craved excitement, adventure and motorcycles, just like he did. But when I was fifteen, I went with my dad to a bike rally and I saw my old man kill someone else."

Eyes wide, she leaned close, clasping his hand. Her touch anchored him, giving him the courage to continue. Not even Rafe, his closest friend, knew everything.

"I saw him get into a heated argument with another biker, and it turned violent. I watched him kill the guy right in front of me. It was brutal, Kara, and I'll never forget the look in my dad's eyes. He looked as if…he regretted it, but it was too late. He got arrested, tried, convicted for second-degree manslaughter.

"After that, my dad was imprisoned, and my mother re-married. She distanced herself from me, probably because she was afraid I'd turn out like my old man." Forcing out the words, he felt raw emotion close his throat. "I was left to fend for myself more or less, so I joined the Army at seventeen. My legal name is Jason Beckett, but started telling everyone my name is Jace. Because my parents always called me Jason. My small way of making my own distance from them."

"Jace, I had no idea. I'm so sorry you had to go through all of that alone."

Nothing but compassion in her blue eyes, compassion and sorrow. Jace felt a surge of pure relief amid his boiling emotions. "Guess I never wanted to tell you because your family was so…perfect. I was ashamed."

"Ashamed?" She shook her head. "With everything going against you, you made something of yourself, Jace. You fought the odds and won. I'm proud of you. That took a lot of courage."

Relieved at her reaction, he studied her expression. "I wanted to make a difference, babe. I never wanted to be like my old man."

Kara cupped his face gently. "We all have our pasts and our secrets. What matters is who you are now, and I see the good in you. I see the man who fights for justice and to protect ordinary people like me. I'm proud of you, Jace, and I'm glad you finally told me."

Longing raced through him. Yeah, life was full of unexpected twists and turns, the kind he enjoyed taking on his bike. You had to lean into the curves, embrace the unexpected and learn to adapt. He'd done plenty of that. So had Kara.

"You know why I love you? Not in the past, but now?"

The question made him blink. He shook his head.

"Because you're many things, Jace, but you make me feel like I'm a better person than I once was—you give me a safe zone where I can tell you my hopes and dreams and the journey is worth it. You make me feel alive again."

"You make me want to be a better man, Kara," he said softly, touching her face. "The kind who can't forget his past but can move ahead of it and embrace every damn little bit of joy in life…like loving you."

Their lips met in a soft, reassuring kiss, sealing a connection that had been fractured by silence and fear. In that moment, Jace felt a weight lift off his shoulders. After facing his past, he felt ready to forge a new future.

He kissed her, leisurely, languid kisses, recalling their tangled past when they couldn't wait to see each other. Jace dropped tiny kisses along her chin, her throat. She made a humming noise of pleasure that aroused him further.

Never had he needed a woman more, not merely for sex, but something deeper and much more significant. If he couldn't have her, he'd lose his grip on sanity.

"Kara," he murmured.

He hardly recognized his voice, deepened by sexual urgency. His cock hardened painfully.

With languid grace, she kissed him back, slowly caressing his bearded cheek. Kara nuzzled him with her own cheek.

"Your beard, it tickles. Feels different," she murmured.

Blood surged to his groin as he envisioned how she'd feel with his beard tickling a different part of her.

Desire cranked up as she kept kissing him. No more leisurely kisses. He was too cranked up, too aroused. Jace pulled her into the bedroom and almost ripped off his shirt.

"Condom," he said, barely managing to get the word out.

Kara shook her head. "Pill. It's safe."

"I want you so much," he muttered. "If you want to back out, do it now."

In answer, she unbuttoned her shirt, her heated gaze never leaving his. As he tugged off his boots and removed his clothing, Jace held on to control with a thin thread.

With a soft sigh, she divested herself of clothing until she stood before him, fully nude.

They fell onto the bed together, kissing.

She'd dreamed of this moment and after years of missing him, it finally arrived. How she'd missed his heat. His passion.

Jace's mouth was as warm and firm, as delicious as she'd remembered. Jace cupped the back of her head as he devoured her mouth, licking and teasing.

Her own desire remained barely leashed, as urgent as the heat in his blue eyes. With a rough growl, he lunged, pushing her naked body back onto the bed.

Kara was the one touching him, her eager hands exploring the body she once loved so well. Her mouth against his skin, trailing tiny kisses over the hard line of his jaw, his throat.

A sharp intake of breath as she saw the silvery stretch of old scar tissue on his chest. "Dear Lord, Jace, what happened to you?"

"Bullet wound. It healed."

"It hurts me to see you like this," she whispered. "I wish I could have helped."

Kara kissed the scar tissue, her mouth sliding over a wound that she never knew he'd had.

She kissed the inside of his thigh, then stroked a finger along the underside of his rigid cock. Jace dragged in a deep breath as she encased his erection in her hand and took him into her mouth.

Closing his eyes, he let his head drop back. He tasted exactly as she remembered—strength and steel. She enjoyed every groan wrung from his throat, the exquisite pleasure she delivered to him.

Then he pulled away, his gaze glittering. Jace rolled onto his back and pulled her on top of him.

Understanding, she straddled him and sank deep into him, moaning with the erotic pleasure of having Jace at last inside her. Strong hands on her hips, he helped her ride him.

Every delicious stroke brought her higher and higher, cranking the sweet tension higher until she was panting. She was so close, close...

His mouth encased one hard nipple. He bit lightly.

Screaming, she shattered, her nails digging into his muscled chest. Then he joined her, his own cries echoing with hers.

Kara fell against him, panting, her perspiration mingling with his, her hands splayed against his rigid chest. She couldn't think about the future or the consequences of what they'd done.

Tomorrow would arrive soon enough.

Chapter 22

Leaden light peeked through the window blinds early the next morning. Jace yawned and rolled over, watching Kara. So beautiful as she slept, her hair spilling over the pillow, a soft smile on her face.

Damn, he'd give anything to wake up to her next to him each day. Maybe they could make it work.

She woke, caught him and her smile widened. "Good morning, lover."

He took her into his arms again.

After they showered and made breakfast, Jace let Darby out for a run in the field. Ankle-high grass hid birds foraging for insects and a curious chipmunk sat up, watching them. The dog chased the chipmunk and then ran to the road, barking.

Sipping his second mug of coffee on the porch, Jace froze at the distant growl of a motorcycle. This was a quiet country road, yeah, and maybe the biker was enjoying the twists and turns…

Or not.

Maybe the Devil's Patrol had found them. Again.

After whistling for Darby, who came running, he ran into the house, the screen door banging behind him. Kara was tidying the kitchen.

"Kara, they may have found us."

She turned, her face pale. "Jace, how? No one knows we're here and this place is so remote…"

"They're tracking us. Or talked to someone in town after tracking us here."

It made no sense. He'd exchanged vehicles with Al, and Al couldn't have had a tracking device on his bike. But somehow, the gang had tracked them down. Unless they'd tracked them a different way…

Jace thought rapidly. Maverick, one of the DP, had worked as a software developer for a large tech firm before getting fired. He'd laughed about it because the criminal life was far more prosperous. Maverick had worked cleaning up people's computers and phones…sometimes placing the malware in the phones himself and then getting paid by the company to uninstall it when the user experienced problems. The company found out what he'd been doing and fired him.

A biker with experience in malware…

"Let me see your phone. This is the same phone you've been using since you spied on the DP the night your jewelry got stolen?"

Kara nodded.

"Have you downloaded anything, anything at all, in the past month? Photos, an app?"

"A game. That's all."

When she told him the name of the game and gave him her phone, he found the game Dylan had sent her. Jace swore.

"Please tell me you didn't download this app from a link Dylan sent you."

Kara's eyes went huge. "That game… I played it with Dylan sometimes in the shop on break and with everything going on…yes, it's the same one. He didn't tell me where he found out about it!"

"Son of a bitch!" He threw the phone at the sofa. "It's

how they've been tracking you, Kara. Dylan told me he got the link for the app from Big Mike. Big Mike must have had Maverick install spyware in the app and you downloaded it to become a sitting duck."

Blood drained from her face. "You mean everywhere I go, they knew where I was?"

"Exactly. It's got to have a location tracker on it. Has your phone slowed down lately? Battery dying sooner than usual?"

She closed her eyes, opened them. "I didn't even think about the possibilities and I'm always careful."

"This business with Dylan threw you off your game. It wasn't your fault. Or Dylan's. But they must have installed a location tracker on your phone and that's how they've been locating you. Lance at the motel after Dylan was arrested. The rest stop."

Jace sucked down a breath. "You're not getting a signal here in the mountains so they can't pinpoint our location. But we have to leave. Right now."

Kara ran into the bedroom and tossed everything into her pack. Jace didn't bother, but grabbed the shotgun and loaded it. He glanced at Darby. It tore him up to leave the dog behind, but they stood a better chance on his bike...

He dumped two cans of dog food into bowls and placed them on the floor. Then he grabbed a steak knife from the drawer and stuck it into his pocket, just in case.

"Sorry, bud. Have to run."

Kara picked up a helmet and went outside. After grabbing his keys, he ran outside to the bike, Darby barking in protest as he followed. Son of a bitch, this was bad, so bad...

"Well, hello there, Jason Beckett. And Kara."

Jace skidded to a halt, staring at the black pistol pointed in their direction.

He blinked. "Oscar?"

His neighbor gave him a nasty smile. "Gotcha. At last."

Kara's pulse accelerated. Jace's neighbor? All this time she'd feared the biker gang and this guy, he looked like an ordinary man, with his bristling crew cut and white shirt and trousers, except for the cruel expression...

"You're Gerald. Aka Marcus." Jace's voice was flat.

Terror skidded through her. This was Marcus, the man who killed the teenagers at the clubhouse?

"Drop the shotgun or I'll put a hole through her right now." Jace complied.

"And your sidearm."

Silently Jace removed the Glock. Still clutching the helmet, Kara stared, too terrified to move.

Gerald/Marcus gestured with the pistol. "That way, in the back of the cabin."

Hands in the air, they walked to the cabin's back, Oscar following, the gun trained on them.

"You never knew I was a biker. I rode here, followed you. Parked my bike up the road and snuck through the woods.

"Typical FBI, all this time you never knew." Oscar laughed. "I had you fooled good. The jewelry, the vague terror threat, it was all to throw you off, Jace. Soon as Lance told me he saw Kara at the Tiki Bar, and better yet, you used to be her boyfriend, I was gold."

"Why me?" she asked, her voice tremulous.

"Ever since I got out of prison, I've been searching for you, you little bitch. A month ago I finally had the chance to find out who you were. Had enough money to bribe a courthouse secretary to unseal the records of the name of the juvenile who killed my father.

"All this time, it was you. Not your goddamn jewelry. Not

your cousin, Dylan. Everything was about you and getting you in front of me so I could experience this moment. My father, Archie Turner. Remember his name? Remember?"

Kara reeled backward. She couldn't think, could barely breathe.

The only son of the man whom she'd killed in the car crash when she was seventeen.

Panic set in as she stared at the gun in his hand, then her gaze traveled up to his cold, dead eyes. Brown eyes. Jace had blue eyes, as sunny as summer skies. Sweat dampened her palms as she clutched the helmet like a shield.

"I found out where you were crashing, Beckett, and rented the apartment next to yours. Changed my name and waited. Waited for a chance to grab her, but you were always there. Always, dammit. Her shadow."

This is all your fault. What you deserve. You deserve to die for killing your brother, for killing his father. You caused so much pain.

The little voice of guilt inside her head echoed the taunts Gerald now said, the cruel, callous words that hurt.

Jace, what had Jace said. *It's not your fault, Kara. It was an accident. Conner should never have climbed into the back seat without telling you. Archie Turner should never have run that stoplight. There was nothing you could have done.*

The niggling guilt inside her eased, replaced with an odd calm.

"I killed those kids because they overheard Mike telling me you were there with Kara and now was the time to come to the clubhouse. I got there and you weren't there, but they were and they told me it was too much, they signed up for fun and stealing jewels, but not murder. I couldn't leave witnesses. Your damn cousin escaped before I could get him."

"Let her go. It was an accident. It's me you want, Marcus." Jace stepped in front of her, shielding her with his big body.

"Oh, you, I'll deal with you, traitor. The guys will be happy to deliver justice. Right now they're planting a welcome-home gift in your parents' house, Kara. Too bad it will blow out half the neighborhood, but I figure they all deserve it, the rich snobs." Gerald laughed.

A scrabble of paws over rough rock, a furious bark and Darby rounded the corner. Snarling, the dog advanced and leaped at Gerald. Cursing, the man raised his gun. Fired.

Kara screamed. Jace stared at Darby, who was whimpering, lying on the ground.

"You shot my dog," he said. "No one shoots my dog."

This was a nightmare, and they were caught in it. No way out. Her terrified gaze flicked to Jace—Jace, who was calm and cool. How could he be so calm?

Gerald kept backing up, close to the porch and wasp's nest. Jace's gaze flicked to beneath the porch, where a few wasps flew around.

Gerald raised the gun again.

"Kara, be good." Jace's gaze flicked beneath the porch. "Be-e-e good."

She nodded. Her only chance. *Please, let me do this…*

Pretending to go boneless with fear, she suddenly lurched forward, and tossed her helmet at the wasps' nest. Angry insects flew outward, landing on the first object of their fury.

Gerald.

Cursing, he fired, his attention shattered by the wasps flying in his direction. Wasps flew at her, stinging, but she barely felt the pain. Jace uncurled his body and struck.

The kitchen knife hidden in Jace's pocket suddenly sank deep into Gerald's shoulder. Clawing at the blade, he snarled at Jace. The two men struggled on the ground, wrestling for the pistol.

Gerald pulled the trigger. The sound was piercing to her ears. Blood blossomed on Jace's white shirt, but Jace curled his right hand around the knife handle and he yanked it upward. Gerald gagged, as blood spurted. Jace slammed Gerald's hand against the ground, loosening his grip on the pistol. The man struggled weakly as blood flowed like a burst dam.

"Kara, kick the gun away," he yelled, straddling Gerald.

Instead, she picked up the gun, and fired, straight into Gerald's leg. The man screamed.

Jace rolled off him, panting, his shirt stained red. Oh, God, so much blood.

"Watch him while I find something to tie him up."

He ran into the cabin and returned with lamp cord, winding it around Gerald's wrists.

Kara handed Jace the gun. "You're hurt, I have to…"

The sound of motorcycles thundered in the air. Kara's breath came in little gasps as Jace sank to the ground, the pistol trained on Gerald, who kept moaning.

Motorcycles.

Gerald's backup.

Bikers. They were toast. But she'd be damned if they didn't go down without a fight.

For Conner. For Jace, who only wanted to protect and serve.

She ran inside, grabbed Uncle Phil's favorite gun, the one he used for deer hunting. Bolt action, she'd used it once while hunting with Uncle Phil years ago.

The box of ammo spilled over the floor, cartridges rolling under the bed. Hands shaking, she loaded the .243 Winchester, praying she could at least give them a fighting chance to make it into the woods. Jace, oh, God, Jace, he'd been hit…

Kara ran to the front porch, steadying the rifle on the porch railing as she bent down and peered into the scope. A motorcycle roared down the incline leading to the field, others following. She had one shot at this, take out the head guy and maybe the others would realize they weren't sitting ducks after all…

Taking a deep breath, she trained the weapon on the first biker pulling into the field. Her finger trembled on the trigger.

Have to do this… I must…

Then she blinked.

Kara went still. Not the snarly face of Mike in the scope. She knew this guy, and behind the bikes she saw several black SUVs and the unmistakable shape of patrol cars…

Standing, she did not lower the rifle, but waited as the bikes pulled up in front of the cabin.

Rafe dismounted the first bike, pulled off his helmet. Clad in black leather and jeans, with a Devil's Patrol patch on the back, he looked the part. Three other bikers dismounted, and she realized from the flash of gold on their belts that they were agents.

He held up his hands. "Don't shoot. We're the good guys. Anyone else here?"

She set down the gun. "In the back. With Gerald, I mean, Marcus. And Jace is hurt!"

Men and women climbed out of the shiny black SUVs, and the local sheriff's office deputies were here as well. And clad in black leather, the woman who'd kissed Jace in the Tiki Bar what seemed like years ago. The woman had a gun in a leather holder on her bike.

"I'm a nurse. My name's Allison."

"Jace." A lump clogged her throat and she began to shake

uncontrollably. "Gerald shot him, he's on the ground in the back."

Grabbing a kit out of her saddlebag, Allison ran to the back. Kara followed, her knees weak at the sight of Jace on the ground, lying so still…

Rafe shrugged out of his leather jacket, placed it around her shoulders. "Easy. You're suffering an adrenaline letdown. Allison will take care of Jace."

Gerald moaned. "I'm dying here. Screw him, I need help."

"Yeah, well, screw you, you ass. Priorities. You can bleed out." Allison began attending to Jace.

Rafe's face tightened. "Dammit, Jace, you have to live. Let Allison treat you."

Jace pushed her hand away. "The dog…my dog…"

Kara ran over Darby, who was lying on the ground whimpering. Rafe squatted next to her.

"Easy, boy," he soothed. He swept his gaze over the dog. "Looks like a bullet nicked him. He should be okay, but he needs a vet."

He removed the bandana from his head and bandaged the dog's wound. Rafe beckoned to a deputy, who lifted the dog with care and promised to take him to a vet who lived close by.

Allison wrapped Jace's arm and staunched the bleeding. Kara kneeled next to him.

"You got stung," he murmured, reaching up to feel her cheek.

Kara touched it. "Doesn't matter, as long as you're okay."

"Everything's gonna be fine, babe."

"Don't you dare die on me," she warned, her eyes filling with tears.

He managed a wink. "Not a chance. Bad-boy bikers never die. We're too tough."

Chapter 23

Six weeks later

"**S**even hundred going once, going twice! Sold!"

Jace lowered his hand. Next to him, Rafe shook his head. "Seven hundred dollars for a vase?"

"Kara likes it." He smiled at Kara, standing next to the auctioneer. She returned the smile. Her auction. Her items from the store. Life was good.

"Wedding gift?" Rafe grinned.

Jace drew in a breath. "Not yet. We've decided to take it easy this time and not rush."

Kara's parents, sitting in front of him, turned around. "Congratulations, Jace. I'm sure it will make a lovely gift for Kara. Wedding or not."

At her mother's soft smile, Jace sighed and her father winked at him.

Rafe looked amused. "Did she give you anything yet?"

Jace reached into his pocket and withdrew the little crystal frog Kara had gifted him, the same frog he had given her years ago. "She wanted me to have this, said it reminded her she was done with kissing frogs because I'm her Prince Charming."

He couldn't believe how lucky he was, how lucky they all

were. After pocketing the frog, he rubbed his shoulder, re-membering the terrible moment Marcus shot him, the horrid fear that he was helpless to aid Kara, keep her safe.

But damn, his girlfriend had proved she could save him instead.

"You're lucky Kara didn't shoot you back at the cabin. Why were you and the other agents dressed as DP bikers?" Jace asked.

"We went undercover, wearing their colors, after we re-alized why Marcus wanted Kara. Figured if he was on his way, we could stop him, but we arrived too late."

Jace nodded. "Thanks for the back up."

"I'll always have your six. It's good to see you back in the office, Jace. You're a terrific agent. By the way, how's Darby working out at your place?" Rafe asked.

Jace smiled, thinking of the beagle who immediately had called his condo home. "Spoiled rotten. His leg's all better, too. I could have killed Marcus, not for shooting me, but shooting Darby."

"Marcus won't be going to trial." Rafe stretched out his long legs. "Someone sank a weapon into his kidney. He's dead."

Jace didn't blink. "Amazing how that happens in prison."

Rafe shot him a look. "Saves the taxpayers the expense, and gives you peace of mind. Wonder how it happened."

Jace shrugged again. Hell, if his father had friends in prison, and just happened to pass the word because he wanted to get even with Marcus for many things, including shooting his son, nothing Jace could do. He'd gotten a cryptic letter in the mail from Al, who said he was leaving Florida and travel-ing out west. Make up for lost time, after tying up loose ends.

Dylan's high-priced lawyer, paid for by Kara's dad, had worked out a deal with the US attorney. Most likely he'd get parole and a pardon. Ten members of the DP were awaiting trial on racketeering charges. Big Mike had the additional charge of murder, as he had helped Marcus kill the young bikers.

Without Lance, without Marcus, the club had lost its leadership, and the last time Jace drove past the clubhouse, it was listed for sale.

At the podium, Kara began pitching the new foundation she and her parents were starting to help at-risk children and teenagers. Conner's Dream was becoming a reality and he couldn't be more proud of her.

Jace glanced at Rafe.

"You never did tell me how Allison managed to join you at the cabin."

"She actually returned to the DP to pick up any chatter after Snake kept pestering her, asking her to go out with him. He promised her a shiny new set of jewels if she did, bragged they were worth about six figures. She got suspicious, knowing about the theft at Kara's, so she followed him to Georgia, pretended to show interest and found out about their destination and the cabin. Snake had threatened Dylan's mom until she gave up the location, so Allison informed me I needed to get to the cabin before Marcus did."

Jace sighed. "I assume Wanda didn't go stay with her friend. I gave her money to leave."

Rafe's mouth tightened. "Found out her husband got home, confiscated the money before she could leave. She was too scared of him. But Jarrett and Lacey stepped in, and she's staying in an SOS safe house now. They're helping her find a new life."

"Allison really came through."

"Yes. Little firebrand, endangering herself like that. I

thanked her and then gave her a long lecture about risking her life with those outlaws. She didn't appreciate it."

Rafe sounded awfully fond of the "little firebrand."

The auction was over and people were dispersing. Jace knuckle-bumped Rafe and strode to the dais.

Beaming, Kara ran down the stairs to him. He went to sweep her off her feet, winced.

"Hey, watch it. You're still recovering. I thought you were resting."

"I came here to bid on a couple of things. And I promised Maria to bid on that ring she wanted. You know, Maria, your friend and neighbor."

Kara's nose wrinkled. "You know her?"

"She's one of us. FBI cyber security agent. She lived in your neighborhood before you moved in. Worked with Rafe, and I met her husband, Hank, at a party Rafe threw. When I found out where they lived, I knew you'd be in good hands with them as your neighbors."

"Thank you for looking out for me," she murmured, sliding her arms around his neck.

"Always will, babe."

"I'm sorry you can't get your diamond necklace or the other jewels back yet. I know they're worth a lot of money," he told her.

"I'll get them back eventually. It's not as important as getting justice for what the Devil's Patrol did."

Kara nuzzled her cheek against his clean-shaven jaw and he felt a surge of pure love, and wonder. They had rediscovered each other, and from now on, he knew they'd forged a new path full of understanding, and secrets laid bare.

"I don't know if I like this new look on you," she mused. "Mr. Federal Agent instead of the bad-boy biker."

"I still have my bike." He searched her gaze. "Okay with that?"

An impish smile curved her mouth. "Come outside. I want to show you my surprise."

Taking his hand, she led him out of the back door of the auditorium into the warm sunshine. He blinked at the sunlight winking off the shiny chrome of a Triumph motorcycle.

Jace ran his hand over the seat. "Yours?"

She nodded. "Guy selling it wanted an electric start. Now, we can go riding together."

He grinned and shook his head. "I can't believe you. You are one of kind."

Her smile dropped. "So are you. You helped me get over my fears. You saved me, Jace."

"You saved me," he said softly. "So you up for a ride in the country with your new bike?"

"Any road you take is fine with me, Jace." Her eyes shone with love for him as she reached up to kiss him. "As long as I'm there with you on the journey."

* * * * *

You'll love the other stories by Bonnie Vanak:

Her Secret Protector
Navy SEAL Protector
Shielded by the Cowboy SEAL
Navy SEAL Seduction

Available from Harlequin Romantic Suspense!

   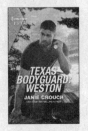

PRAISE FOR NEAL ASHER

"Asher is a modern master of sci-fi." —*Starburst* magazine

"Neal Asher's books are like an adrenaline shot targeted directly for the brain." —*New York Times* bestselling author John Scalzi

"Asher has lit up the sky of science fiction like a new sun." —Tanith Lee

"With mind-blowing complexity, characters, and combat, Asher's work continues to combine the best of advanced cybertech and military SF." —*Publishers Weekly*, starred review

"A wide-screen special-effects extravaganza, a space opera featuring gods and monsters . . . Doc Smith and Olaf Stapledon in a blender, turned up to eleven, with the contents splattering across the ceiling." Russell Letson, *Locus*

"Asher rocks with XXX adrenaline while delivering a vivid future." —David Brin, *New York Times* bestselling author of *Kiln People*

"Asher has an amazing talent for world-building, for writing larger-than-life characters, for weaving gripping plots and for imagining exotic alien races and wonderful technologies. Huge ships! Big weapons! Space battles! Ground battles! Treason! Revenge! This is New Space Opera at its best." —*Sense of Wonder*

"Asher's coruscating mix of epic space opera, weaponised Darwinism and high-stakes intrigue channels the primal flame of deep-core science fiction." Paul McAuley, author of *Four Hundred Billion Stars*

"The world of the Polity explored so far . . . is one as complex and as compelling as any created in the genre, and in the breath of biological speculation almost unparalleled." —Lavie Tidhar, *Dusk Site*

"Violence, of course, is what Asher does best—by presenting a stunning, brutal spectacle and taking his readers right into the middle of it. He expertly ratchets up the narrative tension and excitement with high-tech mayhem and technological razzle-dazzle. And it's a genuine pleasure to watch him." —*Kirkus Reviews*

"Hardboiled, fast-paced space opera . . . Asher's books are similar to the world of Iain M. Banks' Culture universe, but the Polity is arguably a much darker and more vicious environment—and all the better for it." —*The Registers*